THROUGH THE STORM

THROUGH THE STORM

Rosalie Parker

THROUGH THE STORM Copyright © 2020 Rosalie Parker
COVER ART Copyright © 2020 R.B. Russell

Published in November 2020 by PS Publishing Ltd. by arrangement with the author. All rights reserved by the author. The right of Rosalie Parker to be identified as Author of this Work has been asserted by her in accordance with the Copyright, Designs and Patents Act 1988.

The following stories previously appeared as noted:

'The Dreaming', *Black Static* 59, 2017
'Waiting', *A Book of the Sea*, Egaeus Press, 2018
'Chimera', *For Those in Peril*, Black Shuck Books, 2018
'The Moor', *Supernatural Tales* 39, 2019

FIRST EDITION

ISBN

978-1-78636-596-5
978-1-78636-597-2 (signed edition)

This book is a work of fiction. Names, characters, places and incidents either are products of the author's imagination or are used fictitiously. Any resemblance to actual events or locales or persons, living or dead, is entirely coincidental.

Design and layout by Alligator Tree Graphics.
Printed in England by TJ Books Limited.

PS Publishing Ltd / Grosvenor House / 1 New Road / Hornsea, HU18 1PG / England

editor@pspublishing.co.uk / www.pspublishing.co.uk

CONTENTS

THE MOOR	5
VILLAGE LIFE	13
SHOWTIME	25
THE DREAMING	35
DEAR JOHN	45
TOADIE	61
HEAVENLY LOVE	69
COW CITY	79
CHIMERA	91
POACHER TURNED GAMEKEEPER	105
THE WEEPING WOMAN	115
THE CINEMA	121
HIM WE ADORE	127
THE VOYAGER	137
THROUGH THE STORM	149
DEAD LETTERS	155
FEVER	163
HOLY INNOCENT	175

JOY RIDING	183
REALITY TV	193
CHALLENGING BEHAVIOUR	203
CHANGE	211
WAITING	219
TOUCHSTONE	227
THE GROUP	237

THROUGH THE STORM

The author would like to thank Jim Rockhill and R.B. Russell

THE MOOR

As soon as Simone set foot on the path through the heather her spirits began to rise. The red grouse were nesting, but the cries of curlew and lapwing, and the piping of meadow pipits and the trilling of skylarks punctuated the perfect stillness. High overhead, a buzzard soared on the summer thermals. Simone had walked over the moor many times: it was, on a human level, utterly desolate and remote, and it suited her that she seldom met another soul. In the distance the fells slumbered in the heat.

Fine, still days on the moor were rare. In winter it was barren; the heather brown and dormant, lashed by the wind and rain. Often a thick blanket of snow drifted over the path, smothering its contours and rendering it dangerous to walkers. Even in summer, unless you were familiar with the seemingly random twists and turns of the path around the narrow cloughs and rises, it was easy to lose your way. Simone walked carefully over the rough, stone-strewn ground. There was no shelter, no trees, no buildings, just acres of open heathland.

In one of his less taciturn moments Steven had told Simone she was in love with the moor, that it was her refuge (from him). He laughed when he said it, but his eyes were sad. She had long ago given up asking if he wanted to come with her.

A lizard skittered across the path, its supple, striped back glistening in the sunshine. As she walked further, weather-sculpted crags loomed to the north of her, the bare rocks a row of crooked teeth. She flopped down on the heather, basking in the heat. Like the lizard, Simone felt herself awakening from hibernation, her mind and body unfurling like the fronds of moorland bracken. She closed her eyes and stretched out luxuriously. When she opened her eyes some minutes later, a figure leaned over her.

'You were so still I thought you were dead,' he said.

Simone sat up. 'I was resting.'

'I wanted to be sure. . . . '

As her eyes readjusted to the brightness of the day, Simone saw a man dressed in country clothes. He carried a rifle slung over one shoulder.

'I thought it was closed season for grouse.'

He patted the barrel of his gun. 'It's my job to ward off poachers—and other undesirables.'

'Do I come into that category?'

'I don't think so,' he said, seriously, 'although it's not easy to tell at first glance.'

She stood up. The man towered above her.

'Can I take you back to your car? It's easy to become disorientated up here; there's no disgrace in accepting help.'

Simone bridled. 'I've walked the circular path many times and I've never lost my way.'

'Suit yourself,' he said, scanning the horizon, his interest in her evidently waning.

'Thanks for your concern, but I'm fine.'

'Very well then,' he said. 'I won't trouble you any further . . . ' he broke off and began to walk away.

'What were you going to say?' she called after him:

He spoke so quietly she had to lean forward to hear.

'However well you know the moor it can always throw up surprises . . . my advice is, keep your wits about you.' And with that he strode off.

Simone watched until he was a small speck in the distance, then she took a sip from her water bottle and re-joined the path. She needed to speed up: Steven would be anxious if she was late home.

Some miles away, tall cumulonimbus clouds rose above the fells. Later in the afternoon the fine weather would break, but Simone calculated that by then she should be off the moor. Meanwhile, the sun beat down relentlessly and there was not a breath of wind. Even the birds seemed to be seeking shade, their calls infrequent and subdued. Only the bees and crickets were revelling in the warmth. She felt herself overheating and wished she had brought a hat. The water in her bottle was unpleasantly warm.

Nevertheless, it was good to be outdoors, away from home. After another half-mile or so Simone saw two people walking towards her. As they approached it became clear that they were a boy and girl, quite young: she was surprised they were out on their own in such a remote place. The boy was dressed in shorts and a shirt, the girl in a summer frock. Both wore socks and sandals. The girl had pigtails and the boy a very short hair-cut. They were scrupulously neat and clean. As they drew level they stopped. The girl shot out her hand and grasped the hem of Simone's t-shirt. Without preamble the boy said, 'Can you tell us how to get home?'

'Let go of me please,' Simone said.

The girl tightened her grip.

'Please help us,' she said.

The boy hung his head. It was clear they were frightened and upset.

'What's your address?' Simone asked.

The girl let go. 'We're not sure.'

'Do you live in the village? There are no houses on the moor.'

'I don't think so,' said the boy.

'You don't *think* so? Have you forgotten?'

'Yes,' said the girl.

An explanation dawned on Simone. 'I expect you moved house recently.'

'That's not it,' said the boy. 'We've lived here a long time.'

The girl burst into tears. 'Please help us.'

Simone looked at her watch. Time was slipping away. She felt a sharp tug of longing for Steven: later, she would tell him about her unaccustomed encounters on the moor.

'I don't know if I *can* help.'

The distraught faces of the children pleaded with her mutely until at last she relented. 'Perhaps the best thing is for you to walk down to the village with me. We'll find someone who . . . knows you. You can't live far away.'

'We may have been left here,' said the boy miserably.

'What do you mean?'

'It's a sort of game. We're expected to find our own way back.'

'Well that's not very kind of . . . whoever. Come with me and I'll do my best to help you.'

The girl took the boy's hand and Simone led them along the path. The boy began talking about the weather on the moor; he was very knowledgeable about it. He introduced himself—his name was Ryan and his sister Janice. Janice began to skip. They seemed to have cheered up.

'We like the moor,' Ryan said, 'but you have to take care.'

The thunder clouds had spilled over the fells and a weak westerly breeze funnelled along the valley, cooling the air a little. The children began to sing what sounded like a nursery rhyme: Simone did not recognise it. After a while the endlessly repeated refrain began to irritate her, but she fought the urge to ask them to stop: she did not want to jeopardise their good humour. The village was still several miles away and they were making slow progress, the children stopping frequently to examine plants and insects beside the path.

After a mile or so the path skirted round the head of a deep, narrow clough. Without warning, Ryan broke away from his sister, fought through the bracken and stood on the brink of the steep ravine.

'Ryan!' Simone shouted.

Janice gasped, distracting Simone's attention from the boy for a few seconds. When she looked back, he had disappeared.

Making her way through the bracken to the edge of the clough, Simone lay down and peered into its depths: there was no sign of the boy. Again and again she called his name.

'Ryan! Ryan!'

Fighting back the beginnings of panic, she craned her neck as far over the edge as she dared. The bottom of the clough was obscured by thick vegetation: if Ryan had fallen in and was lying unconscious then it would be impossible to see him. She needed to find a way to climb down.

As she was scanning the slopes of the clough for the least treacherous route, she heard laughter behind her. Ryan and Janice were standing on the path, hand in hand, swinging their arms back and forth. Simone stood up, angrily brushing dead bracken from her jeans.

'What on earth do you think you're playing at?' she shouted. '*How* did you disappear like that?'

'He likes to play tricks,' said Janice, as if that explained everything.

'I've a good mind to go on without you. You don't deserve to be helped.'

'We'll follow you,' said Ryan. 'It won't be difficult. Anyway, you promised.'

'I don't think I did . . . you're a naughty little boy.'

Simone marched off along the path. She steeled herself not to look round, but after a few hundred yards couldn't help it. The children were a short distance behind, solemnly picking their way over the uneven ground.

In the distance thunder rumbled and the clouds advanced towards the moor. She would have to hurry if she was to outrun the storm. The birds were silent now, having flown away to lower ground or sheltering in the heather. The moor was infused with an eerie expectancy.

She broke into a trot—so did the children, matching her pace. She heard one of them stumble. After a few hundred yards she stopped to take a sip of water and they quickly caught up.

'Sorry I frightened you,' Ryan said.

'I wasn't frightened, I was concerned. I thought you'd fallen in.'

'You *looked* frightened. I didn't mean any harm.'

'You're old enough to take responsibility for your actions. . . . ' said Simone, although she wasn't sure if he was.

'Please come home with us,.' said Janice.

'Won't your people be looking for you by now?'

'I don't think so,' said Ryan.

Simone sighed. 'Look, what is this all about? If it's a game, then it's a pretty sick one.'

Ryan said, 'It's deadly serious.'

'Explain it to me.'

Simone, after a glance at her watch, walked on. The children trotted by her side.

'What you need to understand,' said Ryan, 'is that the moor has been in existence for thousands of years. Before that it was forest.'

'I know,' said Simone. 'I've read up on it.'

Janice said, 'And we've been walking here for an awfully long time, looking for the trees.'

'We're usually on our own, but sometimes we come across a special person who can help,' said Ryan.

'You mean, help you find your way home?'

'Yes,' said Ryan, 'and in other ways. A few people have been *really* helpful. Will you be one of those, Simone?'

She could not recall telling the children her name.

'I think you will,' said Janice. 'You're the caring kind.'

Simone threw a sharp glance in Janice's direction. Janice was examining Simone's face.

'I'll take you down to the village, then you're on your own. I must go home. I have someone there who needs me more than you do.'

'But we don't live in the village!' wailed Janice.

'What else can I do?' Simone said, with one eye on the thunder clouds. 'The storm is coming. You need to find shelter.'

The children stopped. 'I don't think you understand at all,' said Janice.

Rummaging in his pocket, Ryan took out a pen knife. He pulled the blade open and pointed it at Simone.

'Is this another of your silly games?' she said crossly.

'No,' said Ryan. 'We're not going to the village. You're going to stay here with us. We know you love the moor.' He sliced the knife through the air. 'We've seen you here lots of times.'

The first drops of rain began to fall, the newly dampened earth exuding a pungent, musty smell. Simone would normally be in her car by now, on her way home.

'Put the knife away: you're not going to do anything with it.'

Ryan lunged at Simone, the tip of the blade missing her by inches.

'In order to help us you have to be like us. It won't hurt much,' said Janice.

Simone backed away carefully, aware that there was a steep slope behind her. Ryan advanced, his arm outstretched, the knife pointing at her throat. . . .

Two loud reports shattered the silence. Simone threw herself on the ground. To the west she saw the gamekeeper standing on a low rise, the stock of his rifle tucked firmly against his shoulder, the barrel seemingly trained on her. The children had disappeared, hiding, she assumed, in the tall, shrubby heather which grew on this part of the moor.

'You can stand up,' he shouted to Simone. 'It's not you I'm aiming at.' He lowered the rifle and walked towards her, picking a path through the heather.

Simone erupted into anger. 'What on earth do you think you're doing?' she yelled, 'there are children here!'

'I'd say it's you that had the most reason to be afraid.'

'The boy wouldn't have harmed me, it was just a silly game,' said Simone. 'You might have killed them!'

She called: 'Ryan! Janice! Come out! He's not going to hurt you.'

The gamekeeper was using his rifle barrel to prod around in the heather next to the path. Above them, the skies darkened and forks of lightning scythed through the air. Thunder rolled threateningly and the rain came down so hard it drummed on the ground.

'Come on,' he said, 'you haven't a coat. I'll take you down to the village.'

'We can't leave the children!' she said.

'They'll be fine,' he said grimly. 'Trust me.'

Simone noticed that the rifle barrel was raised in her direction. She had little choice but to go with him. He took long strides and she had to scurry to keep up. Soon she was drenched to the skin; her jeans tight on her cold legs and her hair hanging limply on her shoulders. The t-shirt clung to her. From time to time she looked round, but there was no sign of the children.

'You'll need to stop thinking about them,' he said. 'That can be the worst thing about it.'

'Of course I'm thinking about them. They're on the moor on their own.'

'All the same,' he said. 'You're a good person and they rely on that.'

Simone was too tired to argue. The gamekeeper strode along the stony path. Somehow she dragged on behind him.

At last the village came into view, its gritstone houses huddled together against the rain. Simone could see her car parked on the road next to the church.

'I'll leave you now,' the gamekeeper said. 'You'll be safe here. Just get in your car, drive home and don't stop along the way. I'm sure you have someone at home who'll be worried about you.'

'Aren't you coming down to the village? I could give you a lift.'

He was already walking back along the path

'I have work to do,' he called. 'The moor's my home.'

VILLAGE LIFE

The Robinsons arrived late in the evening, he in black tie and she in a long cocktail dress of sheer red silk. Neither Rachel nor Clive could remember inviting them, but they hoped the couple might enliven what was threatening to become a rather dull event.

Edward and Patricia Robinson were the youngest people at the party, in their late thirties, Rachel guessed, and somewhat overdressed for the occasion. Most of the partygoers were of a certain age and wearing outfits appropriate for an informal evening. The party involved bringing along a simple supper dish to be shared with others—the plates and bowls had long been cleared away—followed by games and dancing. They had moved on to the dancing stage—the games having turned out to be something of a damp squib. A medley of vintage pop songs blared out from the antiquated CD system that Clive had set up at the back of the hall.

The Robinsons were resident in their cottage only during university vacations—he was, it was understood, a lecturer in philosophy and she psychology. They had attempted to fit into the village by drinking in the pub and patronising the shop, and, where possible, attending events such as the annual fête and the church cake sale in the hall. They also went for walks along the footpaths which meandered over local farms, hoping to come across villagers with whom they could strike up a conversation. Acclimatising to country life was proving more difficult than they'd envisaged, as most of the villagers, although friendly, were far too busy for casual socialising, even in the Farmer's Arms, which after 9 p.m. seemed to be largely a male preserve.

'I hope you don't mind,' said Patricia to Rachel, kissing her lightly on both cheeks, 'but we didn't want to spend the evening alone. New Year's Eve is a time for being with friends.'

'What a wonderful dress!' said Rachel.

'I chose it for her,' said Edward. 'It compliments her colouring, don't you think?'

Patricia had made up her face skilfully and pinned her shiny black hair on top of her head. The scarlet dress enhanced the lusciousness of her red lips.

'You put the rest of us to shame,' Rachel said. She indicated a table laden with bottles of wine and spirits. 'Help yourselves!'

Patricia poured two large glasses of red wine and passed one to Edward. He whispered something in her ear: Patricia put her hand over her mouth and suppressed a giggle. Rachel took a gulp of her gin and tonic and regaled Patricia with her views on traffic calming.

Edward, leaving the women to it, approached a group of men standing by the far wall. He recognised some of them, but did not know their names. They were mostly farmers and older farm workers apparently discussing the weather—it had so far been an exceptionally mild and dry winter.

'Aren't you going to dance?' Edward cut in. 'I'd've thought you'd be joining in by now.'

One of the men, eyeing Edward, said, 'There's no hurry. Maybe we'll dance later.' They resumed their conversation, this time complaining about the pot-holed local roads.

Edward shrugged. He re-joined Patricia and, rescuing her from Rachel, who had moved on to the dearth of children in the village (the primary school might have to close), took her hand and whirled her onto the dance floor, where two middle-aged women were attempting to jive to Elvis Presley. It was 'Jailhouse Rock'—very difficult to dance to, Edward found. He clasped Patricia round the waist and they began a jazzed up version of a fox trot. By the time the song finished they were looking into each other's eyes and laughing, a little out of breath. Most people in the room were watching them, including the men at the back of the hall. Rachel clapped loudly. 'Bravo!' she cried.

Edward poured more wine. The music had reverted to an easy listening compilation: even the two women had left the dance floor. Edward and Patricia sat down and Clive joined them.

'How long is it since you moved into Honeysuckle Cottage?' he asked.

'Nearly two years,' replied Edward.

Clive's eyebrows shot up. 'As long as that! How have you settled in?'

Patricia and Edward glanced at each other. Patricia said, 'We're not here as often as we'd like.'

Edward said, 'Perhaps that's why we've found it difficult at times. We miss out on some village events and we're not always invited to others.'

'Oh . . . ' said Clive, shifting on his seat.

Patricia smiled. 'We'd like to retire here. Then we would be able to join in more.'

Clive rose. 'I'm sure that's a long way off. Anyway, retirement's not all it's cracked up to be. You'll have to excuse me, I must see how Rachel's getting on.'

Rachel was sitting next to Julie Oliphant—they were discussing the position of litter bins along the main village street. Clive sat down next to Rachel. When the conversation petered out, he said: 'I think Patricia and Edward feel excluded. I suppose we ought to make an effort to be more neighbourly and ensure they get invited to everything.'

'They're not very organised, though, are they, said Rachel. 'They didn't arrive until after eleven and they forgot to bring a bottle. We couldn't rely on them to be much help when work needs to be done.'

Clive said, 'I feel a bit guilty about it, though.'

Someone had turned up the music and several couples were gyrating to 1970s disco numbers. The group of farmers and their wives joined in—the dancing restrained and stylish. Patricia led Edward back onto the dance floor. This time they abandoned themselves to the music, swaying and twirling, stomping and flinging their arms about, but always in time with the music. Every eye in the hall was on them. Rachel, sitting on her own (Clive was not a dancer), envied their energy, and felt some of her own drain away. The other dancers seemed to have lost some of their rhythm—their efforts feeble in comparison with the Robinsons'. As Rachel glanced round the hall she noticed as if for the first time how old and tired everyone looked. The few young people of the village were enjoying their own no doubt more exciting celebration elsewhere.

Patricia and Edward, she could see, looked more youthful than ever. Patricia's eyes sparkled and Edward was ogling his wife as she swayed sinuously from side to side. Rachel felt tired and upset and wished she could go home. Memories of a wonderful New Years' Eve party she had attended while at university stole into her mind, contrasting with the current, woeful evening. Combing her hair in front of the mirror in the ladies lavatory, she hardly recognised herself. Her face seemed even more lined and haggard than usual. When she re-entered the hall Clive was sitting stolidly on the same chair. Rachel felt a stab of discontent— she wondered if she should have left him years ago, when the opportunity had arisen.

Clive looked at his watch and turned on the radio. They listened to the chimes of Big Ben; another New Year seen in. He gave Rachel a peck on the cheek: he could see she looked tired—he felt weary himself. 'Auld Lang Syne' was sung, and everyone wished each other a Happy New Year. Edward kissed Rachel, his good looks even more evident close up. Most of the men were crowded round Patricia, eager to give her a hug and a kiss. Clive had joined them, Rachel noticed. Patricia seemed to thrive on staying up late: she was looking more elegant and lovely than ever. She accepted the attention of the men gracefully, smiling at each one.

Clive and Rachel decided to leave the bulk of the clearing up until morning. Several people had offered to help, but not the Robinsons, who seemed to have slipped away. Once the lights were switched on (the party had been candlelit), the detritus seemed doubly sordid: half-eaten meals and used wine glasses were scattered amongst soiled napkins and streamers. Food had been dropped on the floor and trodden on. Rachel made a mental note to bring along several refuse sacks for clearing it all away.

The hall was cold and the people who'd agreed to help had not arrived. Clive was muttering bad temperedly to himself when the door opened, revealing Patricia and Edward Robinson, all smiles and friendliness. After the initial greetings they got to work and in an hour or so the room was clean and tidy, the tables ready to be wiped down and carried to the store room, the chairs stacked neatly against the far wall.

Clive turned to Edward. 'I can't thank you enough. Our other helpers must have hangovers.'

'Perhaps they're tired and still in bed,' said Patricia. 'It was a late night for many of them. When you're older it's hard to bounce back.'

Rachel laughed. 'What would you know about that? You're young striplings compared to us.'

Patricia said, 'We have our moments.'

'Perhaps we have more knowledge of old age than you think,' said Edward. 'We believe wisdom and experience to be on a par with youth and beauty.'

Patricia nodded. 'We much prefer talking to older people. You have so many fascinating, life-affirming memories of the past.'

Clive felt rather irritated that he was being included in the older generation. He was sixty-five.

'We'd like to talk to you about the old days in the village,' said Edward. 'Pick your brains about the past. You both went to the village school, didn't you?'

'Yes,' said Clive. 'We've been sweethearts since we were twelve years old.'

Patricia clapped her hands together. 'How lovely.'

'And I bet you could tell us all the village tittle tattle,' said Edward.

'There's no more gossip here than in any village,' said Rachel primly.

'Oh come on,' said Edward. 'I'm sure it's a hotbed of vice and depravity.'

'What on earth makes you say that?' asked Clive.

Patricia put her hand over her mouth and giggled. 'We've heard a few rumours.'

Rachel bridled. 'Not from us you haven't.'

Edward smiled his disarming smile. 'We're planning to write a booklet about the village. Or a book, if there's enough material. Perhaps the shop could sell it, and we'll donate the proceeds to a local charity.'

Rachel and Clive exchanged glances.

'We'll need to include all the juicy bits,' said Patricia. 'Otherwise it might be a bit dry.'

'You'll put local people off buying it,' said Clive.

'I don't think so. Anyway, it's also aimed at tourists,' countered Edward. 'We've already begun research in the local archives. There are some great old maps and photographs, but little in the way of social history. We'd like to talk to the older residents, including yourselves. Every contribution would be fully acknowledged.'

Rachel could feel her antagonism to the idea ebb away: Edward was very persuasive. People didn't have to talk about themselves and their ancestors unless they wanted to, she supposed. She herself had nothing to hide . . . except, she remembered, Uncle Irvin and his fraudulent cheques. There was no reason why the Robinsons should find out about that.

'A penny for them,' said Patricia.

'I suppose we could make a list of people you ought to talk to,' said Clive.

'And have a word with everyone to reassure them it's all right,' added Rachel.

'Excellent!' said Patricia. 'Come round for tea and we'll discuss it further.'

The Robinsons' sitting room was beautifully decorated in William Morris wallpaper and there was a fitted woollen carpet partially covered with antique rugs. The armchairs and sofa were luxurious. Tea arrived in china cups with saucers.

'What a transformation!' said Clive. 'The people who lived here before you did nothing to the place. You've made it really elegant and comfortable.'

'I've compiled a list for you,' said Rachel, handing over a print-out. 'There are eleven older people and three middle-aged, including us. I've told most of them that you'll be in touch.'

Edward's eyes twinkled. 'Thank you Rachel, that's very kind of you. We'll interview them all.'

Patricia came in carrying a plate of biscuits. 'Can we record you today?' she asked.

'I suppose that would be all right,' said Clive. 'I'm not sure we have anything interesting to say.'

When they had finished tea Edward took a small Dictaphone from his pocket. He switched it on and laid it carefully on the coffee table in front of Clive and Rachel. The Robinsons began by asking simple questions: how long had Clive and Rachel lived in the village? (always, except when they'd been at university); what did they do for a living? (they were newly retired); which house did they live in? (Moor View Cottage). Then the questions concentrated on their school days: when they fell in love; the strictness of the teacher and their parents. The questions came thick and fast, and Rachel felt herself losing track of her answers. Inevitably, they asked about notorious ancestors and Rachel found herself explaining about Uncle Irvin. Patricia and Edward's eyes held her: she found she could not look away. Her mouth seemed to be independent of the rest of her and that part of her brain which still reasoned wondered if they had put something in the tea.

Clive, transfixed, watched his wife spill the beans. When the Robinsons turned to him he steeled himself to be discreet, but it was no good, he was soon telling them about an incident in the pub several years before when his neighbour, Jim Fellowes, had hospitalised a young lad as a result of a fight over his daughter. Then he was explaining how funds from the village fête had gone missing—everyone knew who had taken the money but no one could prove it. His own dodgy ancestors included a sheep rustler transported to Australia, and his Great Grandfather William had been a conscientious objector during World War I.

The click of the Dictaphone being switched off brought Rachel and Clive abruptly back to the present. Edward and Patricia smiled at them contentedly. They were slightly dishevelled, Rachel noticed, their clothes and hair disarranged.

'Thank you so much,' said Patricia. 'That was very . . . useful.'

'What just happened?' asked Clive.

Edward frowned. 'What do you mean?'

'Will you use some of the interview in the book?' asked Rachel.

'I should think so!' said Patricia. 'You were very forthcoming.'

Rachel swallowed. 'The thing is, I'm not entirely comfortable . . . '

'Don't worry so much,' said Patricia. 'We'll only make use of stuff that is . . . relevant.'

As soon as they could, Clive and Rachel made their excuses and left. When they arrived at their cottage Rachel burst into tears. They both felt tired and upset. Later, after they had taken a nap, Rachel telephoned Patricia.

'I'm not happy about what went on this afternoon. I'd like to rescind that list of people I gave you. Could you return it to me or destroy it?'

'Too late,' said Patricia. 'We've already contacted everyone and made arrangements for interviews.'

'Perhaps I ought to phone and tell them I no longer approve.'

'I think you'll find that the villagers are very enthusiastic about being in our book. You'll just sound odd if you speak to them now.'

Rachel knew that Patricia was right.

Clive said, 'I don't know exactly what they're about but I feel it in my water they're up to no good.'

'But what can we do about it?' asked Rachel.

On market day in the local town Rachel bumped into Patricia, elegant in a long sheepskin coat, matching hat and gloves and high-heeled suede boots. Rachel, bundled up against the January cold, felt particularly frumpy and old. She had been unwell lately and the icy weather seemed to have reached her bones and joints, making her ache all over. Clive was also below par—like many of the older villagers he was suffering from a lingering cold.

'Hello,' said Patricia. 'The market's wonderful isn't it? I always buy my meat and vegetables here.'

'How's the book coming along?' asked Rachel warily.

'Very well! We've planned the chapters and decided which of us is writing each section. I think we've enough material now for a decent-sized volume.' Her gaze travelled up and down Rachel. 'You're not looking well, if I may say so. Upsetting yourself over things you have no need to is always bad for your health. Edward and I are very experienced at interviewing older people.'

When she got home Rachel told Clive about meeting Patricia.

'I've been thinking,' he said, in between blowing his nose and coughing. 'We could try beating them at their own game.'

'What do you mean?'

'Let's organise another interview—we'll tell them we've had second thoughts and don't want to miss out on the fun. I'll explain the rest later . . .'

Clive and Rachel waited in the Robinsons' sitting room. A coal fire burned cheerfully in the small Victorian grate. They had arrived soon after lunch (earlier than arranged) and turned down the offer of tea or coffee. Patricia and Edward disappeared into the kitchen and Clive and Rachel could hear a muffled conversation. Eventually Edward appeared carrying the Dictaphone; Patricia followed with a jug of water and two glasses on a tray. 'I'm sure you're thirsty,' she said, setting the tray down on the coffee table. 'We're so pleased you've agreed to a second interview. I don't think you'll regret it. We've had some interest in the book from a local publisher, so it may have a wider readership than we originally envisaged.'

'That's good news,' said Clive.

'Shall we begin?' Patricia's eyes shone with anticipation. 'It was so enlightening last time.'

Edward put the Dictaphone on the table. 'Today,' he said, 'we'll concentrate on recollections of your teenage and young adult years. That should get the juices flowing.'

The Robinsons regarded Rachel and Clive expectantly. Rachel thought that they looked in even ruder health than usual; almost indecently so when compared to the ailing older folk of the village. She glanced at Clive and could see that he was making a good job of controlling his nerves. She poured out some water and she and Clive raised the glasses to their lips. . . .

Edward and Patricia began to ask questions, innocuous at first—about Clive's time at secondary school—and then more intrusive. They were sitting on the edge of their seats, Patricia rocking back and forth. Edward's eyes bored into Rachel's. She felt the intoxicating power of him and was for a moment afraid.

'What happened at the dances in the village hall?' asked Edward. 'Was there not a great deal of "courting", of fumbling, of groping, and . . . more? Tell me about it.'

Rachel tried to remember what Clive had told her to say.

'The dances were a real release for us teenagers—there was little else for us to do. They were somewhere we could meet up. One night it all got out of hand. None of the parents were prepared to supervise, you see.

The boys had smuggled in some bottles of cider. They decided it would be fun to swap partners and it ended up in a kind of orgy. Just about everyone was involved. Boy with boy, girl with girl—everything you can think of. Several girls got pregnant—two had abortions, the rest were forced to give their babies away. It was all hushed up.'

Rachel saw Edward run his hand up the inside of Patricia's thigh. Edward asked Clive: 'Were you and Rachel present at the orgy?'

'Oh yes,' he said. 'We were willing participants. In fact it was Rachel's idea that we join in. There were quite a few teenagers in the village at that time and everyone was present. Rachel and I were the youngest. Sometimes we meet up with the others and reminisce.'

The Robinsons listened hungrily.

'We re-enact it,' said Rachel. 'We take it in turns visiting each other's homes. Anything goes.' She turned and looked at Clive. To her surprise he clasped her hand and squeezed it.

'That's not all,' continued Rachel. 'You should see what happens after the fête! The Rev Shawcross holds a Black Mass in the Methodist chapel. Even the children are there. He sacrifices Jeff Goodall's chickens. . . . '

Patricia was sitting on Edward's lap: Her skirt had ridden up to her waist and they were both moaning with pleasure.

' . . . and we take it in turns to curse Jesus and all his followers. I don't need to tell you what happens next . . . '

Clive stood up abruptly, his knees bumping against the coffee table. The water jug rocked and toppled over, its contents spilling onto the rug. 'I don't know exactly who . . . or what . . . you are,' he said quietly, 'but I can assure you that everything we've told you today is rubbish. You've been getting your kicks under false pretences, I'm afraid.' He pointed at the glasses on the tray. 'We didn't drink the water, you see. . . .

'There was no orgy. The village dances were fun, but they never got out of hand. What folk got up to in private was their own business. You don't seem to realise that we're friendly with each other here, most of the time, the same as in any village. There are arguments and disputes, but at the end of the day we're a community. And there are certainly no Black Masses in the chapel.' He laughed 'I can't believe you fell for that.'

The Robinsons looked at each other. Rachel thought she could see in their faces a ghastly deflation and a profound weariness. She almost felt sorry for them.

Age begets wisdom, Edward and Patricia had said. Maybe old age would be something she and Clive could endure—even enjoy—together. It would involve, she realised, an acceptance of mortality. That should not be too difficult. After all, they had, in their own small way, lived through so much.

Honeysuckle Cottage would soon, she felt sure, be for sale. Perhaps another young couple might buy the house, or a family with children. . . .

Rachel and Clive let themselves out of the front door and, arm in arm, made their way back home along the village street.

SHOWTIME

I made quite an exhibition of myself.
I'm usually so shy I fade into the background, take my place at the end of the queue, stand in the corner of the room watching what other people do. It's not that I fear the limelight, but I try to avoid being vulgar or pushy. I expect it's because I was brought up by Methodists. Any displays of youthful *joie de vivre* were dismissed as 'showing off'.

Diffidence, although undoubtedly a curse, is also a form of narcissism: it says, '*I* do not need to join in: *you* can make all the noise. *I'm* fascinating despite my passivity.' Shyness became for me, I suppose, pathological, but at a deeper level I crave attention and have an ego as ugly as the squat chapel in which my father preaches.

But, a week ago I *was* vulgar and pushy, as crazed and crass as any cheap wannabe.

The reading resembled a dull, pretentious talent contest—each poet desperate to delight the audience and outdo the others. Every drop of emotion was wrung from the mediocre material, every gesture imbued with empty significance. Only Tom Pugin rose above the sweaty fawning: it helped that, in my opinion, he was by far the best poet there. Afterwards I stood in line (at the back, of course) waiting with the other fans for him to sign my copy of his latest collection. He smiled graciously as each of us placed *Blue Harvest* in front of him: his agent leaned against the wall, jiggling the change in his pocket, looking through the window into the darkness.

It was my turn and Pugin smiled without really looking at me.

'Who should I inscribe it to?'

'Your greatest fan,' I said, and burst into tears. I leaned forward and touched his fingers. 'You are beautiful.'

The agent, roused to action, slapped my hand away. 'No touching. I think you should leave.'

'Not until he signs my book,' I said, dashing away my tears.

The small crowd of dignitaries and fans remaining in the room stared at the spectacle of the agent's attempts to drag me away. I came close to kneeing him in the groin.

Tom Pugin sighed. 'Leave her alone, Mark.'

Pugin said 'Do you have any idea how often I get propositioned on these tours? I'm very tired, we've been on the road for four weeks. I'm sure you're usually a nice young woman but I'm going back to my hotel room to crash out. We're travelling to Kidderminster tomorrow.'

He signed the book and handed it to me. 'I'm pleased you enjoy my verse,' he said kindly.

Before the agent could stop me I leaned forward and kissed Pugin on the lips, then I strode through the open doors into the square. I looked around—no one was following me. I walked along the rain-spattered streets to the suburb where I live.

Back in my flat I thought about what had happened: I hadn't planned to act in that way. It was wholly spontaneous, an outburst of affection for a man I admired—both for his poetry and his looks. I must confess that I was intoxicated by my behaviour: there were advantages, it seemed, to showiness, to the expression of emotion in public.

That night I dreamed I was pursued by Tom Pugin's agent across the cobbles of the town square. The clock on the church tower said 12. He was mouthing at me, but I couldn't hear what he was saying. Pugin appeared beside him, carrying a book of his poetry, and I ran towards the King's Head. 'We could easily catch you,' the poet called out, 'but chasing is more fun.'

When I awoke I couldn't for the life of me understand why I had run away from him.

At the office on Monday, Katy, my supervisor, reprimanded me for daydreaming. I was thinking about Pugin, wondering if I could engineer a meeting. It would mean travelling to another of his readings—one taking place in a town with a railway station (I haven't a car). It began to seem like hard work, and there was always a chance the agent would recognise me and have me barred or thrown out. It could be an expensive waste of time. In any case I had kissed Pugin, and he made it clear there was nothing else on offer.

I took out my phone and searched for up and coming events. There was another literary evening at the Town Hall the following weekend, with the novelist Mike O'Hare. You'll know his work—a kind of light, hip, comedy, showy but forgettable. I had read his last novel, *Paper Plates*, the previous month. He seemed to have produced a new title, *China Teacups*, in record time, riding the crest of the wave.

In his photographs O'Hare looked older than Tom Pugin, but he had a pleasing face nevertheless. I bought a ticket to the show and realised that this time I could plan my performance rather than rely on spur of the moment inspiration. Or would spontaneity be more exciting? Perhaps I should leave it to happenstance. For the next few days I tried not to think of it.

Besides, I had other things to worry about. After lunch I noticed that the office clocks were wrong. At first they were fast by a few minutes, then by more than a quarter of an hour. By Tuesday morning my alarm clock at home was half an hour fast, according to the time broadcast on the radio news. Every clock in the house, including my wrist watch and those on my phone and computer, was affected. When I arrived at work I asked my colleague Sarah about the clocks, but she claimed there was nothing wrong with them.

I tried altering my watch, but the hands sprung forward immediately. It grew increasingly difficult to stick to my routine. By Wednesday morning the radio and television were affected. I arrived at work before the doors were unlocked. I was unable to determine the time of my lunch hour, and found myself hastily eating a chocolate bar at my desk. This earned me a formal reprimand from Katy (for 'unprofessional behaviour'). When I asked her if a sandwich would have been more acceptable, she said, 'You're already skating on thin ice, don't make it even more difficult for yourself.'

On Thursday I was cannier. Carrying a bundle of files, I climbed the back stairs to the office. This time, Katy didn't notice my erratic timekeeping, and assumed I had been visiting the old records section on the floor below.

On Friday I could not but think of the literary evening with Mike O'Hare. He would be reading from his latest work and answering questions. Perhaps I should formulate some deeply intrusive, probing queries? But that would be unlikely to create much of a spectacle for the audience to enjoy.

I was learning to tell the time by the position of the sun, the arrival of dusk, the darkness of the night. In the evening, just as twilight began to fall, I went for a long walk through the suburbs, before most curtains were closed. Downstairs windows framed tableaux of family life. A breeze stirred the branches of trees which grew through the pavements of the better-class streets, presaging a return to more unsettled weather. I longed for a life more complicated than my own.

That night, as the storm raged outside, I dreamt again of Tom Pugin. I knew it was Pugin, although his hair was combed over his face. He was giving a reading in the library, his agent acting as his bodyguard, pistol in hand. Pugin was dressed in hippy clothes, loon-style trousers and a cheesecloth shirt. Slowly and carefully I lay down and slithered across the floor, aiming to reach and kiss his sandaled feet. The audience, seemingly hypnotised, watched my progress with unblinking eyes. Pugin read his poem 'The Reptile'. On the wall was a clock and I realised there was no way of knowing if it showed the right time.

As I reached Pugin's feet, the agent rose from his chair and pointed his gun at my head. 'Put your hands behind your back,' he ordered. But I could feel that I no longer had limbs, only a long sinuous body. My forked tongue flicked over Pugin's toes: he did not move his foot away.

I spent Saturday afternoon searching for a dress to complement my blue velvet jacket. Eventually I found one in the shop on the High Street which sells 'vintage collectables'. The dress was an animal print; snakeskin—a fortuitous cast-off—long and clinging. Early in the evening I put on the dress and jacket, and dug out a pair of high-heeled shoes. I took a taxi to the King's Head, ordered two Martini cocktails and drank them in quick succession. Across the square, the Town Hall lights blazed—a few people were gathered outside. Assuming the event was imminent, I left the pub and joined them.

Standing at the back of the queue was a middle-aged man in a duffel coat, carrying a plastic shopping bag.

'We're early,' he said, 'but it's worth it to get the best seats.' He took his hand out of his pocket and popped a sweet in his mouth. 'It should be a good evening. Have you read all his books?'

'No,' I said.

'You should. He's a great stylist as well as a fine comic writer.'

I looked at the ground, then the clear sky. I thought about giving up on the reading and going home.

'My name's Keith, by the way.'

He held out his hand and I was forced to shake it.

The queue had built up behind us. Keith chatted about Mike O'Hare until eventually the doors opened and, as he had suggested, we were able to sit on the front row. I chose one of the less desirable seats, at the far end, hoping to deter Keith, but he sat down next to me without asking if he could.

'It's quite exciting,' he said, pulling a handful of slim volumes out of the carrier bag. 'These are a complete run of O'Hare's first editions. I'm hoping he'll sign them for me. A signature will make them more valuable.'

The hall echoed with loud chatter. I imagined Mike O'Hare behind the scenes, the adrenaline beginning to kick in.

'That's a nice outfit, if I may say so,' said Keith. 'Perhaps I should have dressed up. Not that I own any evening clothes.'

He had bought a programme. A close-up of Mike O'Hare's face graced the front cover, the definition so sharp I could see each silver thread in his hair.

Keith put on a mock Irish accent. 'He's a fine looking fellow. I expect that's why there are more than a few ladies in tonight.'

He laughed, then took out his bag of sweets and offered me one. I shook my head.

'You don't say much,' he said.

I looked up at the clock on the wall. It said 9.15, although I knew the performance was scheduled to begin at 7.30. The stage was set up as a facsimile of an Olde Worlde library, with books on shelves, a leather sofa and a standard lamp.

The house lights dimmed and Mike O'Hare walked onto the stage. He smiled graciously as the audience burst into applause. In real life, he wore glasses. He sat on the sofa, crossed his legs and began his rather banal opening speech:

'Thank you for coming this evening. I expect some of you have travelled rather a long way, others not so far. You're all very welcome.

'I've visited this town before, on a day-trip with my family. There are some fine buildings, the church and the Town Hall especially. But you'll know that already, those of you who live here.

'I've been invited along tonight to read from my latest novel, *China Teacups*. I'm going to read three longish extracts, and then I'll answer any questions you may have. The first piece is from the opening chapter—in fact it's the very beginning of the book. So here goes . . . '

He opened *China Teacups*, found his place, and as he began to read Keith whispered in my ear: 'I don't know about you but I find it difficult to concentrate when someone is reading aloud.'

I agree with Keith, as it happens—I'd much rather read a book than hear it, even when it's read by the author. Keith popped another sweet in his mouth. The aroma of pear drops hung in the air. 'You haven't told me your name,' he said.

I put my index finger to my lips and shushed him. The audience was laughing at the jokes in the book and O'Hare did not seem to have noticed Keith's whisperings. Keith put on a hurt face and took refuge in looking through his pile of first editions, randomly opening each one.

Uncrossing his legs and leaning forward, O'Hare gestured with his free hand. Despite his enthusiasm I found that I was not really listening. I glanced up at the clock. Its hands were whirling round the pivot, a black blur against the white of the dial. When I dragged my eyes away, after what felt like only a few seconds, I was surprised to find O'Hare already finishing the last excerpt. As he closed the book, the audience broke into wild applause. To my mind it resembled an Evangelist meeting.

'Any questions?' he asked, when the noise had died down. There was a brief silence. 'Come on, don't be shy!'

Several hands were raised. O'Hare pointed to a woman near the back.

'When did you know you wanted to be a writer?'

Mike O'Hare laughed. 'I often get asked that one. I knew from a very early age. As a child I read all the time. When I was seven I wrote stories for my brothers. . . . '

The questions were as dull and sycophantic as I had feared. The hands on the clock whirled faster.

I stood up and climbed onto the stage. I took the toy gun from my bag and pointed it at O'Hare. He shrank back on the sofa. I could hear Keith shouting, 'Don't be a fool!' A woman screamed. Keeping the gun trained on O'Hare I half-turned to the audience.

'Everyone keep calm. This is a performance—"Fire and Brimstone". No one will be harmed by this installation.'

I took out a bag of glitter and sprinkled it over the stage.

'Sparkle, sparkle, quite a show
Tell them things they do not know.
Challenge their complacency
All from watching little me
Sparkle, sparkle, quite a show
Tell them things they do not know.'

'For instance, Sir,' I said, pointing to a man sitting in the middle of the front row, 'you are desperate to be a hero, but you haven't the balls. And you, Madam, if you don't make it to the ladies in the next thirty seconds, you'll wet yourself.

'Ask yourself why you are here. You are worshipping a false prophet. Mike O'Hare's writing is nothing but a cheap magic trick—a technical exercise.'

I heard a gasp. O'Hare attempted to stand up but his legs betrayed him.

'Is that gun real?' he asked.

'As real as you are,' I replied.

'What do you want?'

'Don't you get bored with this? The endless, empty self-promotion? Spouting self-satisfied drivel you think people want to hear? I'm giving you the opportunity to do something extraordinary. Something you'll be proud of for the rest of your life. You can take the chance and . . . '

'I don't believe it *is* real,' he said.

Keith chose that moment to rugby-tackle me to the ground. He lay across my body in the most ungainly fashion. I managed to keep hold of the gun and pointed it at him. He grabbed for it, but I kicked him in the head and he fell back. I crawled from under his dead weight, then slithered across the stage towards O'Hare, my legs sheathed in my skin-tight, snakeskin dress.

'You're the only one who can stop me,' I whispered. 'Think about the newspaper headlines. It would be fabulous publicity. You could write a book about it. Call it *Showtime*.'

I looked up at the clock. It said 9.15. There was no way of knowing if the time was right.

THE DREAMING

Dusk is some way off and I stand at the bar, waiting to be served. I've been here often on my way home from work—It's half-empty on early summer evenings, and the staff are efficient and not averse to passing the time in conversation. I like the cool pale green of its walls; the lack of music; the unmatched tables and chairs.

I'm usually alone when I come here and sometimes I indulge in people-watching: I'm a connoisseur of eccentrics and their friends. They're more common than you might think, especially in obscure little bars like this one. Take the man sitting in the alcove, with the long slicked-back hair and the brown pin-striped suit. His deeply-grooved face is expertly made up, and two young women are hanging on his words, their gaze never leaving him. I'd like to listen in but if I stand any closer he'll realise what I'm doing, so I have no idea what is making him so attractive to his companions. Perhaps he's a good talker. For all I know he has the conversational skills of Oscar Wilde. One thing among many I've learnt recently, which goes against the axioms of the great man, is not to judge by appearances.

Beer is something I'm supposed to have given up, but as it's a special occasion, I'm risking a pint. I'd forgotten how good it tastes. I agreed to stop drinking alcohol as a condition of being accepted for the course.

Tonight, all my self-denial and hard work should pay off—although there's no fail-safe way of knowing exactly what will happen. Things have a habit of unfolding in their own manner. But you can heal, and influence the future, I do believe that. If I didn't then I wouldn't be here now.

It's been a beautiful afternoon, very warm, with a slight breeze to leaven the heat. Now, in the evening, it's cooler. I drink the beer—the magical draft is swiftly absorbed. I am the most relaxed I've been all day.

It's brewed by a couple I met at a trade fair. I was there to support my friend Howard, who was pedalling his latest invention (a silent juicer). The couple, Phil and Mary, were handing out free samples. I drank one and talked with them about the labels on their bottles. It's one of my areas of expertise. They call their beer 'Goathland' (they moved to London from North Yorkshire) and brand it with a picture of a goat. The label is a poor piece of graphic design, and the name awful, but it seems not to have held them back—last year they won 'craft beer of the year'. I have invited them tonight, and they promised they would come. Their beer is truly the drink of the gods.

I'm hoping that all my friends and most of my relatives will approve of my new direction. It has to be better than working in advertising. Prudence has outweighed enthusiasm so far and I have refrained from resigning from my job, but the soulless promotion of pointless products will not detain me for long. I have discovered that I have better things to do with my life.

Suddenly I'm so excited my fingers are tingling and I can't stand still. I finish the beer and order another. The barman says 'I thought you had an ulcer or something. You usually drink water.'

'Today's special . . . ' I say, but he's moved on to serve someone else.

Freddie from work walks in. He seems tense and I offer to buy him a beer, which he accepts, rubbing his hands.

'So, tonight's the night!' he says, slapping me on the back so hard that I nearly spill my pint. 'Who else is coming?'

'A select crowd,' I answer. 'I've arranged for us to use the back room. It's quite small, so we can't fit many in.'

'You're being very mysterious about this.'
'You'll find out about it soon enough.'
'It's a surprise for everyone?'
'That's the idea.'

The others begin to arrive: Margaret from the art studio we use for most of our campaigns, Jonathan Hallows (my old school friend) and his sister Clarissa. There is my brother Leo, Davy from the squash club, my neighbour Miss Collins (I don't know her first name) and Phil and Mary who brew the beer. When they are all assembled I introduce them to each other: there is much frank curiosity and good-natured joshing at my expense. Then I excuse myself. After a word with the barman I let myself into the back room. The curtains are closed and ten chairs have been arranged in two rows facing an armchair at the front. It's warm and stuffy and in the evening light shining through the thin green curtains the room looks as if it is at the bottom of the sea.

I open my bag and paint the symbols on my face, then change into the costume. It has been made for me by a skilled seamstress, working from photographs in a book. I have tried to make everything as authentic as possible, but the outfit is a composite, the embroidery her own design. I carefully tie the laces of the tunic and arrange the sleeves and trousers. Even though I have rehearsed this moment many times, I am fearful. I light a joint and inhale deeply.

I sit on the armchair, and as I smoke the joint down to the roach the door opens and the invitees file in. There is some suppressed laughter as they see me, and several of them knowingly sniff the air. I begin to tap on the little drum with my fingers. Moira, my course leader, slips into the room and sits on the last empty chair.

I close my eyes and sing the song of the reindeer herders. The room falls silent. Before long the trance enters me, the drum a heartbeat, the song a conduit for the spirits. I stand up and begin the dance. Soon the sweat drips from my face and armpits, producing dark stains on my costume.

The spirits of the wolves and wild reindeer guide me into the deep trance. Now the healing can begin. I open my eyes. Through the eyes of the wolf I see the pain, the heart-ache of my friends. Freddie, the spirits tell me, is suffering from a malaise of the soul. His case is the worst. I put a hand on his shoulder and whisper the incantation. His eyes open wide, his chair scrapes back and he stumbles from the room. I work my way round the chairs. Miss Collins is lonely; Leo is permanently stressed; Margaret has an abusive partner. Phil and Mary are last. I see that their business is in trouble and I bring out the telling bones. I crouch down and spin the bones on the floor, they fall outwards, leaving a rough circle at their centre. 'All will be well,' I say to them. 'There is symmetry.'

I feel the spirits retreating. I sit in the armchair, my head resting on my chest. The drum is discarded, the dusk advancing so that the translucent green light is gradually giving way to semi-darkness. Moira stands up and begins to clap. The bewildered audience follows her lead.

I find the energy to raise my head, open my eyes. Moira comes to the front and congratulates me on my graduation. 'A competent performance,' she whispers, 'but cut out the beer next time. It drains the energy.'

The invitees file out, avoiding my eyes, and I change back into my everyday clothes. I pack the costume into my holdall with the drum, remove the grease-paint with cold cream and go back into the bar. Freddie is halfway through another pint, he eyes me warily.

'I don't know what you think you were doing in there.'

'Attempting to help,' I say.

His disdain is obvious. He turns his back on me.

Phil says, 'At least you tried. Mary and I appreciate it.' He grasps my shoulder briefly.

The others are drinking at the far end of the bar. My brother moves his hand minutely from side to side in an acknowledgment I gather he doesn't want the others to see. I take a deep breath and join them. It is awkward; no-one mentions what has happened.

The next Monday I resign. Ian, my boss, calls me into his office.

'Freddie tells me you've got yourself involved in some form of crackpot magic. Do you really think you can make a living at it? We have noticed that your mind has been wandering off the job for the last few months.'

'I hope I can do some good in the world.'

'Good doesn't put food on the table,' answers Ian. 'How will you manage?'

'I already have a few bookings. I expect to pick up more by word of mouth.'

'I wish you the very best of luck,' says Ian. 'You'll need it.'

My first professional engagement is at the home of Caroline and her mother, Edith. They live in a Victorian house in Wimbledon in old-fashioned shabby gentility. I imagine they have a small private income inadequate for their needs. The ornate plaster ceiling of their enormous drawing room is discoloured and cracked, and the sofas and chairs are threadbare. A yellow-eyed cat sprawls on a cushion. Despite the fact that it is another sunny day, the curtains are closed.

I placed an advert in the *Evening Standard*: Edith telephoned to make the appointment. She did not want to tell me what the trouble was. When I arrive, Caroline shows me into the drawing room, then goes out to make tea. I begin a conversation with Edith—she is hard of hearing. I ask her how long she has lived in the house and eventually she understands.

'I was born here. Before the war. I'm eighty-one.'

'Do you like living here?'

'Not much. I haven't any choice, have I? I'd rather live in the countryside. Suffolk, or Norfolk.'

Caroline returns with the tea in bone china cups with saucers. I set mine down on the rickety occasional table beside me.

'I need to change,' I say, indicating my bag. 'Can I use your bathroom?'

I catch the horrified look which passes between them.

'Or another room?'

'You can divest yourself of your garments in the entrance hall,' says

Caroline. 'We'll close the drawing room door so your modesty will be preserved.'

I put on the costume and paint the symbols on my face. I take out the drum and begin to tap on it. When I open the door into the drawing room the ladies are sitting together on the sofa. Edith coughs.

'We are plagued by a spirit, Mr Carmichael. It is entirely malevolent. For a number of reasons we can't move house, so we need an exorcism of sorts. We cannot abide the female vicar that has been foisted on us by the Bishop, so we are relying on you.'

I nod, close my eyes and begin the dance. Edith sits expectantly, Caroline leans back on the cushions. I sing the song of the reindeer herders but the trance will not come. I am frozen in the gaze of Edith, the surliness of Caroline: the joint lies unsmoked in the bottom of my bag. As a last resort I stare at the sprawled cat and gradually its yellow eyes become the eyes of a wolf. I enter the body and mind of the wolf and at last dissolve into the sacred trance. The spirit of the reindeer flows around me and the drum is the life-beat of the tundra. I dance and dance and the sweating begins. I look at the two women, see the murderous impulse in the face of one, the tricks and pranks of a desperate woman who wishes to frighten her mother to death.

I bring out the divination bones, crouch down and spin them. They fall here and there on the carpet.

'You will live a long life, Edith. At the end you'll be at peace with the world.'

I look up at Caroline. 'You must learn to be patient, otherwise there will be trouble for you. You still have time to mend your ways.'

For an instant I see the anger rise in her, then her features compose themselves into their habitual mask.

'I'd like you to leave now' Caroline says. 'Mother is upset.'

'I'm perfectly all right,' says Edith.

I lie down on the floor and close my eyes. When I open them again, Edith is standing over me. Caroline is nowhere to be seen.

'Has it worked?' she asks. 'Will the evil spirit return?'

I say 'I don't think so,' although in truth I'm not sure what will happen.

'Here is your money,' Edith says, handing over a bundle of notes. 'I've enjoyed meeting you.'

I change in the entrance hall and let myself out. On my way home I fall asleep in the tube train and miss my station.

Leo comes to see me at my flat. He asks if I'm okay.

'I'm fine,' I say, 'I'm averaging four consultations a week.'

'I've no idea how much you're charging.'

'Enough. I live frugally.'

'Well, if you need something to tide you over . . .'

'How's work?' I ask.

'They've advertised for an assistant. It should take some of the pressure off me.' He pauses for a moment. 'Have you seen Freddie? He's a changed man.'

Seeing my face he nudges me in the ribs. 'Don't flatter yourself. I'm sure it's something that would've happened anyway.'

I keep myself pure. I forgo alcohol. I smoke and practice the trance. I live at one remove from my friends and relatives. Word trickles out and I have plenty of work.

The most heart-breaking clients are those who are terminally ill. I can't always cure them, but I help them accept death as the next step along the way. In the jargon of my former job, I manage expectations.

A broken relationship, or the loss of a loved one, is the most common reason for a consultation. Often I see new love on the horizon, and steer the clients towards it. Not all of my consultations are successful. One man loved his dead wife so much he wanted me to help her manifest in the room. I danced and sweated and sang, but still she would not come. He was angry that he had not seen her. She spoke through me, told him he must let her go. He refused to pay my fee.

Soon I am so busy that my life spirit drains away. I am exhausted. I avoid bookings for a few days and sleep, walk in the park. It's late autumn—the leaves brown and curl and scatter beneath the trees. Geese swim on the pond. I live for each moment, each hour, each day. I meet my brother and he tells me I look tired.

'This new direction of yours doesn't seem to suit you.'

'It's my life, Leo.'

'I'm glad you're taking some time off.'

After a week I am ready to resume. My energies are renewed, and all seems well. I feel the need for company and revisit the little bar near the park. I ask for sparkling water and a young woman approaches me. I've seen her there before.

'You're the Shaman guy,' she says. 'I may have a job for you.'

I hand her one of my cards.

'My sister's stopped talking. I mean, she doesn't talk to anyone. We took her to a therapist but he hasn't helped. We don't know what else to do. You're our last resort.'

Later, she phones and makes an appointment.

'I'm Shelly,' she says. 'My sister is Farrah. We're relying on you.'

They live in a London-brick terrace in Islington. Shelly answers the door and ushers me into the living room. In an armchair sits a pale woman in a dressing gown. She makes no sign that she has seen me. I go up to the bathroom and paint my face, change into the costume. On my return I drum, sing and dance. This time the spirits come quickly, the wolf looks at Farrah but there is nothing to see except a haggard young woman in a chair.

The heartbeat of the drum is strong, and for the first time the dreaming comes. I am in the forest, I can smell deer in the distance. Farrah sits in a chair; next to her stands Shelly, lithe and beautiful. Farrah has a gag in her mouth; tears spill from her eyes. The deer call me—I am hungry—but I know I must stay for Farrah's sake. She is dying of a lack of beauty. Shelly strokes her hair, and I see that she is fond of her sister, but she cannot see the gag.

Shelly says, 'Speak to me.'
Farrah's tears roll down her face and drip onto the ground.
I pad closer. I say, 'Shelly, you must remove the gag.'
'There is no gag.'
'I can't do it. It must be you.'
'If she speaks, what will she say?'
'That's up to her.'
'I want to protect her.'
'Don't you want her to be free?'
Shelley stands behind the chair and unfastens the gag she cannot see.
Farrah rubs her mouth and looks at me fearfully.
'Your sister will look after you.'
The two women return to the world. I am called by the scent of the deer and with my pack I chase them through the forest.
Later, I wake, the tang of fresh blood on my breath. Farrah strokes my hair.
Shelly says, 'We were going to call for an ambulance.'
'I'm all right,' I say, sitting up on the sofa.
'The dreaming was deep,' says Farrah.
Shelly's mouth hangs open.
I change in the bathroom, hearing muffled conversation from the room below. When I return, Shelly says, 'Farrah's getting dressed. Then we're going for a walk.'
At home I sleep.

I sleep for a long time, then go to the park. It's a crisp afternoon, there is still ice at the edge of the pond. I breathe in the cold air. Ahead are the trees, bare branched, their arms open. I walk through the wood, winding around the girth of the tree trunks, shuffling in the deep litter of fallen leaves. But it is all ashes. I feel nothing, and can no longer make things happen. Where is the beauty in this world? The dreaming has entered my bones.

I am the wolf who dreams in dreams. Freedom is the forest, with my brothers, hunting under the moon.

But I am tied to the world with a gossamer thread, spun by those who would keep me here. I am called from the dreaming to dance and heal.

'Where are my brothers?' I cry. I am sick, and in the dreaming the wolves leave the forest, following the reindeer. I am abandoned, a captive of my own heart.

In despair I descend the thread, bite it through and fall into the forest. My brothers return to heal me. We sleep beneath the trees, and hunt under the moon.

DEAR JOHN

There are times when something affects you deeply and alters the way you look at the world. It's happened to me on several occasions—when your father and then you were born; so vulnerable yet full of possibilities; and last year when I learned of my illness. But the thing I'm going to tell you about now took place when I was in my late forties and living comfortably and happily, and it grew out of something so simple it took me unawares. For a while I was lost to myself. Time has passed, but I think, and dream, about it still. I'm hoping that if I unburden myself to you, you will, with your scientific training, help me arrange what happened more comfortably in my mind. I've been unwilling to tell anyone about it before, even Peter, who has been my best friend since I was five.

You're too young to remember John. I thought of him as a quiet man, somewhat shy, with hidden depths. I only wish that he had been more forthcoming. I did my best to bring him out of his shell but there was always something that seemed to hold him back. The events that I am about to describe changed my view of him entirely.

We found the letters in the bottom drawer of a filing cabinet in his study.

His personal papers needed looking through before the clearance firm took away his nearly worthless furniture and effects. Anything of value, and there was little enough of that, had been sold at the auction house in town. John's home of thirty years was also to be auctioned, although it could hardly be considered desirable. It was a badly maintained Edwardian terrace and the kitchen and bathroom were damp. Rain had dripped through the roof into the attic, staining the ceiling of the bedroom beneath.

Peter and I were, in the absence of any close family, John's executors. His estate—what there was of it—had been left to a second cousin once removed, an orphan who was only six years old. Her parents were killed in a car crash, and John took pity on the little girl, who was living with her grandparents.

We had two piles of paper—one for discarding and the other for keeping to look through. The pile for discarding was by far the larger of the two.

Peter said, 'Not much to show for a life, Justin. Not much at all.'

I waited until Peter went to the bathroom, then retrieved the slim bundle of letters from the keeping pile and put them in my pocket. I was at that point little more than mildly curious, and Peter might have thought me unnecessarily nosy if I'd read them there and then. They were the only letters John had kept, so they must have been important to him. When Peter returned he got stuck into the filing cabinet and didn't seem to notice that the letters were missing from the pile.

Once we had finished with the papers we moved to John's bedroom, stuffing clothes from the chest of drawers into black plastic bin liners for the charity shop. A flimsy modern wardrobe stood in the far corner; at first I thought it was empty, but when I pulled out the bottom drawer I found a pair of women's shoes. I had always thought John was what they call a 'confirmed bachelor', but the shoes gave me pause for thought. They were gold and had open-toes and sling-backs—the shoes of a young woman. Despite, or perhaps because of, the platform heels, they were sexy and elegant, showing few signs of wear.

I was reluctant to put them in the charity bag, but couldn't think how to explain to Peter why I might want to keep them. Peter is a very down to earth sort of man, things are black and white to him. So I put the shoes in the bag and hoped, in vain as it turned out, that I would be able to retrieve them later.

John had always been a bit of a mystery to us. We were friends because we went to the same school, and I knew he worked as a clerk in the job centre in town, but the rest of his life was a closed book. Even at school he was secretive, and had few friends apart from Peter and me. Like us he hated sport, and we often bunked off and hung out behind the sixth-form building. One thing I knew about John was that he was quietly determined to follow his own path—he didn't much care what other people thought of him. I admired him for that, knowing that it was a quality I lacked. As was expected of us, Peter and I went to university; John left school in the middle of his A levels and got a job in what was then the labour exchange. He stayed there until his death (of a heart attack, at work), never seeking promotion or pastures new.

The three of us met up every few months in the Red Lion, John usually content to listen to Peter and me rabbiting on about our jobs and families, the latest films and exhibitions. He enjoyed classical music, however, and sometimes talked about his occasional attendances at concerts in Manchester and Leeds. We met regularly for twenty-odd years, and John never once mentioned a girlfriend or partner. I assumed he was one of those asexual people who choose not to enter into close relationships. Once or twice I introduced him to single women friends, but he never showed any interest.

When we had finished disposing of John's clothes, we called it a day and went home, each with half of the keeping pile of papers to look through. After dinner I shut myself in my study, opened the briefcase and took out the letters. To be honest I felt quite excited, being about to find out something of John's private life without him being there to put the kybosh on it. I suppose curiosity got the better of me. He must in any case have known the letters would be found.

There were ten of them, nine hand-written in an elegant, forward-sloping script. They seemed to be in date order. Naturally, the letters John must have written in return were missing. At the bottom of the pile was a sealed white envelope, addressed to me. They're in my desk drawer. If you'd be kind enough to fetch them, I'll read them to you.

6th June 1975

Dear John,

It's quite funny, isn't it, that this is a 'Dear John' letter. As if we were at the end of our correspondence rather than the beginning.

I'm intrigued that you have chosen me to be your pen pal—without even a photo to guide you. For all you know I could be an old woman, or a forty-year-old man. Oh dear! Have I sowed the seeds of doubt in your mind? I promise that I am the girl whose details you were sent by the Pen Pal Club.

The only things I know about you, Dear John, are that you are male and eighteen, and I have been warned not to give you my telephone number. The organisers seem very cautious, but I suppose they know what they're doing.

Are you still at school? I have two weeks of my summer term left (study leave, mainly), and then I'll be free! I've a place to read English at Durham University so my freedom won't last long. It's quite exciting and scary at the same time. No one in my family has ever been to university, and I'm held up by my aunt and uncle as a role model for my poor cousins, Elaine and Joe, who have every intention of leaving school at sixteen. I won't be disappointed if you're a trainee gardener or a barber or something—after all, the Pen Pal Club is about bringing different kinds of people together.

You probably want to know more about me. I'm pretty ordinary—medium height, medium-length brown hair, average looks. I'm not a girly-girl or a tomboy, but somewhere in between. I live in a semi-detached house with my parents and my little sister Bryony. She's spoilt rotten. We moved here when I was five, and I can't remember our previous house, which was in another town. I don't have any particular vices (except ice cream!). I like reading and I play hockey for my school—it's a girls grammar—and on Friday nights my friends and I go to a disco or on a pub crawl (my parents don't know about that). I've been to France on a school exchange trip, and it's the only foreign country I've visited. We usually go to Devon for two weeks in the summer.

It's really warm here in Sussex and I'm spending a lot of time reading in the garden. I have quite a sun tan! It's very quiet in the house—Mum and Dad are both at work in the daytime and Bryony is at school—I don't always like being here on my own. Sometimes I meet up with friends, but most of them have stricter parents than mine, and they're supposed to be on study leave too. I suppose it's all right so long as I don't spend too much time in the house.

My favourite things:—ice cream (I've already mentioned that), dancing—moonlight—books—shoes—Mum and Dad and I suppose Bryony—walking on the Downs.

Now I've come clean about myself, I think you should too!

I hope the above isn't too dull—or brainless. I refuse to mention politics, philosophy or music until I've heard from you and know where you stand. Don't let it be too long before you write. I'm looking forward to it very much.

All best wishes
Ruth

12th June 1975

Dear John,

Thank you so much for your letter, and I'm glad you liked mine: I'm not sure it deserved your fantastically long reply, but you should know that you've cheered me up no end. I've been a bit down in the dumps lately, but perhaps I'd better not burden you with that.

I'm not especially clever. Most of the girls at my school go to university; it's expected of us. I imagine it wasn't the same at your school. I respect your reasons for getting a job instead, although I'm not sure I understand them. From what you say you were perfectly capable of getting top grades. As long as you're happy it really doesn't matter.

You've lost me with the classical music references—I'm mostly a David Bowie fan, but, hey, whatever turns you on! On the philosophy front you're well ahead of me—I've never read Marx or Engels—so far I've concentrated on fiction. Dickens is my favourite, and some spooky authors, like M.R. James. I'm hoping it will be different at University and we'll read a wider selection of books. I'm looking forward to leaving home now, it'll be a new start. Blow some of the cobwebs away.

I've been taking long walks on the Downs—the air is clearer up there and the views are amazing. You can see the whole of the Weald and nearly as far north as the southern edge of London. Do you walk in the hills? I know many people in the North do. I'd never been further north than Birmingham until my university interview at Durham. The scenery flashing past the train carriage window was breath-taking.

You asked for a photograph. I suppose I could send one, although I'm worried you'll go off me when you see how I look. I have one my father took last winter in the garden. Perhaps I'll put it in the envelope with this letter. You must promise to find a photo of yourself, though—it's only fair. I'm dying to know what you look like.

It's extraordinary that you're saving to buy your own house. I can't imagine being in that position. Perhaps you could describe it to me in your next letter. It must be lovely to have your own money to spend. All I'll have to live on is my poxy student grant.

It's getting late now and Mum, Dad and Bryony are still not back from Aunty Daisy's. She must have made some of her lethal fruit punch. It's too dark to go into the garden so I'm stuck inside on my own. I'm writing to you, Dear John, on the dining room table, trying to keep my mind off scary things. Mum says I worked too hard for my 'A' levels and am now 'a bit nervy'. I'm sure that's all it is. I'll be able to sleep properly again soon. I'm telling you this because I already think of you as a friend. Do you believe in spooky things?

Mum and Dad and Bryony have just arrived home (Bryony is asleep in Dad's arms), so I can safely go to bed. Do write soon, and be kind about the photo.

       Ruth

            21st June 1975

Dear John

I hardly know what to say!—how can I react to descriptions like 'nymph in jeans,' and 'ethereal beauty'. I'm very flattered but are we really talking about the same photo? I was about to go to the youth club disco when it was taken, so I'm wearing my favourite platforms (I think I told you I have a thing about shoes). They make me look taller, but otherwise I'm as wispy and scruffy as usual.

Thank you for sending your photo. It's a shame it's blurred, but despite that I can see that you have a lovely smile. Is that a wedding suit? Seriously, though, I feel that I know you a bit better now. And you go for long walks too! How well 'suited' we are, Dear John, although all that political stuff you write about is lost on me. My parents vote Conservative. Perhaps you could educate me and help me decide who to support. I think I can work out where you are coming from.

Your house sounds great—two bedrooms means you can have friends to stay. I hope you save enough for the deposit before anyone else buys it. Even if they do, you'll probably find somewhere just as good.

I wish my parents would move house. Although I'm going away to Durham soon I'll still have to come home for vacations. I'm trying not to let it get me down but it's proving difficult. This probably sounds overly mysterious and I'd like to explain it to you properly, but I'm afraid you'll laugh, or think I'm crazy. If I don't tell someone soon I think I *will* go crazy. I've told you I'm a bit nervous and down in the dumps. Well, it's rather more than that.

I'll take a deep breath and just come out with it: When I'm in the house reading, or writing to you, I feel as if someone is looking over my shoulder. I can't always see them, but I hear them breathing. Their outline is very faint, just an impression, but I think it's a man—a middle-aged man. And it's always my left shoulder he's peering over.

I haven't been able to tell my parents about it, because they'd insist I see the doctor. I could really do with some advice. Am I just a bag of nerves and seeing things because of it? It feels very real and creepy at the time. If I sit still and stop what I'm doing he eventually fades away. He's not overtly hostile, but seems to have a goggling kind of curiosity about me which is really quite repellent.

I'm writing this in the garden as he doesn't seem to venture out here. Will you write to me soon and tell me what you think? I'll try to take it on the chin if you're entirely sceptical.
    Love
    Ruth

2nd July 1975

Dear John

Thank you, thank you, and thank you again for your kind reply! I'm so glad you're taking me seriously—but you think it might all be an hallucination. Perhaps you're right, and I'll gradually get better as the summer wears on. It makes me a bit crazy, though, doesn't it? I hope I haven't put you off.

It's interesting that you're not a believer in the supernatural—I suppose it's because you're a materialist and not into any kind of religion. 'The opium of the people!?' What does that make spooky stuff? Marijuana? I'm not sure where I stand, especially since my goggling man came on the scene. I'm seeing him more often now; I've even glimpsed him in the living room and the kitchen, just as I leave the room. He frightens me, Dear John, even if he is a product of my own brain. I'd do anything to be rid of him.

You're right that a change of scene might help me get a fresh perspective on things, so I'm going to take you up on your invitation, even if it's against the Pen Pal Club rules! It'll have to be just a day trip though—my parents would never let me stay overnight. I'll leave very early in the morning so we can have a long day. If I come on the date you suggest, will you be able to meet me at the station? I suppose you'll have to take a day off work. Would that be all right? Oh dear, I'm very excited, as you can probably tell!

Perhaps you can show me around York, or shall we go out into the countryside? I don't even know if you own a car.

I'll see you in a few days. I can hardly believe it. It'll be a real adventure.

        Ruth

11th July 1975

Dear John

Things have changed, the world is subtly different. A connection has been made that can never be broken.

I was beside myself with excitement on the train, and it was a joy and a relief to see you waiting on the platform. You made everything so easy and natural. Walking round York was a treat—the city a revelation to me, and the Minster—Divine! (pun intended). It was silly of me to wear my beloved platforms, though, and so much more comfortable once I'd exchanged them for the espadrilles you bought. I was probably trying to impress you. I must've left the shoes in your bag—at least I hope so. Returning them will provide a good excuse to meet up again.

Writing to each other has made us friends; meeting has made us good friends, I hope you agree. I enjoyed talking to you in the Museum garden—you are so passionate about the things you believe in—but I have to admit that I was distracted because I could see my tormenter, standing at the end of the bench, listening to everything that was said. You've made it clear how you feel about this apparition, and I tried to stay calm, but I can't seem to do anything to make him go away. I haven't any dark secrets, nothing to feel guilty about, and if that makes me squeaky clean then so be it. I'm sure I'm not hysterical, and I'm desperate for some kind of resolution. I'm not sure what I'm going to do next, but I'm grateful to you for letting me write to you about it and for giving me such considerate advice.

I don't mean to spoil what was otherwise a wonderful day. Even the weather was kind to us. Being immersed in the history of the city, with such a knowledgeable guide, was my favourite part of the day. The city walls, the overhanging timbered buildings in the narrow streets, the gargantuan meal in the Golden Lion—these are things I will remember for a long time. Stepping into the railway carriage and leaving you on the platform was a sobering moment. It would be easier if we lived closer together.

Write soon, and look after the shoes for me (they're very precious).

Ruth

18th July 1975

Dear John

I've waited four days before picking up my pen. I haven't known what to say; how to deal with this. It was completely unexpected.

I've been a fool. I've opened up to you in a confiding sort of way and must have given you the wrong impression. You're kind and sympathetic and intelligent, and I like you very much, but I never meant to stir up romantic feelings in you.

You say you love me, but, in truth, we don't know each other well enough for that. I can't help feeling that your declaration, coming so early in our friendship, might spoil things for the future—if there is a future. It would be better if you could take it back! Perhaps if we never mention it again, then everything would be the way it was? I've felt so free and natural with you and I don't want that to be spoilt.

I can't help but be hurt that you're suddenly so dismissive of my troubles, as if they are an inconvenience to you. Even if the apparition is just a product of my stressed-out brain, he's causing me a lot of unhappiness. It's as if you've run out of patience with a part of me that doesn't fit with your ideal. You want me to be the perfect woman, unreal, without flaws.

Shall we try to go on as before? I'm not sure we can. I feel uncomfortable and upset and I don't know if I trust you anymore.

I suppose I'm very innocent. I've had a sheltered upbringing, and I've never had a serious boyfriend, so you must forgive me if through inexperience I've inadvertently led you on. I know I should be flattered by the compliments, all the lovely things you've said. But I'm not the goddess you make me out to be. She's a figment of your imagination. I'm ordinary, I'm human; I'm not some woman in a poem or a film. I make mistakes. I'm beginning to think I made a mistake confiding in you.

All the time my tormenter is getting bolder, more intrusive. Right now he's leaning over my shoulder, reading every word. I can't go on like this. I never thought of myself as highly-strung before. But you don't want to read this, do you John. You'd rather fantasise about some woman who only exists in your head.

Prove me wrong, step back from the brink. Write a letter to a friend who cherishes you, but can't yet think about love.

           Ruth

25th July 1975

Dear John

You saw him in York? Why didn't you say so at the time? You let me get angry with you; I thought I had lost my only confidant. I was in despair.

You did see him, didn't you? You're not just making it up to please me?

I'm even more scared than I was before.

Why has he chosen me? The only interesting things in my life are you, Dear John, and him.

His eyes follow me everywhere; in the house, in town, even in the garden. I can almost feel his breath on my cheek as he leans over my shoulder, spoiling everything. My thoughts are stolen from me, all my movements tracked. There is no part of my life that is my own.

You give me a modicum of hope, Dear John. Apart from you he's all I think about, night and day. I have seen the doctor and he has prescribed Valium and some other pills. I didn't tell him what the real trouble was. When she is home, my mother watches me like a hawk. There is talk of postponing university for a year. My life is falling apart: only you can save me.

Please, please write soon.

           Ruth

30th July 1975

Dear John
You haven't written.
I'm sorry things have to end this way.
I hope your life is long and happy and that you quickly forget about me. As I've explained to you before, I'm no one special. You'll find someone who is the perfect match for you.
I know you tried to make me feel better by pretending you had seen him in York. I forgive you for that; you were only trying to help. But it has not relieved any of my suffering.
Goodbye Dear John
        Love
            Ruth

2nd August 1975

Dear John Butler
I am writing to let you know that two days ago Ruth took an overdose of tablets. She died yesterday in Brighton Infirmary. She wouldn't have suffered in any way; it was very peaceful at the end.
Looking through Ruth's things I found your letters to her. I must say I am shocked and angry that you wrote to her in the way you did: it is clear that she confided in you, and you did nothing to alert us to the delusions from which she was suffering. I would have thought that any other intelligent young man would have acted with more compassion. My poor daughter was obviously very sick, and you did nothing to help her, even, at the end, encouraging her in her beliefs.
We had no idea how advanced her illness had become. I thought she was merely suffering from stress. You could've saved her and

you didn't. The whole family is distraught—we can't believe we have lost our daughter in this horrible way.

You will not be welcome at the funeral, so please keep away. And do not reply to this letter.

Marjorie Smith

20th August 1975

Dear John

It's so calm here, in the green of the garden, alive with late flowering plants and the chirruping of the birds.

I hope you are well, Dear John, and I must apologise for the note I wrote to you. I was in anguish and could think of no other way to escape. Here they look after me as if I were a fragile piece of porcelain.

I think I could have loved you and I accept now that you love me. It is probably the case, though, that we will never write to each other again. You will have noticed that there is no address on the top of this letter: Isolation is the price I pay for peace.

They will be calling me in soon.

Live well, Dear John.

Love
Ruth

Now open the envelope addressed to me and I will read it.

5th April 2005

Dear Justin

I know that it'll be you, not Peter, who'll read the letters. You're always so curious about me, asking questions I usually manage to deflect. I don't know why you're so interested; you have a pretty full life yourself. Despite all that I still count you as a kind of friend, because of our school days, because there's no one else except Peter, and because I want to keep you close.

I had a health scare (my heart: you don't know about that) and it made me realise that I need to write to you before it's too late. You'll read Ruth's letters first—I know how methodical you are—and I expect you will be all agog that I fell in love once in my life. And she was the love—the only love—of my life. I have been waiting for her to write again for thirty years.

Do you like the letters, Justin? They answer some of your questions about me. You'll never find the letters I wrote to Ruth; her mother will have seen to that, so don't go chasing after them. You'll have to be content with one side of the story.

I really did catch a glimpse of Ruth's goggling man in York. He looked just like you—as you are now—a middle-aged man, asking me intrusive questions that I don't want to answer. You were leaning over the bench, inspecting me. It was only recently that I realised it must be you, smarming all over her, making her feel spied upon, spoiling her life. Her letters to me were private, but you couldn't stop yourself from gloating over them.

Wherever she is I hope she is happy and free. I will never be able to forgive you, Justin, for making her life a misery, for tearing us apart, for enjoying the letters so much. Not that my feelings will mean anything to you.

You've had your fix.

John

TOADIE

Clarinda stared open-mouthed at the squat little creature, its amber eyes gleaming in the afternoon sun, its moist, warty skin taut over the rubbery flesh beneath.

'It's time you set us free,' said the toad, looking her in the eye. 'Then I will live in your garden and talk to you whenever you like.'

The other toads were half-buried in mud at the bottom of the dilapidated water trough.

'You've kept us captive long enough,' the toad said. 'There was some excuse for it when you and your brothers were younger and ignorant of the distress you were causing. But now you're almost adults you should know better. Anyway, you'll soon leave the farm for your own spawning grounds and there will be no one left to look after us.'

Clarinda rallied. 'I've already asked Mother to feed you some worms when I'm gone.'

'We're not pets,' it said. 'We belong on the outside. There's not even a puddle in this trough: you're keeping us in an unnatural state.'

'You're well fed,' said Clarinda, 'and safe from predators. I'd have thought that would count for something.'

'We've been picked up, poked and prodded: it's undignified. And there are too many of us in this small space. It leads to bickering and fights.'

The toad crawled over to one of the worms Clarinda had dropped into the trough. 'The diet's pretty monotonous, too.'

Clarinda reached out her hand, scooped up the toad and stroked it with her index finger.

'Come on, Toadie, I've looked after you all these years and you've never complained before.'

'Enough is enough.' The toad squirmed out of her grasp and plopped back into the trough. When it had righted itself it said, 'You could set us free straight away.'

Clarinda frowned. 'I suppose I could. . . . It would save Mum the trouble of looking after you when I'm travelling, and to be honest Basil and Dylan lost interest in you a while ago. I'll have to ask them, though. I won't mention the talking, they'd never believe me. Are you sure you'll be able to cope with the big wide world?'

'Quite sure,' said the toad.

Basil and Dylan were watching a film and showed no emotion when Clarinda suggested that the toads should be liberated.

'Yeah,' Dylan said. 'I suppose they should. They were fun when we were younger, though. You see to it Clary.' Basil didn't look away from the screen.

Clarinda fetched a garden trowel and a bucket from the shed and began carefully to dig the toads out of the mud. In all she counted fifteen. She slid each one into the bucket and carried it to the field next to the farmyard where there was a pond.

A voice said, 'Don't forget that I'm to live in the garden.'

The talking toad was sitting on top of the muddy mound formed by its brethren.

'That was the idea,' it said, calmly.

She tipped the toads onto the edge of the pond. They sat where they landed, blinking in the evening light. One made slowly for the water. The talking toad crawled back into the bucket.

'You can take me to the garden now.'

Clarinda considered carrying it into the house to show her mother. As if reading her thoughts the toad said, 'If you exhibit me to anyone else I will stop talking. They'll think you're crazy.'

'Where do you want me to put you?' sighed Clarinda.

'Let's go and see,' said the toad.

It wasn't a particularly large garden, but it had a lawn, apple trees, flower beds and a small pond. Clarinda walked around the perimeter, holding the bucket on its side to give the toad a good view. She stopped at various points, but the toad was silent; its throat pulsing gently. When she reached the pond it said, 'I could live in the plants at the back. There are plenty of places to hide.'

Clarinda picked it out of the bucket and slid it into a patch of yellow irises.

'Will that do?' she asked.

'Come and see me tomorrow,' said the toad. 'Because I'm a magic toad I can reward you by granting a wish. I know it's a cliché but it should be worth your while.'

It was perhaps reasonable to believe that a talking toad could also perform other kinds of magic, but as Clarinda made her way down the garden to the pond after breakfast the next day, she decided that none of it was real. Toads didn't talk, and it would almost certainly be the case that her toad, if it existed at all, would have left in the night, seeking a more congenial home. Or it would have buried itself deep in the soil so that she would never be able to find it. As she neared the pond, a knot of disappointment formed in her stomach.

She parted the irises and saw the toad sitting there, its eyes mocking her all too evident relief.

'Hello, Clarinda.'

'I didn't think you'd . . . be here.'

'I keep my promises.'

Clarinda stooped to pick up the toad but it shuffled to one side.

'None of that,' it said sharply. 'I'm a wild creature now.'

'What kind of thing can I wish for?'

'Anything,' said the toad, 'as long as it's centred on you or your loved ones. I can't do "world peace", etc. But I'd think very hard about it, if I were you. You know what they say, "be careful what you wish for . . . " '

'All right,' Clarinda said irritably. 'I know the score.'

Pacing around the garden Clarinda was well aware of the absurdity of the situation. Nevertheless she thought hard about the kind of thing she wanted. Although her family were reticent to the point of taciturnity and didn't often talk to each other about important things, Clarinda knew that after agricultural college her brothers would take over the farm, leaving her to make her own way in the world. She had some vague hopes of teaching abroad. Being well aware that she was essentially a dreamer only exacerbated her panicky dread at being cast off into the unknown. She had hoped that travelling for a year with a group of friends would build her confidence and make the idea of leaving home less daunting, but just thinking about it made her anxious.

'What is your wish?' asked the toad.

Clarinda took a deep breath. 'I wish that my worries about leaving home will disappear.'

The toad blinked. 'Granted,' it said.

At first, Clarinda didn't feel any different, only a little more restless than usual. She was sitting in the field under the oak tree, watching cotton-wool clouds drift slowly by. The fourteen liberated toads had disappeared into the pond or under the hedge. She hoped they were enjoying their freedom.

Putting aside her vacation reading she fetched the keys from the house and took her mother's car out for a spin. It was a beautiful early summer's day, a warm breeze ruffled the fat-fingered leaves of the horse chestnuts lining the farm track. She opened the window and drove faster along the lanes than usual, taking risks on blind corners and speeding up on the straights. Without thinking where she was going, she found herself on the outskirts of the nearby market town. An almost overwhelming desire to carry on took hold of her, to drive onto the motorway and follow the wide grey ribbon down to the green hills and sparkling seas of the West Country. She had to remind herself how impractical that would be: she had no money and her mother would be needing the car.

When she returned, Basil and Dylan were making pancakes. Clarinda was offered one, drizzled with lemon juice and honey. The kitchen was indescribably messy, with spilt flour over every surface and egg shells on the floor. She refused the pancake, wrinkling her nose.

'You'd better clear up,' she said. 'It's disgusting in here.'

'Where have you been?' asked Dylan. 'You left your phone behind. There was a call for you earlier. Something about your student loan.'

Clarinda trailed through the house. Every room seemed dowdy and messy, in dire need of cleaning and tidying—no longer the lived-in, comfortable home she was used to. She found she could take no joy in it any more. Minor idiosyncrasies—the creaking stairs and the antiquated central heating system—had become major irritations. Even her bedroom seemed sordid, the carpet from her childhood an eyesore, the furniture unmatched and unloved. It distressed her to admit it, but the farmhouse was badly maintained and shabby, and she couldn't see how she had not noticed it before.

Restlessness took hold of her again and she longed to jump back in the car and drive wherever the wanderlust took her.

The toad crouched in the irises.

'Hello, Clarinda,' it said. 'What would you like to talk about this afternoon?'

'The wish isn't working out as I thought it would. Can it be reversed?'

'I'm sorry, but it can't. There's no going back, that's why I told you to think carefully . . . '

'I know, I know,' said Clarinda. 'I thought I had.'

'You're not denying you feel less anxious about leaving home?'

'No, but . . . '

'Well then. Concentrate on that.'

'I didn't know there would be such an unpleasant side-effect. I can't stand being at home anymore.'

'Everything has its price. Look at me, stuck here on my own. You can have another wish, if you like. You get three, like in the fairy stories. It's all very conventional.'

She lay down on the lawn and closed her eyes. The grass was cool on her back, although the afternoon heat drew beads of perspiration onto her forehead.

'I wish,' she said, after a few minutes, 'that I could love my home again.'

'Granted,' said the toad.

Sitting up and looking at the old farmhouse, Clarinda felt her heart swell and open like a rosebud.

'Thank you, Toadie. I think everything is going to be all right.'

'Remember, you have a third wish, although you don't have to use it if you don't want to.'

'I'm hoping I won't need it.'

Clarinda lay back on the lawn, her arms under her head, and contemplated the clear blue sky.

The toad sighed loudly.

'What's the matter?' Clarinda asked.

'I thought you wanted to talk to me. I'm rather lonely, you know.'

'What would you like to discuss?'

'You could ask me some questions. Everyone likes to talk about themselves.'

'I suppose I don't know much about you. Where were you born?'

'In the pond in your field. That's where I swam as a tadpole. When I emerged from the water I lived happily under the hedge until you captured me. I was just a regular toad then: I couldn't speak your language. That happened after you and your brothers imprisoned me. I listened carefully to your prattle until I came to understand it, then I practiced on the other toads, but they didn't share the facility I seem to have been born with. Of course I don't know who my parents are: perhaps I am like them.'

'Are there many other magic toads?'

'I don't know. I've never come across one. But, as I've explained, I've led a sheltered life and my powers are limited.'

Clarinda sat down on the grass. 'Have you talked to other humans?'

'I didn't think your brothers would be sympathetic.'

Clarinda stretched her arms above her head. 'What would you like to do with the rest of your life, Toadie?'

The toad sighed. 'I thought I wanted to live in your garden, but now, after a few days of it, I'm bored. I'd like to be with my brothers and sisters in the field. I'd like some female company and to spawn in the pond and see a new generation of toads populate the farm. It seems I have ordinary instincts after all.'

'Then that is my third wish,' said Clarinda. 'That you should lead the life you desire.'

The toad suffered her to pick him up and carry him to the field. She put him carefully under the hedge near the pond. It seemed he was so overcome he couldn't say a word.

'Goodbye then little Toadie. I hope to see you again before I leave.'

Clarinda's anxiety about travelling had passed and she was looking forward to going to France with her friends. On most of her remaining days at home she walked over the field in an attempt to find the toad, but he had disappeared from under the hedge. Occasionally she came across one of the mute toads. She missed her toadie, but hoped he was enjoying his sociable life.

The day came for her to leave. She had packed her rucksack the night before—Dylan was to drive her to the station. Saying goodbye to the house and garden was a sentimental indulgence, as was, in a non-tactile family, the long hug her mother gave her.

'Take care, Clarinda. Keep your wits about you and don't do anything silly.'

Dylan dropped her off on the station forecourt. As she walked into the building, she thought she felt a strange squirming in her rucksack. She took off the heavy bag and unzipped the main compartment. There, sitting on top of her underwear, was the toad.

'Hello, Clarinda,' it said. 'Nice to see you again.'

'What on earth are you doing?'

'I'm afraid I soon got bored in the field. The limited communication I am able to enjoy with other toads is so unsatisfying. And I couldn't find a suitable breeding partner. I decided to give travelling a try. I thought you wouldn't mind: I'll hide away from your companions whenever necessary.'

'But I thought . . . my wish . . . '

'That I should have the life I desire. This is it. I can be quite useful to you. I've a very good instinct for trouble and my sense of smell is excellent.'

Clarinda sighed and gently stroked its head. The toad blinked contentedly.

'You better nestle down in the rucksack, Toadie. Keep still though. We have a train to catch.'

HEAVENLY LOVE

Finding a suitable father for your babies is a haphazard business; there are usually several false starts before you fall in love, move in, get married. If you're lucky, children follow swiftly. Then, without warning, you discover that your husband has done something that hurts you to the quick, destroys your spirit, sears your soul. It's a betrayal of everything you have built together . . .
. . . But you have a secret of your own. . . .

When he first appeared I had dreamt of it for so long I wept with joy. Now he's mine I feel I cannot live without him.
I loved him long before we met—I knew he would come to me eventually. He shines so beautifully that all the longing is transfigured into bliss. My angel means more to me than any other lover; I'll never tire of looking at him.

After the initial upset and anger, you try to shut your eyes to what your husband has done. You go through the motions of daily life. But the injustice of the betrayal eats into you, despite the justifications, the apologies, the fevered, empty love-making. Eventually you're a sobbing heap of confusion and self-pity, begging for everything to go back the way it was, because you would do almost anything for the children.

His smile is so ravishing it hardly matters that he doesn't speak. One day I may find the courage to caress his alabaster limbs, but for now I am happy just to look, to breathe him in and draw strength from his perfect smile.

He is as tall as I imagined. His wings fold around the contours of his body. He stands straight, a soldier on guard: I know he will never let me down. I wish he could stay with me all of the time.

I have banished myself to the spare room and he arrives before I go to sleep. If only he would come earlier, when the children have gone to bed and the quarrels begin. He could guide me through the storm. I'd know he was there, I'd feel his steadying hand on my shoulder, clearing my mind of the fuddle of past happiness, sharpening my reasoning, strengthening my will.

You maintain a façade of family life, but the children are aware of the tension in the house. They hate you both, because they are scared (rightly as it turns out) that their world may be about to change. Their behaviour deteriorates and letters are sent home from school. Then comes the sit-down moment when you explain that Mummy and Daddy are going their separate ways: it's 'not your fault', you say, we will be 'there' for you, and, through gritted teeth, 'we'll always be friends'.

Your old love moves out. Bowed and bitter you promise yourself that you will never again enter into a human relationship. Homesickness brings your husband back and for a few days you sleep in the same bed, but both of you know it's over. The children cling to false hope, and you have to explain all over again that Daddy's moving out.

He appears by the window, raises his arm and points.

'Am I to go out into the world?' I ask. 'But I'm sick of it. My life is here with you, my angel, and the children.'

I thought he realised that I would rather be with him for one second than re-join the human race.

Seven months later, you meet Francis.

Parties are not your thing but you go because it's Gudrun's birthday. Gudrun stuck by you when the divorce was mired in endless disagreements about the custody of the children. Now the process has ended, both you and your husband are vaguely unhappy with the settlement, but at least the children live mainly with you.

You're standing self-consciously by the buffet, drinking your third glass of wine, trying not to catch anyone's eye, when Francis approaches.

'I've never seen anyone look so uncomfortable,' he says. His grin lifts his face into something close to handsomeness.

'I'm shy, that's all,' you reply.

'Are you party phobic?'

'No . . . well, not really . . .'

He offers you another glass of wine.

'I think I've had enough.'

Some guests have left and you sit on the newly vacated sofa. Francis tells a story about a friend who went to the wrong party. You laugh. He leans over.

'You look happier now you've relaxed a bit,' he says. 'How about I take you back to my flat and work off some more of that tension.'

For a moment you are shocked, but that doesn't stop you from getting in his car and being driven to an apartment building on the expensive side of town. You follow him into the lift and up to his flat. It's smart and modern, with abstract paintings on the walls, even in the bathroom. He shows you into the living room and you take off your dress and lay down on the rug.

While I put the dishes away and the children play in the living room, my angel spreads his wings and shakes out the feathers. It makes the kitchen seem very small.

'Where do you go,' I ask, 'when you're not here?'

To my astonishment, he speaks. 'I'm here to look after you,' he says, avoiding the question, and he enfolds me for a moment in his cool embrace.

Sandra and Simon run into the room, wanting me to settle some dispute. Half-hoping that I can introduce my angel to the children I look round, but he has gone.

During the week, Francis proves elusive. You phone him several times, but your calls go straight to voicemail. Driving to his flat seems too much, and you don't know where he works. You're not in love, but you're obsessed by the memory of his love-making—the warmth of him, the taste of him. . . . You hardly bother with your children and at the weekend you are glad to pack them off to their father.

On Friday, Francis answers your call.

'I've been away.'

'All week?'

'Pretty much. At a conference. Shall we meet up?'

'I'll see you in Teacher's Bar at eight.'

You last for all of half an hour before driving to his flat. This time you make love in his bedroom; ultra-masculine (all straight lines and dark colours) and very comfortable. Afterwards he lies on his back with his eyes closed and you stroke his hair.

'We should meet at your house next,' he says.

'I don't have the children this weekend . . .'

He opens his eyes. 'Perhaps I should come when they're at home. You can introduce me to them.'

So you find yourself reheating a meal for him on a school night, the children yawning and ready for sleep when he arrives, an hour late. He is charming and boisterous and they respond by refusing to go to bed. The miniature robots he has brought toddle across the carpet. While he eats his food the children run out of steam and you persuade them to go upstairs. 'Goodnight Uncle Francis,' says Sandra sleepily.

His limbs are glistening ice, his face adamantine, the wings scarcely visible, folded away behind him. 'I love you,' I say.

Francis makes love to you in the kitchen among the unwashed pots and pans. Halfway through, your phone rings. Afterwards, it rings again. It's your ex, wanting to know why you didn't answer the earlier call.

'I need to talk to you about the maintenance payments,' he says. 'Can we have a moratorium for a couple of months?'

'No,' I say firmly. 'You can't back out now, just because you've other things you'd rather spend your money on. Like your girlfriend.'

'Fiancée,' he says.

Francis hands you your skirt. 'He sounds like a complete wazzock.'

'Please don't go! You promised you would look after me.'
'You've chosen your lover,' he says. 'You have Francis.'
'But I want you!' I wail. 'Why can't I have you both?'
He's looking out of the window. His wing tips flutter.
The next day, there is no trace he has ever been here.

Your old love knocks on the door. He looks tired and upset and wants to see the children. You take pity on him and soon he has his feet under the table, coming round two or three evenings each week, as well as having the children at weekends. Sometimes he babysits while you sleep with Francis at his flat. Your children are ecstatic that they are spending more time with both parents. The arrangement works well until you realise that your ex is becoming complacent: he sings in the bath and kisses you on the cheek when you leave the house. He is still with his fiancée but one evening he admits that she is unhappy about the new arrangement.

After a bottle of wine he begins to cry.

'The thing is,' he says, 'I love you, and I miss the kids. Can we get back together?'

You try not to shout. 'I have someone else, and so do you.'

'We were a good family. You can't deny that.'

'It was you who threw it away.'

'Give me another chance,' he pleads.
The old feelings stir and you feel yourself weakening.
'I need time to think about it. You'll have to get a taxi home. I'll see you on Thursday, we'll talk about it then.'

Francis laughs. 'What a nerve, after all he's put you through. I hope you told him to get lost.'
'I couldn't. He's the children's father.'
'He gave up all rights when he slept with that woman. How can he marry her *and* live with you?'
'He says he's going to dump her.'
'I bet he's just nervous about the wedding.'
'I think he's serious.'
'You're not going to agree, are you? Just because he was drunk and feeling sorry for himself. He'll have changed his mind by now. Or forgotten about it.'
'I need to consider what's right for everyone—it's not just about my preferences.'
'Which are?'
'Oh shut up, Francis. You know how I feel about you.'
'No I don't. Not really.'

His wings brush against me. As he folds them away I wrap my arms around his neck and lay my head on his chest where his heart should be.
He says, 'Which of them will you choose?'
'If you were to stay I'd be happy. I wouldn't need anyone else.'
I hold him until I drift into sleep, just as I'd dreamed when I was a child. The next morning I wake, fully clothed, on the bed.

Francis doesn't ring for several days, then asks you to meet him at his flat. He pours two glasses of wine.
'I'm hoping to impress you. Look, if you want me, I'm in this for the long haul. But I could do without your ex trying to mess things up. I

understand that he has to see the children, but I'd like him to keep to the agreed times. None of this staying over on week nights . . .
'I love you,' he says, and puts his arms around you.

Your ex is heartbroken. 'I was about to split up with Sheila. We've already called off the wedding.'
'It's confusing the children to see so much of you. Make up with your fiancée and move on. That's what I'm trying to do. You can still come round, but not so often.'
So your old love and his woman get back together, and you and Francis become fixtures in each other's lives.

For days I pretend I haven't made my choice: the angel is silent, waiting. In desperation I look into his eyes and take his hands, then I kneel and kiss his feet.
'Take me with you', I beg. 'Don't leave me behind.'
'You have Francis,' he says. 'He'll look after you.'
'I don't love him the way I love you.'
He looks down at me.
'Could you live without your children?'
'Take them too!'
'Put your trust in Francis.'

Sandra and Simon are fascinated by Francis, who buys many presents and never talks down to them. At the dinner table he candidly discusses his job and complains about colleagues. He is willing to play video games and takes the children to the park for real-life adventures. They are settling into a routine in which fatherly duties are shared by your ex and Francis.

A positive pregnancy test confirms what you have suspected for several weeks. Days pass before you find the courage to tell Francis. He is delighted, opens a bottle of champagne and takes you out for dinner. You realise he is assuming that you will move in together.

Where is your angel now? Jealousy claws inside you. You feel unwell and rush to the bathroom: on your return, Francis strokes your hand.

'You'll need to see your doctor and find out when the first scan's due. I'd like to come along. It'll be a wonderful adventure.'

I am grieving for my love, he's someone else's angel now. Waiting for him is the hardest thing I've ever had to do.

Will he ever come back?

I'm sick at heart and would gladly give up everything to see him once more.

Cradled inside you, the baby is healthy, and you are blooming. Six months in is the best time, before you grow uncomfortably large. Francis fusses, makes sure you are eating well, and runs warm baths. You have resisted his attempts to move in: he is hurt, but seems to think you will change your mind once the baby is due.

Your ex and his new wife are putting on a brave face but their relationship is fragile. He is moping over your pregnancy. You harden your heart and try to concentrate on the baby. The children are looking forward to meeting their new sibling.

I dream of my angel: he is with a child whose father is in prison; an old woman who fears she will die alone; a man snowed in and running out of food. By comparison my problems are insignificant. I realise I should think myself lucky that he came to me at all.

A week before my due date and I dream that he hovers outside the window. When I wake I lift the sash, but there is only the apple tree, its gnarled limbs stirring in the breeze.

I take myself back to bed and the baby twists and kicks.

You gave birth to your children in a small maternity hospital with minimal intervention, but Francis books you into the hi-tech ward at the district hospital. He thinks you and the baby will be safer there. The delivery room is full of alien instruments and machines.

In the event it's a swift labour—all is well with you and the baby. You call him Alec, after your grandfather. Francis buys a beautiful bunch of flowers and a diamond pendant, which you suspect you will never wear.

Through the night you feed and comfort your baby. You fall in love with him. In the morning your other children come to visit, excited and affectionate towards the new arrival. Francis has prepared them well. You are to stay in hospital for one more night and then you'll be going home. Francis insists that he will be there with you, 'for the first few weeks at least,' he says.

My angel bends and touches my cheek, then, to my surprise, he picks up the baby and, wings outstretched, raises him to the ceiling.
'Blessed be,' he says.
He hands Alec to me and I lay him in the cot.
All will be well with my baby, whatever happens to me.

Francis fusses—he has taken paternity leave and assumes most of the baby's care. You're expected to recline on the sofa, feed Alec and 'regain your strength'. If you were in a better state of mind, you'd be moved by Francis's cooing over the baby: unlike you, he seems happy and contented.

When you dream, you're unsure if you're awake or asleep. The dreams are nightmares, and you try not to dwell on them. In fact you hardly sleep at all, as the baby needs feeding twice each night. You insist on occupying the spare room with Alec, arguing that you do not want to wake Francis.

As the days pass the nightmares take hold; your head is full of monsters and you are the worst of them. In your more lucid moments you pray for your angel to save you and he comes into your thoughts, shining sword in hand.

The battle rages through the day. Safe in your room you pray for his victory, sing songs of bravery, wrestle with your fears.

Francis is 'phoning for the doctor.

You throw up the sash and spread your wings. The sill is narrow but you balance for a second and then launch into the air, your baby clutched in your arms. You gain a few metres but your wings are so new they are unused to flight and you feel yourself plummet until . . .

Your angel catches you and bears you up into the night.

COW CITY

The wind-whipped grass rippled in the field. Spring had come early, the sunshine and showers producing a tall, healthy crop. Tomorrow, all this luscious ripeness was to be mown and gathered, stored and fed over the coming year to the captive cows in their perpetually lit sheds. It would be the first cut of the season.

Silaging is a brutal business; the grass harvested down to stubble, stinking liquid slurry spread to force-feed the regenerating shoots. The grazing regime it replaced was more benign: at least the cattle spent their summers out in the meadows. Leonie smelt the cloying sweetness of the sap as she rolled over and stood up. The low sun burnished the fell-side above the fields and she knew she would have to hurry home to be in time for supper. She re-joined the footpath that led up to the stile and the village street beyond.

At the front of the cottage were two south-facing rooms, warm even in winter, in which most of the family's life was lived. The larger of these was a comfortable sitting room; the evening meal already laid out in the smaller room when Leonie flung open the side door and kicked off her walking boots. Grandfather called out:

'Just in time! Come and eat while it's hot.'
'What's it like out there?' asked Grandmother.
'Blowy. It may rain later.'
'Let's hope it stays dry for the silage cutting.'
Leonie forked up cottage pie.
'And it's a big day for you too,' said Grandmother, 'I hope that lass'll not mess it up again.'
Leonie fetched her book and read while her grandparents watched television. Tired after her long walk, she soon made her excuses and went up to bed. Outside, the moon was a bright sliver and the rain had kept away. She closed the curtains and climbed into bed.

Going out into the fine morning Leonie fetched the old tennis racquet and hit the ball against the side of the garage. The farmer's dogs slunk into the yard and circled round, eager for a game of chase, their eyes fixed on the ball as it thudded against the wall and bounced on the concrete of the yard. In the distance she could hear the whirr of grass cutting machines at work in the fields.

The gate opened and Tanya jogged in.

'Is it today?' she asked.

'What?'

'You know!'

Tanya caught the ball and threw it into the paddock. The dogs hurtled after it.

'I thought you might like some help.'

'I have to do it alone. You know that.'

'But I'm in the drama society too!' said Tanya crossly.

'I know, but they chose me.'

A collie returned, carrying the ball. The dog dropped it at Leonie's feet and looked at her expectantly. Tanya wore much the same expression.

'There's nothing exciting about it,' Leonie said. 'Kay's a normal person. Last time was a bit of a shambles; something distracted her and she broke the connection. We didn't get any work done. That's all it is: a job of work.'

'But you get to talk to her.'

'Look, something nice will happen to you. You'll see.'

Leonie cheered Tanya up by promising to go with her to the annual funfair. It was a favourite of Tanya's: she was in love with the vivid, cacophonous anarchy of it—Leonie, who, despite having enjoyed the fair as a child, found it dirty and noisy and vulgar. Nevertheless it had to be done. She would be able to persuade Grandfather to drive them into town.

On the screen, Kay Simon was perfectly groomed, her skin flawless.

Leonie said, 'What would you like me to do?'

'Read something so I can listen to your voice, then I'll repeat it.'

Leonie took a copy of *Jane Eyre* from her bookshelf. She opened it near the end, where Jane hears the blind Rochester calling her. After reading a paragraph she stopped. Kay repeated the last sentence in an approximation of a North Yorkshire accent, her Texan drawl reasserting itself halfway through.

'You have a great voice, Leonie,' she said. 'I can see why they chose you to help me.'

Reading the same passage, but slowly, Leonie emphasised individual words and phrases. After a few runs through, Kay began to make a better job of it: she was a good mimic. As the end of the hour approached, Leonie asked about the film they were preparing for.

'I know it's set in Yorkshire, but they haven't told me anything else.'

'It's about the people and the farms and the country. There's a young woman who wants to leave, but she has family ties. It's not a rural romance, though, it's a kind of horror movie. I can't say more 'cause it's under wraps.'

Grandfather parked on the High Street: with increasing age his driving had become cautious and there was plenty of time for Tanya to extract information.

'What's she like? Did she mention Jeff Fellows? You know they're an item.'

'I can't say anything about what happened.'

'This is me, Leonie! Are they paying you?'

'Yes.'

Tanya sulked until they approached the town, then the sound of the fair revived her and she grabbed Leonie's arm.

'Let's go on the dodgems!'

Tanya bought candyfloss and bit into the sugary cloud. After the dodgems, Leonie pleaded vertigo and refused to go on any more rides. She held the stick of candyfloss and watched Tanya on the Big Wheel and the Waltzer, thinking how old-fashioned the fair was, even though families and younger teenagers still flocked to it. None of her other friends or contemporaries were there. As they zigzagged from ride to ride, Leonie felt the blaring pop music and diesel fumes from the generators meld in her aching head. She had to lean against a barrier as Tanya flew down the Helter-Skelter. At last Tanya had had enough and they walked back through the attractions to Grandfather waiting in the car.

As they passed the Ghost Train, Leonie was surprised to see, above its entrance, a crudely-painted image of Kay Simon. It was from the closing scene of *Outsider*, the horror film that had made her famous. Her hands were clasped either side of her face, the torn dress clung precariously from her bare shoulders. Looming behind her was a blurred figure, a bloody knife clutched in its raised hand.

'Now do you appreciate what a big deal she is,' said Tanya.

Leonie had withheld the fact that she was being paid a small fortune for what were now daily Skype sessions with Kay. As far as Leonie was concerned, Kay's accent was already pretty good, but Kay, she had come to realise, was a perfectionist. Leonie had been given the job partly because she was the same age as the character Kay, five years older, was to play in the film. Kay was determined to sound exactly like Leonie.

Since university Leonie had settled for an indolent life: her grandparents were only too pleased to have her back home and made few demands on her. This was her first paid job since graduation.

As she walked through the fields Leonie saw that the grass, fuelled by the slurry, was already sending up energetic green shoots. At the other end of the dale the cows were being milked to exhaustion. In the fully automated parlours they were unaccustomed to close human contact. Some people in the dale believed this made the cows more like wild beasts than domesticated animals. Leonie felt that her little patch of heaven was being spoiled, the unreflecting acceptance of childhood a distant memory. She longed for the anonymity of the city, tasted in her years at university, tolerated then, desired now. She would be able to find a job there; earn enough, with her savings, to pay the rent on a shared flat.

Once my work with Kay is finished, she told herself, *I'll go to the city*.

Grandmother and Grandfather were weeding their vegetable patch, the air full of insect buzzings, the sun warm on the old people's hats and shoulders. Grandfather stretched his back.

'Leonie's restless,' he said.

'That film star has unsettled her,' said Grandmother.

'She's usually a level-headed girl.'

'I suppose we're not lively enough for her.'

'And there's no young man on the scene: at least not one who would keep her here.'

Grandmother leant on her hoe and thought for a while. 'I'll have a word with her. See if I can find out what's really the matter.'

Kay was far busier than the other cast members—as well as being leading lady she was also reading the voiceover.

'You must promise not to tell anyone about this,' she said to Leonie. 'The script is still embargoed, but I want to be word perfect when rehearsals begin.'

Kay raised her iPad and read the first lines.

'Looking back, there was little sign of the horrors to come.
'We were quiet folk, feeding our stock, tending our gardens, sending our children to school. We got along with each other—mostly. . . .
'But all that was to change.'

Her accent was perfect.

'There's not much more I can do for you,' Leonie said.

Kay's reply was drowned out by a loud crash. Jeff Fellows blundered into the room behind her, swigging from a bottle. Leonie saw the look of mortification on Kay's face.

'Haven't you finished yet?' he slurred. 'I thought we were going out to dinner. . . . '

The call was ended.

Grandmother smoothed Leonie's hair. 'I know something's bothering you. Can't you tell me what it is?'

Leonie said. 'The dale's changed.'

'What do you mean?'

'There's no joy in it any more. The cows are just machines for milking.'

Grandmother said, 'You're leaving because of the cows? The city is no bed of roses.'

Leonie shrugged.

'I'd like to give it a try.'

Grandmother stood up. 'I suppose you're old enough to make your own decisions.'

Kay insisted on the Skype sessions continuing at least until she flew over to the UK a few weeks before filming. They concentrated on the voiceover:

Every morning and evening my father checked on the sheep, making sure there was nothing to hinder the ewes from looking after their lambs.
I was hoping to go to university, but my plans were put on hold.
When Father came back to the house he found it hard to speak. I don't think he ever fully recovered. All the lambs had been beheaded and the ewes disembowelled. This was no frenzied dog attack. It had been carried out by someone who knew exactly what they were doing.

Kay never mentioned the incident with Jeff. She seemed focused on the film but was happy to chat about other things whenever they took a break from work. Leonie found herself telling Kay about her plan to leave for the city.

'You can always go home if it doesn't work out,' Kay said. 'You're lucky to have a supportive family. I ran away to Hollywood when I was sixteen.'

Father could not bear to face the truth: that a farmer in the dale, probably someone he knew, was responsible for the mutilations.
Always a brittle stick he broke in two. He'd spent the last thirty years honing his breeding stock and improving the quality of his lambs. Now, because of one despicable act, all was ruined.

The mowing machines were cutting the second crop of the year. Leonie watched from her bedroom window, unmoved by the beauty of the warm summer day.

In the evening was her penultimate session with Kay. Kay was still in Los Angeles: rehearsals were to take place in a studio in Bradford in the UK and they arranged to spend a day together in the city when Kay was able to take time off. Towards the end of the call Jeff Fellows appeared behind Kay and waved.

'Goodbye, little Leonie,' he said. 'We'll see you in Yorkshire.'

Kay met Leonie at the station: she was unrecognisable in a silk headscarf and oversized sunglasses. The two women soon fell into easy familiarity. Over coffee, Kay, aware of the native speakers around her, began to talk in her new North Yorkshire accent. To Leonie's ears it was perfect.

'No one will be able to snipe about you being American. You sound like a local.'

Kay said: 'The rehearsals are going well, but I need to work on the voiceover. Would you be willing to help? We could go to the studio. Everyone else is having a day off.'

The studio was surprisingly small, but the acoustics were wonderful.

Knowing that someone local had killed our sheep ruined everything for us. Father was a nervous wreck.

Michael was going away to start an apprenticeship on the other side of the county. As far as he was concerned Father should take the insurance money and restock.

I longed for the city, but my parents needed me at home. . . .

The silage wagons roared through the village, the drivers desperate to get the third cut of grass undercover before the rain came. As the first drops hit the ground, Leonie, on her way home from her walk, found shelter in a derelict field barn: the roof sagged and the walls had been robbed of stone. A man without a coat ran along the footpath towards her. Calling out, she beckoned him into the barn. He was out of breath and it was some time before he could speak.

'Changeable weather!' he panted.

'I like it when it rains,' Leonie said. 'As long as the sun comes out afterwards.'

They looked out at the heavy shower. In the next field cut grass was still being harvested.

'They're working hard,' he said.

His name was Mark. He was staying in one of the holiday cottages in the village, writing his PhD thesis.

'My thesis is about modern agricultural methods. I had no idea when I came here that farming in so remote a dale would be so intensive. Where have all the old traditions gone?'

The rain stopped abruptly. Mark asked if Leonie would like to meet him in the village pub that evening. 'I'll buy you a drink to thank you for finding me shelter.'

It took only a few seconds for her to agree. The machinery roared behind them as they hiked up the hill to the village.

As Mark and Leonie walked along the road towards the cottage, Grandfather and Grandmother nodded to each other.

'It's worked then,' said Grandfather. 'She'll stay with us?'

Grandmother said, 'The spell may be temporary, but it'll do for now.'

In Bradford Leonie had tentatively invited Kay to visit the dale. Kay seemed keen on the idea, in fact she was positively enthusiastic. One day, just before filming was due to start, she arrived unannounced in a shiny 4x4, Jeff Fellows at the wheel. Fellows sat in the car while Leonie introduced Kay to her grandparents. They went for a walk along the village road and bumped into Mark, who was aiming for the pub.

'This place is beautiful,' said Kay to Leonie. 'I can't believe you'd rather live in a city.'

'That seems to be on hold.'

Kay eyed Mark speculatively. 'Well, good luck to the two of you!'

'How does the film end?' asked Leonie. 'Are you allowed to tell me now?'

'I don't see why not. As you know, the girl has to stay on the farm to look after her father. She meets a man, an outsider, and falls in love, but he finishes with her. Then the horror element kicks in . . . '

'Come on,' interrupted Mark, 'I'll buy you a drink in a real country pub.'

Jeff Fellows got out of the car and walked towards them.

'Where can I get a beer around here?'

'You're driving,' said Kay.

'I'll have a beer if I want one.'

Mark said, 'the police are pretty hot on drink driving around here.'

Jeff turned to Mark: 'And you can shut up too.'

With a helpless glance at Leonie, Kay linked her arm in Fellows' and steered him back to their car.

Mark asked, 'Why does she stay with him?'

'Because he needs looking after,' said Leonie.

Mark was witty and kind and Leonie soon became fond of him. Her grandparents seemed to like him and he was often invited to the cottage.

He settled into the dale, and even though the academic year was about to begin, he said he had few teaching commitments and was being allowed time to finish his thesis. After that he would have to return to his university.

Leonie wondered if she should follow him when the time came. Mark avoided talking about the future, he said he was enjoying the present too much to worry about it. As autumn cooled and they walked over the moors and along the banks of the tumbling peaty river, Leonie dreamed of a time when the city would be their home.

Grandfather watched as Grandmother twisted the dried herbs and sang the incantation.

'This time make it permanent,' he said. 'Mark has done his job but now he may lead her away. It's for her own good. She has to stay in the dale: she'd never survive in the city, we both know that. Look what happened to her mother.'

Filming was about to start. At the end of their final Skype session, Kay thanked Leonie for her hard work and told her she would receive a credit on the film. It was an emotional moment for them both and entirely inappropriate when, like a stage villain, Jeff crept up behind Kay and pretended to stab her with a kitchen knife. He even managed to smear fake blood over the blade. Leonie caught a brief glimpse of Kay's shocked face before the connection was terminated.

Leonie, unsettled, walked to Mark's house. She knocked and knocked on his door. Through the window she could see that the living room was unaccustomedly tidy—bare, even. He'd put away his laptop, books and papers. The kitchen was similarly sparse and clean. His car was not in the drive: he must have gone into town.

She decided to walk to meet him. It was a dry, early autumn morning and the leaves were beginning to fall. For once the road was quiet—the last grass cut of the year was due in a few days' time. The raw beauty of the dale tugged at her heart—the high fells, the heather-topped moors, the dry-stone walls enfolding the silky green fields. She was in danger of falling in love with it all over again.

At the point where the road climbed to the watershed before plunging down into the next dale, the buildings of Highacres Farm huddled under the fell. The cows in their giant milking shed bellowed, their hooves clattering and sliding on the concrete floor.

As Leonie drew level there was a loud clanging and a sudden shout. A group of cows barged through a half-open gate and bolted into the yard, kicking and bucking. The stockmen raced out of the building, cattle prods at the ready, but the cows easily outflanked them, picking up speed until they were cantering up the track towards the road.

Leonie, unfazed, stepped onto the verge, but the cows were unstoppable, flailing and stamping: they had scented the open moor and were determined to reach it. The last thing Leonie saw before the cows veered towards her was the silage clamp beside the barn, the sickly sweet aroma of fermenting grass rich in her nostrils. . . .

Grandmother and Grandfather tend the family plot beside the church. The grass on the most recent grave is clipped short and there are fresh flowers in a vase.

They have their wish. Leonie will remain in the dale.

The old people try not to think about the fact that all there was left to bury of her was a mangled mess of hair, flesh and bone.

CHIMERA

Chimera—A fire-breathing female monster with a lion's head, a hair-covered body, and a serpent's tail, or, a thing which is hoped for but is illusory or impossible to achieve.

The incoming tide nudged gently at the line of seaweed and broken shells. Her eyes were on the horizon, her bare toes dug into the sand.

It was entrancing, the first light soft and pure. Julie scanned the far waters, hand shielding her eyes, but the sea's green glassy surface mocked her, a carapace over the murky depths beneath. She took some photographs, but they could not capture the beauty of the day. Once more she had a presentiment that the thing so desired would not show itself, and, after a while she headed back to the hostel. Despite a flicker of disappointment, hope resurfaced. She had been unlucky today, but there was always tomorrow, or the day after that. . . .

The room was small, a single bed the dominant feature. In one corner stood a rust-stained enamel sink. Julie took her camera from her bag and scrolled again through the photos she had taken. She hung her jacket in the flimsy wardrobe and continued with her daily routine—breakfast, then down the hall to the shower. There was a queue.

Christine said: 'It's only just been fixed.'

Above the spray of the shower they could hear singing.

'His benefits came through,' said Christine. 'Lucky him. I went to the food bank yesterday. You'd be amazed at the kind of people who were there.'

After her shower Julie walked through the awakening town to the library. She looked for jobs on the computer, then searched the shelves for something to read. As she reached for a book, another flashback hit her: She was on the landing, screaming as the fire burnt through her front door. The fireman shouted at her to get back, and smashed the door down with his axe. Inside was an inferno, the heat indescribable.

Julie sat down and took deep breaths. Three months before, a fire had destroyed her flat and possessions, including her books and laptop. Stored on the computer were four years' worth of films and photographs. The flat was rented and she had no insurance, and it was her good fortune that she had been out with her camera when the blaze first took hold. It was thought that a petrol-soaked rag had been lit and stuffed through her letter box, although no traces of accelerant were found. She couldn't bear to think about who could have done such a thing or why. The horror and uncertainty of it gnawed at her.

Julie knew she should be grateful that the council had found her a room in the hostel. Her estranged father, away on an extended visit to her brother in Australia, had so far failed to stump up the loan that would help get her back on her feet. Her only hope was to take and sell more photographs. She had built a reputation for unusual subjects beautifully shot: there were plenty of picture editors happy to consider her work. But to be able to afford her own place she needed something special—a picture or piece of film associated with a great story. Then her agent could orchestrate a bidding war and her troubles would be over.

She had some modest successes. On a twilight walk along the cliff path she took a photo of lightning striking a hawthorn tree. It appeared on the front page of the *Daily Telegraph*. There was always a market for pictures of extreme weather, and animals. But, despite living cheaply, Julie had been unable to save enough money for a deposit on a flat. The hostel was shabby and noisy and she had to keep her door locked because of the drug taking and pilfering that went on.

The Red Lion was as good a pub as any in which to drown her sorrows. Nestling in the Old Town it had oak panelled walls and an open fire, and was frequented by real ale enthusiasts and tourists, as well as locals. As Julie nursed her beer she listened in to a conversation between two men at an adjacent table. They were fishermen: she recognised one as Michael Duggan.

'. . . It rose up in front of me, then dived back under, too quick for me to make out much,' he was saying. 'It was big, though; the head was massive, like nothing I've seen before. I asked my father about it. He said to talk to one of the old timers. According to Jimmy Laidlaw there've been a few sightings over the years. Never very far out. They keep it quiet. It's supposed to be bad luck if you see it.'

'You're pulling my leg,' said his friend.

'Believe what you like. I'm a pretty sceptical person, but I know I saw something. The next day one of the flats went up in smoke.'

Julie was intrigued, and the reference to the fire which had destroyed her home was troubling. Researching in the library she found a paragraph in the *Victoria County History* that described the local myth of a 'great fire-breathing beast' living in the seas around the bay. The earliest recorded sightings dated to the seventeenth century. It was said to have been seen before the devastating storm of 1854, and was supposed to have, pretty comically she thought, the head of a lion, a hair-covered female body and a snake's tail. Perhaps there was some garbled truth in the myth: the creature could be a whale or a basking shark seen from an unusual angle. That would still be of interest. She sniffed the beginnings of a story.

So Julie began her daily trips to the beach. If she could photograph the creature, whatever it was, or better still film it, the story might go global.

Part of her knew it was a sign of her desperation that she gave credence to Michael's tale, but the potential rewards made her visits worthwhile. It wasn't as if she had anything better to do.

Only Christine knew about Julie's pilgrimages to the shore.

'You're wasting your time. It's a fisherman's yarn: he was winding up his mate. You'd be better off doing something useful.'

'Taking photos is the only thing I want to do. Anyway, I've been applying for jobs for weeks. No one wants to know. If I can take one amazing photo or shoot an earth-shattering film I'll be set up for life.'

Every morning Julie kept the faith. On stormy days tall clouds massed to the west. Pummelled by the wind, she struggled along the shore, her cheap coat failing to keep out the rain.

One day, in despair, she flung out her arms and yelled:

'Where are you? Show yourself! Raise your head above the water!'

A stray gust of wind snatched her words away.

It was easy to track down Michael Duggan. A few enquiries sent her back to the Red Lion. Julie approached him and asked if they could talk. The pub was busy, there were no tables free so they stood at the bar. He accepted her offer of a pint.

'I'd like to pick your brains,' Julie said. She explained that she had heard his conversation in the pub several weeks before.

'What do you want to know?'

'Tell me what happened.'

He repeated the story. There were no embellishments.

'I don't expect to be believed,' he said.

The latticework of lines around his eyes came into sharper focus as he leaned towards her. His face was weather-beaten and although he looked weary, his eyes flicked over her.

'Why the interest?'

'I'm a photographer. If there's a new species out there, I'd like to get it on camera.'

Michael laughed. 'It would make your fortune.'
'I'd cut you in if you'll take me out in your boat.'
He leant back. 'Really? You believe me then?'
'We could prove the doubters wrong.'
He considered, then shrugged.
'I could use the money. What do I have to lose?'

They had chosen a still afternoon and the waters beyond the bay were relatively calm, the usual swell soothed by the tranquil weather. Julie took out her camera and cleaned the lens carefully, then rechecked the battery, even though she knew she had charged it earlier in the day.

'Ready?' Michael called from the wheelhouse.

Julie, standing at the bow, waved her assent. She felt adrenaline surge through her. Switching the camera to video mode, and, focusing on the middle distance, she panned around the boat, her finger ready on the zoom.

Ahead, a flock of gannets had gathered, diving and resurfacing with fish in their beaks. Other seabirds circled overhead. Michael reined in the throttle and the boat slowed to a crawl. He joined Julie at the bow.

'There's a shoal of pilchards down there. It's not just the birds that take them. You sometimes see dolphins, sharks, even whales.'

'And the occasional unidentified sea creature?'

'It has to eat something.'

'Do you think we'll see it today?'

Michael laughed. 'You'll have to be patient. I would've thought that's a necessity in your job.'

The gannets dived again and again, folding their wings against their bodies as they pierced the water.

Michael returned to the wheelhouse and cut the engine.

'Why did you call your boat *Monster*?' Julie asked.

'It's a bit of a beast. I named it a long time before I saw the creature.'

The gannets rose from the water and flew eastwards.

'The shoal's moved on,' Michael said.

Monster followed the coast, Julie's eyes on her camera screen. Apart from the seabirds, there was no sign of life. After several hours' fruitless searching, they called it a day.

As they entered the harbour, Michael said, 'We'll go out again at the weekend.'

That night Julie dreamt she and Michael were scuba diving: they were at some depth, just above the sea bed. She was filming with a waterproof camera. Michael, swimming beside her, steered them towards a shoal of curious-looking fish. As they swam closer she could see they had lions' heads, hair-covered bodies and snakes' coiling tails. The strange little fish began rooting in the sea bed, stirring up detritus so that it was impossible to see more than a few metres ahead. Michael grabbed her arm. There was a surge in the water and a huge shape swam past. It was impossible to see the thing clearly. When she looked down she saw that she had gripped the camera so hard it had broken in two. . . .

She woke, got out of bed and checked her own camera. It was in one piece. But the dream stayed with her and it was nearly dawn before she went back to sleep.

The worst of the storm had yet to hit, but the sea was already raging and waves thundered onto the beach. Julie took photographs of the surf and the dark distant clouds. Everything was lit by a numinous glow; the air brimmed with expectation. Suddenly the light changed. She looked through the photos: they were disappointing, grey and indistinct, lacking the energy of the day.

Julie was hungry; she had been on the beach since dawn. Christine would be waiting for her in the Old Town. One last time Julie looked out to sea, then slipped the camera into her rucksack.

Christine was waiting outside the Town Hall. They headed for the market and ate their sandwiches sitting on the War Memorial steps. After a few moments Christine said:

'They're threatening to throw me out of the hostel.'

'Why?'

'Apparently, I've had my room long enough and should be trying to get my own place. I told them that's not going to be easy, but there's a long waiting list and they have to think of others. I don't know what I'm going to do.'

'Surely they'll help you find somewhere?'

'You know how few vacant flats there are. And they're expensive dumps.'

'I expect I'll be next,' said Julie. 'I've been there nearly as long as you.'

Christine said, 'We could get a place together.'

Julie smiled. 'I'd like that.'

It would take a miracle for them to find the money.

Time, she realised, was against her.

Julie had not sold a picture for weeks: her agent was becoming impatient. Even the thought of tomorrow's boat trip with Michael could not distract her from self-pity. Last weekend they had gone out on rough seas. She discovered that she was a bad sailor, and had been relieved when they turned for home. Apart from her seasickness the trip was uneventful. Even the many porpoises that visited the bay eluded them.

Calls to her father were unanswered. Funds were running low, and she could not claim benefits until her money was as good as gone. Christine was about to move out of the hostel into a run-down bed and breakfast on the sea front. As Julie had predicted, the hostel manager had approached her and asked if she too would start looking for somewhere else to live.

She took her camera out of her bag and studied the film she had taken during the rough trip out. Grey water churned, seagulls squawked. There was not a spark of interest in it, except for some incidental shots of Michael in the wheelhouse, looking out to sea.

The storms had given way to a sullen, overcast day. *Monster* skimmed over the calm waters of the bay. As they reached the open sea Michael opened the throttle a little and they cruised in wide circles. Julie attached her camera to the tripod, but her heart wasn't in it. Sensing her depression, Michael put his hand on her shoulder.

'We'll find the bloody thing,' he'd said. 'It can't hide for ever.'

'I'm in trouble, Michael.'

'Something will turn up.'

Porpoises raced each other in *Monster's* wake. Gannets dived in the distance.

'There's a shoal,' Michael shouted, and steered the boat towards the birds. Julie prepared the camera for close-ups. As they neared the feeding area she spotted something floating in the water.

'Cut the engine!' she yelled at Michael. She leaned over the side.

A grey shape bobbed on the waves.

'It's a porpoise. Or it was.'

Blood darkened the water.

'Just the tail-end, poor thing.'

Michael surveyed the remains.

'Look at the way it's been savaged.'

Julie turned to him.

'Are we on to something?'

'I don't know.'

He went back to the wheelhouse and the boat picked up speed. As they neared the birds Michael cut the engine and Julie took shot after shot of the gannets diving. When she reviewed the pictures they seemed to her hackneyed, but Michael praised them.

'I can tell you're a professional,' he said.

She thought, *He's being kind.*

Just then *Monster* began to yaw.

'Hold tight!' Michael shouted.

Julie grasped the rail. Something swam underneath and brushed against the keel: the boat shuddered. The gannets rose from the water and flew silently away.

Julie cried out, more in triumph than fear.

The Red Lion was almost empty and they chose a table near the fire. Julie watched Michael as he bought drinks at the bar.

'We were so close to seeing it . . . ' she said, when he returned.

He sighed. 'It could've been a humpback.'

Julie reached for his hand.

'We're going to see it, aren't we?'

He gently removed her fingers.

'There are no guarantees. Look, Julie . . . '

'Are you bored with it?'

'I should never have raised your hopes.'

'We were close,' she said fiercely. 'I want it so much, Michael.'

The party began in the late afternoon and continued for most of the night. Julie gave up trying to sleep and read her library book in bed. From time to time the night manager asked for quiet and the decibels lessened, only to rise again when he retreated to his office.

Julie watched from her window as night shaded into morning, then dressed and let herself out of the building. She saw no one. The brief walk was equally free of human activity, although the seagulls called out from their cliff-face perches. As she stepped onto the beach she stopped to take off her shoes. Cool sand trickled between her toes.

The rising sun gave light to a calm, clear day. She pulled the camera from her rucksack and walked to the gently foaming surf, where a cluster of empty shells rolled in its ebb and flow. She took photographs and some film. The thought came to her that she would rather die than move away from the sea.

Her father rang, only to announce that he was staying in Australia for as long as his visa allowed. He said, when she asked him for a loan, that she was old enough to fend for herself; it would do her good, and she should find a cheaper town in which to live. Julie could not bring herself to beg for money. When she explained about the dire straits she was in, he said, 'You'd better find yourself a boyfriend.'

The shock of it rearranged her thoughts. She felt that for the first time in months she was thinking clearly. The myth of the monster was just that—a legend to spice up an evening tale, a story passed down through the generations. The power of suggestion had bewitched Michael and the old fishermen, conjuring false sightings. She had stupidly allowed herself to believe that it might be true.

I've been a fool, she thought.

Julie sold some photographs. Christine found a job waitressing and managed to slip her a few free meals. Julie saved a little money.

Michael offered to take her out again in *Monster*. She aimed to spend the trip taking a series of photographs of the coast from the sea. Her agent had pitched the idea to a Sunday supplement and they expressed an interest in publishing the pictures.

Michael looked exhausted. When she commented on this he said: 'Fishing's a tough way to make a living.'

'I thought you enjoyed it.'

'I used to,' he said.

'What's changed?'

He shrugged. 'Fish stocks are falling. I'm getting older, I suppose. . . . '

Julie watched him—surreptitiously filmed him—took a photo or two.

They spotted a school of porpoises, leaping over each other in their haste to reach the open sea. The seagulls were flying back to land.

'Is there bad weather on the way?' she asked.

'The forecast's good.'

She took some pictures of the cliffs.
Michael said quietly, 'You've stopped believing, haven't you.'
'No . . . It's just that . . . '
'I've been thinking that we might as well give up.'
She found herself saying, 'I enjoy these trips. I enjoy being with you.'
'Julie . . . '
She put her hands over her ears.
The sea lapped against the hull. Michael opened the throttle and turned the boat for home.

As they entered the bay *Monster* began to rock violently. All around them, the water churned.

'Grab the rail!' Michael cried, cutting the engine. It was too late. Julie tumbled over the side and into the sea. As she surfaced the cold made her gasp and she inhaled more water. She swam aimlessly around, remembering at last to inflate her life jacket. Michael threw in a life ring with a rope attached, but she couldn't reach it. *Monster* was drifting away. He called out, 'I'll get help.'

He picked up the radio handset.

The air was still, the sky cloudless, but the sea threw her around like a doll. Panic seized her as she felt her strength drain away. She had swallowed a great deal of water.

Michael shouted, 'I've called the coastguard. The life boat'll be here in a few minutes.'

Julie turned over and floated on her back. The cold ate into her bones. She knew she would not have long before hypothermia set in. Michael started *Monster's* engine and the boat inched towards her.

'Hold on,' he said. 'Don't go to sleep.'

The sea boiled and out of it rose the creature. It writhed, exposing its hair-covered torso, and, thrashing its scaly tail, shot tall plumes of water into the air. Fire flared from its nostrils, illuminating the snarling leonine face. It dwarfed the crazily rocking boat where Michael searched frantically for Julie's camera. The beast reared up and opened its jaws, revealing scythe-like fangs. Finding the camera, Michael took photograph after photograph as the creature swam toward Julie. As its eyes locked on hers, she slipped into unconsciousness. . . .

Michael sat by the bed while Julie slept. They had warmed her carefully and a touch of pink suffused her cheeks. She woke slowly, stretching her body before opening her eyes.

'Michael,' she said, and smiled.
'I didn't think you'd make it,' he said.
'Well, here I am.'
She rested for a while.
'Did you take some photos?' she asked sleepily.
'I was too busy helping to pull you out of the water.'
'Not of me! . . . The creature! . . . '
'What are you talking about?'
'It was there!'
Michael shook his head. 'I'll come clean. I'm sorry. I bet my friend I could persuade you the thing was real. It got out of hand.'
'But I saw it!'
'Hypothermia does funny things to people.'
'You're saying it's all in my head.'
She thought for a moment.
'I don't believe you. Where's my camera?'
'It went over the side with you.'
Julie, exhausted, closed her eyes and drifted away.

It was best to make sure. Lifting her head he slowly pulled out the pillow. She did not wake, and he laid it gently on her face. The nurse had shut the door on her way out and it should be some time before she returned. He took hold of the pillow and pressed down hard. Julie barely stirred.

When it was over he replaced the pillow beneath her head. She was beautifully still, an angel in her white hospital gown. He sat down and waited for the nurse.

After he had answered their questions, they sent him home.

He uploaded the pictures. They were astonishing, incontrovertible.

It was time to find himself an agent.

POACHER TURNED GAMEKEEPER

Clive was right to suspect there would be trouble when he set up his computer consultancy. Just as he began his publicity campaign, the local newspaper ran an article about him entitled: 'CAN YOU TRUST THIS MAN?' with a police photo of his younger self. He supposed he should be grateful they had made an attempt to balance the piece by printing an interview with a retired probation officer. She said that people make mistakes and should be given a second chance, especially when they had paid their debt to society and lived a blameless life ever since. In his heart Clive knew that it wasn't remorse but cowardice that had made him live so quietly. He was constantly afraid that he might be outed. But now it had happened, he had nothing to lose. It was time to come out fighting.

He changed the name of his firm to 'Poacher Turned Gamekeeper' and promoted himself as a fraud spotter, problem solver and financial wizard. This in-your-face approach, along with the fact that his was the only computer consultancy in town, bore fruit: he gained several small business clients and a woman called Michelle Furnival hired him to set up her new laptop. Michelle was single and glamorous, older than Clive: she seemed to like him and was curious about his younger years.

'I suppose you had a deprived childhood,' she said. 'Abusive parents, etc.'

'Actually they're pretty respectable.'
'So why did you go off the rails?'
'Temptation. It's easy to part people from their money and I thought I was clever enough not to get caught.'
'Was it awful in prison?'
'I was in Meadowfields most of the time. It's like an enlightened boarding school.'

Michelle knew very little about computers and it would have been easy to take advantage of her. Clive was careful when setting up a spreadsheet for her household expenses, building society accounts and stocks and shares to look away as she keyed in the amounts. He liked to think that she was reckless because she trusted him.

Several small businesses had contracted him to sort out their computer problems and seemed pleased with his work. Most paid on time and Clive was soon earning a reasonable income. After a few months the local newspaper sent a reporter to interview him. They ran a human interest piece with a photograph of him in his best suit. The report concentrated on the turnaround in his life. It was sympathetic, a 'bad boy makes good' story, and brought him several new clients.

Michelle Furnival began to make a nuisance of herself, phoning him at all hours with minor queries, asking him to come to the house. It took a proper talking-to to make her leave him alone. He had fewer problems with business clients, who called for his help only when a computer crashed or data were lost. After a few days he went back to Michelle's flat and apologised. Then he seduced her. Because he could.

A few months' later Clive's consultancy was so successful that he was planning on hiring staff. He allowed himself to believe he'd transcended his earlier problems. The business was his baby and he was determined to make a go of it. Even if they knew about his past, his clients seemed not to care that he had ripped off a few hapless pensioners. It was hardly the crime of the century. Anyway, most of those directly affected would be dead by now.

The phone call was a surprise, and a nasty one. It started with a silence of some seconds, which made him think it was a nuisance call attempting to sell him double glazing or a funeral plan. Then a man's voice said:
'Hello, Clive.'
There was another silence.
'Who's that?'
'I'm not sure you'll remember me, even if I tell you my name.'
'What do you want?' Clive asked.
The silence that followed was uncomfortably long.
'I haven't got all day,' Clive said. 'Spit it out, or I'll end the call.'
'We're concerned you're up to your old tricks,' said the voice.
'Who are you?'
'You should be aware that we're watching your every move. One step out of line and we'll be on to you.'
Clive ended the call.
He told himself it was a prank, but it was still worrying. Someone had threatened him, knowing he wouldn't go to the police.

To distract himself he opened the file containing the business plan he was preparing for the bank. Working out of a bedroom at his parents' house, where he had lived since prison, was becoming increasingly impractical. He had applied for a loan so he could rent an office and buy a flat. Michelle, who was an estate agent, would be able to help him find somewhere suitable.

Clive was good with numbers. He knew how to make them work for him. It helped that Poacher Turned Gamekeeper was turning a decent profit. There was the little matter of his past, of course: Clive was hoping that the bank would overlook that once they had seen his account balance and projections.

He worked into the night, forgetting to close the curtains. The winking of the stars distracted him, and he went to the window. Under the street light was an elderly man, spindly, in a loose overcoat. He looked up and Clive could see blank, mottled-green pulp where the man's face should be.

Clive recoiled, then looked again. It was horrible, the skin squirming as if maggots burrowed under it. Clive retched. He closed the curtains and made himself go down to the kitchen for a glass of water. When he found the courage to look out of the living room window, the figure had gone.

He calmed himself (he had learnt the technique in prison), then took a sleeping pill. He slept through to the early afternoon and when he woke he thought about his strange encounter. The mind, he knew from first-hand experience, could play strange tricks. It had become so bad in Meadowfields that he'd asked to see the shrink.

Michelle made him very welcome that evening, cooking a meal and opening a bottle of wine.

'You seem distracted,' she said.

'I want to sort out some premises, then I can hire staff. I need that loan.'

'You'll manage it somehow.'

It was a warm night. Clive opened the window. Standing on the pavement was the figure with the green squirming face. Its hand was raised and an ivory finger pointed at Clive. Clive stepped back in horror.

'What's wrong now?' asked Michelle from the bed.

The thing disappeared.

Clive said, 'Is this a practical joke?'

'I don't know what you're talking about.'

'Someone's trying to scare me.'

'Why would they want to do that? Go to the police if you're worried.'

On the way home Clive's mobile rang. There was silence, then came the insinuating voice.

'You've had some worrying encounters I hear.'

'Leave me alone,' said Clive.

'I'm afraid we can't do that.'
'I have no idea what you want from me.'
'You know what you've done.'
'I've paid my debt . . .'
'You didn't pay enough.'

Despite the heat of the day Clive put on his best suit and most conservative tie, only to find the bank manager in an open-necked shirt and slacks. On Graham Cross's computer screen was Clive's completed business loan application form. On the desk were printouts of his spreadsheets and projections.

'This is very impressive,' said Graham. 'You obviously know how to put together a good case. It's one of the best I've seen. It says a lot about your competence, and given your customers' positive feedback, your computer skills are obviously up to scratch.' He cleared his throat. 'Trust, though Clive, is vital in business, I'm sure you agree. You say you've turned a corner and put your . . . indiscretions behind you. But the stain on your character will always be there. That's the dilemma. Should we take a risk on you?'

Graham tapped his teeth with his pen. 'I'm sorry Clive, but I think we need to give it more time. Let's say a year. Prove we can trust you and you'll get your loan. You have my word on it.'

Michelle was phlegmatic.

'You must have enough income to rent a small office somewhere. Everything else can wait.'

'I need staff to take on some of the work.'

'Hire freelancers.'

Clive sighed. 'It's not what I wanted.'

'All you have to do is wait a year, then you'll get your loan and you can do what you like.'

The small, dingy office above a newsagents was all that Clive could afford, but at least he had somewhere to invite prospective clients. He fixed a sign on the door, bought flat-pack office furniture and painted the walls white. Even so modest a premises made him feel more professional, but when several of his contracts came to an end, Clive found that, with the extra expense, his profits halved.

Running the business was still fun, however, and through it he met several women. Michelle didn't know about them. His relationship with her had always been relaxed and casual.

After a few months, Clive's spreadsheets showed that profits had fallen again. Tightening his belt was tedious, and he was unable to pay freelancers who would help his business grow. A larger office and flat were out of the question.

One morning Clive received a phone call from the IT manager of TEC, an international corporation that made aeronautic components. He had been recommended to them by one of their suppliers. TEC wanted him to design, among other things, a new stock-control system. The work would take around three months. To say that the phone call saved Poacher Turned Gamekeeper was an exaggeration, but the job would hopefully keep his head above water until he found new clients.

Phoning round the small business community, Clive had discovered there was a new reluctance to give him work. He told himself it was because of a dip in business confidence, but he could detect an unmistakeable wariness in some of the voices when he mentioned the name of his firm. One Human Resources manager explained that they had received a phone call warning them off Poacher Turned Gamekeeper.

Relying on one large job was not part of his business plan. He aimed to spread his efforts and risk over several smaller contracts. It didn't help that he was expected to send an invoice to TEC only when the work was complete. Over the next three months his cash flow crisis heightened, and he had trouble finding the money to pay the office rent.

Michelle could see how worried he was.

'Hang on in there,' she said. 'Just keep doing your job well, and everything will come good.'

Clive finished the software design for TEC before the three months were up. When he asked for payment he was told to submit an invoice to the accounts department for the agreed amount. Clive's financial worries were continuing; even the money from the TEC job would not tide him over for long. As he created the invoice, an idea came to him. TEC was a massive organisation and his fee would barely register. Adding a nought to the end of the amount was easy, and, he reasoned, would probably not be queried by the accounts department processing the payment. If it was, then he could claim he had made a simple error.

He checked his balance every day and at last the full amount was transferred to his account. He felt an enormous weight lift from his shoulders. Poacher Turned Gamekeeper would be safe until the bank loan came through.

The TEC work led to several new contracts and Clive hired John, a freelance programmer. Clive asked Michelle to find him a larger office. Things were back on track.

After spending the night with Michelle, Clive had overslept and was in danger of being late for an early meeting at his office. Hurrying through the sleazy part of town, he decided it would be safe to take the short cut. As the alley narrowed he found his way blocked by a nearly stationary man.

'Excuse me,' he said.

There was no reply. The man shuffled on. Clive tapped him on the shoulder, his fingertips sinking into the overcoat and continuing down into the pulpy flesh beneath. The man turned and Clive saw a seething, mottled-green mess. . . .

When Clive came to he was alone in the alley. His phone was ringing.

'Back to your old ways, Clive?'

'How are you doing it? Is it some kind of mask? . . . '

'Your mind is playing tricks on you.'

'I've not seriously hurt anyone . . . '

'Are you sure about that?'

Clive ended the call. Had TEC found out about the money? He felt his stomach lurch.

True to form, Michelle had cooked him a roast dinner.

'You look a bit peaky, Clive.'

'I've had a bad day.'

'What's wrong?'

'Just some trouble over a payment.'

'Large amount, is it?'

There was something in Michelle's tone that made him cautious.

'Nothing for you to worry about. I'll get it sorted.'

They ate in silence. Clive drank most of the wine. When they had finished, Michelle washed up.

'You've never asked me much about myself, have you Clive?'

Clive, who had been dozing in the chair, sat up.

'I'm always interested in anything you have to say.'

'All right then. Here's a story about my family. My father got into financial difficulties a few years ago. He went into a decline and took an overdose. My mother found him, but it was too late to save him from serious kidney damage. He's really ill. Neither of them have been the same since.'

'That's very . . . '

'Yes,' said Michelle. 'It is. You see there was a conman who bamboozled him with computer speak and inveigled his savings from him. My father was an intelligent man and it destroyed his pride. I'm surprised you didn't hear about the overdose.'

'It happened when I was in prison . . . ' said Clive, then stopped abruptly.

There was a long silence, then Clive asked shakily, 'Did you arrange the phone calls, the masks?'

'I gave you every chance. You'd no need to cheat, but it was only a matter of time before you did. You were careful, though, I'll give you that.' Her face contorted with anger. 'Do you think I wanted to sleep with a nasty little crook like you? I had to get close to catch you out. You think I'm a fool, but I know how to read a bank statement.'

Before Clive could reach her the door opened. A number of blank-faced figures shuffled in and gathered around Clive. Michelle stood up.

'They're here to remind you of your obligations. Give their families what you owe them.'

Clive backed towards the window. 'They're not real,' he shouted. 'Leave me alone. I've paid my dues.'

Michelle smiled.

'Are you sure, Clive? You of all people should know when you've tripped the trap.'

THE WEEPING WOMAN

Penny's survey of Luscombe Manor, a honey-toned, seventeenth-century house with Victorian additions, was taking much longer than she'd anticipated. The owner, Percy Davington, didn't seem to mind, however, and, going into the warm kitchen to eat her packed lunches, she often found him waiting for her with a glass of good dry sherry.

She had discovered Luscombe and its owner on one of her long hikes in the country. Penny approached her supervisor who agreed that the house would make a good subject for a dissertation. She was to produce a comprehensive chronology and a set of detailed plans to back it up. Percy Davington agreed that she could visit two days each week. It was only on her first day that Penny realised they had failed to take account of the garden pavilions and the extensive range of outbuildings that formed an integral part of the manorial complex. The dissertation was to be completed by the beginning of April, and as February drew on Penny began to suspect that she had bitten off more than she could chew.

It was an exceptionally cold winter. On some days the harsh white rime of a hoar frost covered the garden and Penny's hands were chilled beyond usefulness. She was forced to break off from the survey of the house and warm herself in front of the Aga. Percy Davington often joined her there and they talked about the building and its history. Apart from the kitchen, the house, although very beautiful, was cold as stone.

Percy (as he insisted she call him), ran an investment company from one of the nineteenth-century extensions. Having explained that she would need to measure every inch of the buildings, Penny was allowed free rein. Each room of the manor house, even the attic, was clean and tidy. Of the outbuildings, only the old dovecote, a large and interesting example of its kind, was in a state of disrepair, although Percy said he had plans to renovate it. It would be quite a job as the building needed reroofing and repointing and most of the timbers were rotten.

By the beginning of March the survey of the main house was complete. Percy was impatient to see the results, but although Penny had begun to generate plans, she could not make a start on the chronology until she had finished surveying and researching the whole complex. Time, she was well aware, was slipping away from her.

The gardens and grounds of Luscombe were looked after by Si Shurrock. In order to speed things up, Si helped her measure the house. Penny suspected that he offered to do this only because he had been asked to keep an eye on her. They got on well enough, however, and one crisp morning she asked if he would assist her with the outbuildings. His cheerful demeanour fell away.

'I'll help you with everything except the dovecote,' he said.

'It won't take long.'

Si looked at the ground.

'It's at night you hear it. She weeps, you see, and wails.'

'What do you mean?'

'I've never been in there and I won't start now. Mr Davington did some research in the county archives. Not long after the house was built, the daughter of the squire was caught with a local farmer. Her father had them strung up from a beam in the dovecote. She's been weeping in there ever since. If Mr Davington had known about it he'd probably not have bought the place.'

Penny supposed that every old house had its legends. She was surprised that Percy and Si took it so seriously. Surely someone who'd heard the story was playing games, pointless though it might seem. Someone with a grudge. She resolved to visit after dark one night with a torch and flush out the culprit. It was the least she could do after all Percy and Si had done for her.

So one clear March evening Penny found herself creeping across the moonlit courtyard towards the dovecote. Somewhere, a solitary dog barked. As she approached the dilapidated entrance there came the sound, faint at first, of hopeless sobbing. It increased in volume as Penny tiptoed inside. She switched on her torch and flicked the beam around the interior. There were no hiding places. The dovecote was empty.

That night the desolate weeping Penny had heard kept her from sleep. Her thoughts ranged over the possibilities. Could some kind of sound system have been installed in the dovecote? What motive would provoke such a thing? How might a hoaxer produce something that sounded so genuine?

The next day, Percy was waiting for her in the garden.
'Si tells me you've been investigating our weeping lady.'
'I wanted to get to the bottom of it.'
'And?'
'Do you know anyone who has a grudge against you?'
He laughed. 'You heard her, didn't you?'

The only building left to survey was the dovecote. In daylight, it looked merely gloomy and unloved. Penny hurried herself along, stepping quickly over the detritus, estimating measurements where the interior walls could not be reached. It was damp and chilly; weirdly shaped fungi grew on the fallen beams, and Penny, despite telling herself that there was nothing to worry about, experienced a great surge of relief as she finished and went back to the house.

'No falls from the roof?' asked Si.

'I didn't spend long inside.'

Si said, 'She must like you.'

Percy frowned at him.

'You're very dedicated, Penny. It's a dangerous building. I really ought to get the contractors in.'

Penny worked frantically to finish her dissertation, producing a meticulous plan of the whole manor complex and a comprehensive chronology. In due course she was awarded her Masters degree, with a distinction. Percy invited her to dinner at Luscombe to celebrate.

Candlelight made the dining room more intimate and the fire had been lit. Shadows danced on the wainscoting. Percy had cooked dinner and dressed the table himself. Si carved the pheasant. They raised a glass to Penny's achievement, and Penny handed a copy of her dissertation to Percy. They began to eat.

After a few mouthfuls Si said: 'She's still weeping and wailing. If anything it's worse than before.'

Percy sat back.

'She's a lost soul,' said Si.

There was an enormous, rumbling crash. The plates and glasses rattled on the table. After a moment of shocked silence they hurried out to see, on the other side of the courtyard, the dovecote reduced to a pile of rubble, a cloud of brick dust rising from the ruins. Penny was puzzled by the look of triumph that flitted over Percy's face.

There was a terrible wailing. The outline of a woman unfurled from the rubble; the keening ceased as she regarded the devastation around her. A second figure, taller, emerged from the stables and grasped the woman's hand. There was a disturbance in the air and they disappeared, a breath of breeze cool on Penny's cheek.

Si said, 'She's gone!'

It was some months before Penny went back to Luscombe: Percy had not contacted her since the dinner party. There was bound to be some awkwardness after their extraordinary experience—she hardly knew what to think about that—but she felt they shared a bond because of it. She was old-fashioned enough to believe that the first overture should come from Percy. Perhaps he assumed she wanted to put everything to do with the Manor and its ghosts behind her.

On the strength of her dissertation Penny found a job with a conservation architect, surveying dilapidated historic buildings. The work was interesting but demanding and ate into her evenings. She was so busy that Percy, Si and The Weeping Woman faded from her mind.

Then she heard from her supervisor that Luscombe Manor was for sale. When she looked at the description of the house on the estate agents' website she found it borrowed heavily from her work. The asking price was astonishing. The fact that the manor had undergone a full historical survey was presented as a selling point. Penny felt sick. Why would Percy have done this without even asking her? She resolved to go to Luscombe and find out.

As she parked in the outer courtyard she saw the ugly estate agents' board. Si was in the garden.

'Hello, Penny. What brings you here?'

'I came to see Percy.'

'Let yourself into the yard and I'll fetch him.'

The rebuilt dovecote, clad in scaffolding, towered over her. Only the conical roof was missing. Penny felt a shiver run through her as she remembered the demise of the old building. Percy appeared from the house.

'What do you think?' he asked.

'You haven't been in touch.'

'I've been busy . . . ' he gestured at the dovecote. 'Impressive, isn't it?'

Penny saw that the building had been furnished with several small windows and a solid-looking door.

'It's going to be a holiday cottage. I've Listed Building Consent for all the other outbuildings to be converted—by the next owner, probably. Your survey really helped. It'll be a small holiday village.'

'You let the dovecote fall down, didn't you? You hoped it would get rid of the Weeping Woman.'

Percy laughed. 'I'm so glad you didn't mention her in your dissertation. People dislike *real* ghosts on their property. I've several interested buyers and I don't want them put off.'

'You used me! I thought we were friends. . . . '

'The survey was your idea. I thought you'd be glad I've put it to good use.'

Penny said, 'I'll tell your buyers about the Weeping Woman. She may yet come back to haunt you.'

'I don't think so,' said Percy, twisting Penny's arm behind her back and frogmarching her to the dovecote. He opened the door and pushed her inside. The Yale lock clicked behind her. Imprisoned in the bright new interior, Penny wept and wailed in vain.

THE CINEMA

Despite the argument they held hands until they reached the cinema, then she felt his fingers slip away. Next to her she saw not Callum but a man taking a photograph of the Art Deco building. Callum was nowhere to be seen.

Losing an argument was a poor reason for leaving her on her own. It had been an unimportant spat about where they would next go on holiday. These sorts of discussions had become a habit, a way of asserting their separateness: cute coupledom appealed to neither of them. Anne had plumped for Madeira, and although she did not feel strongly about it, she'd argued for her choice until Callum gave in. He'd favoured Budapest.

Anne leant against the cinema's frontage, waiting for Callum to return. She reached for her bag then remembered she'd left it in their hotel room, along with her phone, cash and credit cards. Wearing a tight-fitting dress without pockets, she had not wanted to spoil its line. Vanity, she thought ruefully. She was somewhat ashamed that, although it was her turn, she had let Callum pay for the drinks and meal.

Anne attracted some inquisitive looks from passers-by. The evening cooled and she shivered in her thin dress. If Callum was not coming back, then it was time to return to the hotel. The trouble was that, having a poor sense of direction, she had no idea how to find it. Callum had arranged the booking and this was the first night of their stay: she was not even sure of the hotel's name.

Perhaps Callum *was* still looking for her. She vaguely remembered reading that you were supposed to stay put if you wanted to be found, but she decided that it was best to set out for the hotel. The receptionist might remember her and let her have a room key.

The crowds had doubled in size and, attempting to retrace her steps across the square, she brushed against several people. Finding herself in a street of unfamiliar pubs and night clubs, she knew she had taken a wrong turn. She returned to the haven of the cinema.

A woman approached, her pink face framed by an immaculate hairdo. Hanging from her shoulder was an expensive-looking handbag.

'Are you all right, dear?'

'I'm okay,' said Anne automatically. 'Well, actually, I'm not. I'm lost, I don't have any money and I'm not sure of the name of my hotel.'

'Come down on the train, have you? Don't worry, I've helped plenty of girls like you. I'll find you somewhere to stay and we'll take it from there.'

She grasped Anne's hand. Anne shook herself free and kicked the woman hard in the shins. The woman swore and hobbled away.

Shaken by the encounter, Anne decided that she would have to make a more determined effort to find the hotel. She pushed her way through the crowds until she reached the other side of the square. Around the corner was a row of high-end shops selling clothing and accessories. It was less crowded there. Anne walked warily, looking over her shoulder in case the woman was following her. The street joined a busy road, cars and buses nose to tail in a seemingly endless line of traffic. Although there were some hotels on the far side, none of them resembled Anne's, which, she recalled, was a smaller, older building.

It was beginning to get dark, but there were lights everywhere: the cars, the shops, the streetlights. Unused to the city at night, Anne tried to stay calm, picking her way along the street, turning the corner back into the square. Callum would be worrying about her, frantically searching for her, thinking about calling the police. Perhaps she should put him out of his misery and approach a kind-looking person with a phone she could borrow.

A long queue snaked from the cinema. After her experience with the pink-faced woman, she couldn't bring herself to beg for a phone. In any case, she would rather Callum found her himself. It might make him think twice about abandoning her in future. Also, she could picture the delicious, tearful reunion. . . .

The cinema doors opened and the queue began to move. A doorman in a smart uniform sold tickets. There were no posters outside the cinema, but whatever was showing was obviously popular: it was difficult to see how so many people could fit into what must surely be a fairly small auditorium.

Anne caught sight of the back of a dark-haired man at the front of the queue. He looked a lot like Callum. She called out his name, but the man bought his ticket and disappeared inside. It couldn't have been Callum, though the resemblance was strong: why would he be going into the cinema when he should be looking for her?

Leaning against the wall attracted more unwanted attention. A man wearing a large sandwich board approached her, 'JESUS SAVES' in large lettering printed on both sides. He handed Anne a leaflet.

'You look lost.'

'I am. I can't find my hotel.'

'You're lost in the wilderness. Come to our church and be saved. All your sins will be forgiven.'

He looked her up and down, slowly.

Anne bridled. 'I'm not a working girl.'

'Everyone's welcome. You can come with me now; I've nearly finished my shift.'

'No thank you.'

'You'd be doing me a favour. I'm new to this and I haven't made any converts.'

'Go away,' said Anne.

The man looked at her sorrowfully.

'I said go away!'

He was soon lost in the crowd.

The cinema queue filed in and the doorman closed and bolted the doors. Several latecomers rattled the handles, turning angrily away. The lights in the foyer were switched off and shortly afterwards she heard music, too quiet to identify, drifting out onto the pavement. A short man approached her, but when his friends began to jeer at him, he thought better of it. The group wandered on. Anne tried not to worry: Callum would be here soon, she was sure of it.

Night settled on the city. Revellers spilled from the pubs, jostling and calling: Anne felt uncomfortable, vulnerable even. She shivered uncontrollably. After a while a large middle-aged woman came up to her.

'Are you all right? Only you look rather cold.'

'I'm lost. I have no money. I think the name of my hotel is The Metropole, or The Majestic. It begins with M, anyway, and it's not far from here. Can you help?'

The woman tut tutted. 'I don't approve of beggars, especially when they try to entice you somewhere else. But, because you've probably been coerced into it, and you're genuinely cold, I'll give you my cardigan.'

The woman took off her coat and handed her cardigan to Anne.

'There are shelters you can go to,' said the woman, re-joining the passing throng.

Anne put on the oversized cardigan and immediately felt less exposed. It was made of fine wool, soft against her bare arms. Within a few minutes she had warmed up sufficiently to feel more comfortable. Would Callum spot her in the crowd now her dress was partly covered by the cardigan?

The bolts were drawn and the doors of the cinema opened. The doorman stepped out and beckoned to her. She unpeeled herself from the wall and walked towards him, careful to keep some distance between them.

'Come in,' he said. 'We don't bite. Your loved one is here.'

Anne felt a wave of relief wash over her. She let the doorman usher her into the dark foyer.

'You'll be safer in here,' he said.

'Where's Callum?'

'He has a few things to clear up, then he'll be with you. I'll come back to check you're all right.'

He smiled reassuringly and disappeared into the gloom. Somewhere close by, a door banged shut. The music Anne had heard outside resolved itself into an ambient drone. She could just make out a swing door at the rear of the foyer. At its edge was a gap through which knifed a narrow beam of flickering light.

Had Callum involved the police after all? Was there paperwork to complete? Would she be expected to confirm Callum's story, and if so, what would she say? That he had accidentally let go of her hand, when she knew he had relinquished it deliberately? Anger boiled in her, obliterating the relief at being found. What a low trick he had played.

After some searching she eventually found the light switch on the far wall. The foyer was painted a dull red. Apart from the swing door at the end there was only one other door. She knocked on it, hoping to find Callum and the policeman. She shouted, 'Callum! . . . Callum!' When she tried the handle she found the door was locked. There was nowhere else to go but the auditorium.

Anne pushed open the swing door: it was surprisingly heavy. Except for a dark-haired man sitting in the middle of the banks of seating, the auditorium was empty. On screen, to the soundtrack of the ambient music, a fully-clothed man appeared to be gnawing the arm of a naked, disembowelled, woman. The man watching was Callum.

Callum turned and saw Anne standing there. He stood abruptly, bounded up the stairs and took her in his arms.

'What have you been doing Callum? Where are the police?'

'Why would we need the police? I knew you'd be cool about it if I just popped into the cinema for a few minutes.'

'It's been hours, Callum! I've been at the mercy of every nutter who took an interest in me.'

'Is that where that horrible cardigan came from?'

I'm grateful that at least one person was kind.'

'I would have told you, but . . . I just wanted to be let off the leash for a while.'

'What does that mean?' Anne said. 'You didn't have to abandon me in the street.'

'Look,' he squeezed her tight. 'I love you, that's all that matters.'

'No it isn't,' she said quietly.

Blood-curdling screams came from the speakers.

'We could have two holidays,' said Callum, 'Madeira *and* Budapest.'

'We can't afford it.'

Callum let her go.

'What are you watching?' Anne asked. The disembowelled woman had staggered up and was busily strangling the man. 'Where are the others? There was a queue.'

'What others?' he said. 'It's just some . . . fake snuff movie. Nothing for you to worry about. Shall we go back to the hotel?'

Anne was close to tears. 'I couldn't find it, Callum. I was completely helpless.'

'Well never mind, my darling, you're with me now,' said Callum, taking hold of her hand.

HIM WE ADORE

She assessed the damage. The coffee-stained duvet, charred by cigarette burns, was stuffed in the wardrobe. Ranged around the rubbish bin were several empty beer bottles lying on their sides. Unrinsed mugs and glasses stood everywhere and damp towels had been dumped on the couch. Worst of all were the brown footprints where chocolate from the trashed minibar had been trodden into the carpet.

Marta opened the door to the en suite bathroom. The shower curtain hung from one ring. A newspaper had been stuffed down the toilet and water, dripping from the walls, puddled on the floor.

It was Marta's job to bring order to the chaos. She regarded her work as a form of magic: the tools of her trade a cartful of cleaning potions, a Hoover and every kind of mop, cloth, and scourer. While she dusted, vacuumed and polished, the laundry trolley appeared in the corridor with fresh sheets and towels; the dirty mugs and glasses left outside were whisked away and replaced by spotlessly clean ones. Making the bed was her final task and she smoothed the duvet in its pristine white cover until it resembled newly-fallen snow.

Guests trashed their rooms in an infinite number of ways; cleaning and tidying demanded, for each one, a unique plan of action. In addition to a thorough going over, this room required the copious application of carpet cleaner and the ministrations of the maintenance team. The duvet was dispatched to the tip. Marta was valued by her employers for her speed and attention to detail, but she knew a cleaned room was rarely perfect. There was often a tiny stain, a crease in a pillow slip, a speck of dust left behind.

The room next-door, however, was immaculate. To her practiced eye the bed was expertly made, clean mugs stood on the tray and dry towels were neatly folded on the bathroom shelf. How could a guest make so little impact? Thinking that a mistake had been made, she phoned her supervisor. The girl insisted that the room had been slept in and must be cleaned. Here was a dilemma. Marta could shut the door and walk away, or clean a room that didn't need it.

Marta considered the problem. She was well aware that most of her colleagues would be cleaning the adjacent room by now. Sighing, she wheeled in the cart and polished the unsmeared surfaces, scoured the shining bathroom, vacuumed the dust-free carpet. Nothing was out of place.

As she folded back the duvet, she saw a small object lying on the bottom sheet. Marta picked it up warily: it was a gold-coloured ring. As she turned it over she was confronted by a skull with rose-red eyes. A horrible thing. Inside were some engraved letters. They were worn, but she could just make out: Him We Adore.

Marta placed it on the bedside cabinet while she finished changing the bed, then picked it up and put it in her pocket. She would hand it in at reception when she had finished her shift, but chatting with Brendan in the lift made her forget all about it.

The ring didn't surface again until Marta was at home putting her overalls in the washing machine. It fell out of the pocket and landed with a ding on the floor. She found a small velvet-covered box for the ring and put it in her handbag, resolving to take it back to the hotel the following day.

She slept badly that night, her mind crowded with dreams of her old life in Poland. In the morning she realised she was ill with a fever. It was a rare thing for Marta to take time off work but she had no choice. She phoned in sick and went back to bed.

The following day she felt well enough to sit in the armchair with her laptop. On it she researched the ring. She found several similar examples. It was something called a memento mori, probably dating to the early nineteenth century, the skull a grim reminder to the wearer that life was finite. She shivered a little, though the fever had passed, and fetched the ring. One of the gems was loose in its eye socket. The skull grinned up at her, the yellow gold worn and scratched. Had it slipped off the finger of the sleeper in that perfectly made bed?

She should have handed in the ring on the day she found it. If she gave it to her supervisor now, questions would be asked. Her researches had suggested that the ring was valuable. The owner, discovering his loss, might phone the hotel. Records would show that she had been responsible for cleaning the room.

Marta liked her job and did not want to lose it. Her wages enabled her to send money back to her parents in Cracow. If she were dismissed for stealing, she would be unemployable and might have to go back to Poland with her tail between her legs.

Then it came to her. If the bed had not been slept in since she cleaned the room, she could put the ring back where she had found it. The next guest would find the ring and it would be their decision whether or not to hand it in. If they did, then the worst that could happen was that she would be reprimanded for not changing the bedding.

It was easy to persuade her supervisor to let her have the card key; Marta explained that she thought she had left a bottle of bleach in the bathroom. The room was as she had left it, and it was the work of a moment to place the ring back under the duvet. She was out in the corridor in less than a minute. It was a great relief to know that no-one would lose out or get into trouble because of her actions. Her job was safe and the guest could get his ring back if he wanted it. She had decided it was a man's ring because, although she had not tried it on, it looked far too big for a woman's finger.

Back at the flat she took the velvet-covered box from her pocket. Something, maybe the heaviness of the box, made her open it. The skull ring lay inside, the inscription, Him We Adore, on display.

Had she forgotten to replace the ring in the bed? Were the after-effects of the fever affecting her memory? Confused and upset, Marta thought about it for most of the night. She decided to keep the ring and hope its owner would continue to be indifferent to its loss, although she found it hard to believe that he would let it go so lightly.

So the skull ring remained in the velvet-covered box in the dressing-table drawer. Its owner did not contact the hotel, and Marta went about her work and almost forgot the ring. Almost, but not quite. Every so often it would steal into her thoughts.

Nevertheless, some months went by before, one rainy Sunday afternoon, she fetched the box and took out the ring. As her fingers turned it over she realised that she had failed to notice before the sheer quality of the workmanship: the skull was beautifully fashioned and the cabochon eyes as red as blood. Slipping it onto her ring finger, she found that it fit perfectly. She must have been mistaken about its size.

Marta took to wearing the ring around the flat. She looked at it often, was reassured by the weight of it, appreciated it more every day. Its history intrigued her and she wondered often about past owners. The inscription looked like a quote, but her researches came to nothing.

One evening she found that the ring would not come off. She attempted to twist it, and lubricated her finger with soap. In the morning she tried again. Late for work, she stuck a dressing over the ring and ran to the bus stop. In her lunch break she went to the jewellers, only to find that having the ring cut off and expertly repaired was beyond her meagre means.

She took to wearing latex gloves to hide the ring from her colleagues, but she could not stop others from noticing it. The woman on the checkout at the supermarket thought it was an unusual engagement ring and asked Marta where it had come from. Her hairdresser was similarly intrigued. It was a relief that both seemed under the impression that the ring was a modern reproduction.

Marta worried that wearing the ring all the time would damage it. Already there were additional scratches on the skull. She decided that, despite her misgivings, she must have the ring cut off. Reducing her household expenses would be difficult, but it was the only way she could fund the work.

Over the months it took Marta to save the money, she felt a growing sense of pride that she was the ring's custodian, part of its long history. The ring looked good on her finger, she felt elegant wearing it. Once the money was saved, she made excuses to herself for not going to the jewellers.

On her days off Marta visited various churches in the city. In most were memorial stones decorated with sculpted skulls. The best examples resembled the skull on the ring, although they never surpassed it for craftsmanship and beauty. Marta used some of her savings to have the loose ruby fixed in its eye socket. The jeweller looked at her strangely when she asked him to carry out the work with the ring still on her finger. She was pleased to have made her mark on its history.

One lunchtime Marta and Brendan sat on the bench at the rear of the hotel. The autumn sunshine was warm enough for them to have taken off their coats.

'Why are you still wearing gloves, Marta?' Brendan asked. 'Aren't you hot?'

Marta peeled them off carefully. She tried to hide the ring but Brendan saw it.

'You're engaged!' he cried.

'No. Nothing like that.'

He picked up her hand and looked at the ring more closely.

'Is it gold?'

'Of course not.'

'Are you sure? He's gruesome, isn't he?' Brendan touched the skull, then pulled his finger away. On it was a bead of blood.

'It bit me!'

'Don't be silly.'

'I tell you, it bit me with its horrible yellow teeth.'

The next day Brendan was not at work. Marta was told by her supervisor that he was in hospital with an infection. He was very sick; only his family were allowed to visit him.

Marta didn't know what to think. Brendan must have cut himself on some rusty metal, or a dirty piece of glass. How could it be anything to do with the ring? The ring was as snug a fit as ever: the ruby eyes glimmered and she could see her reflection in them, the scratches on the skull were less noticeable than before.

Brendan recovered slowly and eventually returned to work. He kept his distance from Marta, who sorely missed their chats. He was one of the few people who talked to her as if she were a real person.

It was on one of her lonely walks through the suburbs that she came across St Michael's, a church she hadn't visited before. Its exterior was in the provincial Gothic Revival style, but the interior suggested that the Victorian architect had remodelled a more ancient church. Marta inspected the memorials on the aisle walls, admiring the skulls and putti that decorated them.

One plaque caught her attention. Unlike the others it was polished and unchipped, the veined grey marble beautifully chamfered. Underneath the name of the deceased was a single line of script:

Him We Adore

The inscription above read 'Abel Watson, Gent, departed this life 5th October 1829'.

There were no other memorials to anyone by the name of Watson in the church, and no family graves in the churchyard. Marta made a note of the name and date and hurried back to her flat. While she sat at her computer her fingers traced the features of the skull, its ruby eyes, chiselled cheek bones, rows of even teeth. She could find no information about Abel Watson. 'When,' she whispered to the ring, 'will you give up your secrets?'

Marta's supervisor left for another hotel and, much to Marta's surprise, she was interviewed and given the job. No longer would she wheel her magic cart along the corridors; she would be drawing up rotas, motivating and disciplining the cleaners, reporting back to management.

'There is one thing, though,' the manager said, pointing to her hand. 'Lose the ring.'

Marta swiftly raised her hand to look at it and the ring grazed the manager's wrist. Pin pricks of blood rose from the wound. He put his wrist to his mouth and sucked.

'It's dangerous as well as frightening! You could injure one of the guests and we'd be facing a law suit. Take it off, Marta!'

Marta explained that the ring was stuck.

'Have it cut off. In the meantime, put something over it.'

The manager took some time off work with what was rumoured to be blood poisoning. Marta stuck a fresh plaster over the ring every day— the deputy manager didn't say anything about it. When the manager returned he was preoccupied with catching up with his work. Every evening Marta took off the plaster and gazed at the ring.

One Saturday she returned to St Michael's. As she looked up at Abel Watson's memorial she was approached by a woman in clerical black.

'You've been standing here for some time. I'm Jill, the rector. Can I help you?'

Marta said, 'I don't suppose you know anything about Abel Watson? It's the inscription below his name I'm most interested in.'

'Ah,' said Jill. 'There is a story about him. Let's see if I can remember it.

'He was a God-fearing man, attending this church every Sunday. It was countryside then, before the city spread this far. He insisted that his tenant farmers act soberly and fairly in their dealings. Abel was also known for his good husbandry: he was an expert on horses and their ailments and was often called in by other landowners when a valuable animal was sick.

'One winter evening a messenger arrived at Abel's door. He asked Abel to attend a racing stable several miles away, where some of the horses had come down with colic. Abel had his fastest horse saddled and rode behind the messenger through driving rain. Despite Abel's efforts it was too late: four of the horses had to be shot. Two survived, but would never race again. If the messenger had been sent earlier, things might have been different.

'The stable owner, a man called Grice, was well known for his thrifty ways. He grunted at Abel, and, as Abel was about to mount his horse, handed him something, muttering that it was to thank him for his efforts. In the light of the servant's lantern, Abel saw a ring. On the front was a grinning skull. Inside was an inscription—Him We Adore. Abel slipped the ring onto his finger, meaning to examine it more closely the next day. But when he arrived home and tried to remove the ring it would not come off.

'From that day forward Abel was obsessed with the ring. He refused to have it removed and his wife soon noticed how much time he spent looking at it. She persuaded him to let her prise it off, but in the attempt she nicked her finger on the sharp edge of the skull's teeth. The next day she felt unwell and took to her bed. She died some days later. Abel was heartbroken and at last consented to have the ring cut off, but the jeweller was careless and Abel's finger was badly injured. He had the ring repaired, so that you would never know it had been damaged.

'Abel's finger never fully healed. When he died, not long afterwards, he cried out, at the moment of his passing, "Him We Adore." The rector of that time thought this was a pious invocation and so it was carved on the memorial.'

'What happened to the ring?' Marta asked.

'His son gave it to the jeweller, who was only too pleased to sell it to a lady customer with macabre tastes.'

Jill, seeing Marta's face, laughed. 'It's just a story. Who knows if it's true?'

'Where is Abel's grave?' asked Marta.

'Well that is rather odd. There isn't one, at least not in this graveyard, and there's no record of him being interred in the church.'

Jill collected herself. 'Look, why don't you come along to the next service. I'm sure you'll find it interesting.'

Marta made her excuses and left.

The jeweller had some difficulty sliding the cutter under the ring. Marta winced and looked the other way.

'Sorry it's taking so long,' he said.

At last there was a loud snap and the ring flew to the other end of the bench. Marta screwed up her courage and looked at her finger. Apart from a white indentation where the ring had been, there was no sign of injury. The jeweller was examining the ring under his jeweller's loop.

'It's a fine thing,' he said, 'but it's been cut off and soldered many times. You'd like me to repair it for you?'

'Yes,' said Marta.

It felt strange now the ring was off her finger. The weight of it still seemed to be there and she looked down at her hand often. She missed the ring terribly, and wondered if she had done the right thing.

The next morning she woke up feeling hot and unwell. She was too weak to phone for the doctor. Later, her manager knocked on the door. Marta crawled over and unlocked it. He took one look at her and said:

'You need to go to hospital. I'll take you there in the car.'

Marta became delirious soon after her admittance. No-one was sure what was wrong with her—she was treated with intravenous fluids and antibiotics. Her speech was garbled—a mixture of English and Polish—and although she often mentioned the ring, it was difficult to make sense of her words.

Brendan visited her and brought the news that her parents were flying over from Poland. Marta, in a lucid moment, asked him to collect the ring from the jewellers. He promised he would.

'Don't try it on,' she croaked.

Marta found the energy to open the velvet-covered box. The ring lay on its side, the skull half-buried in the plush lining. She picked it up. The jeweller's repair was invisible—the inscription intact. It would be easy to slip the ring on her finger; assuage the longing and the skull's unrelenting gaze. She fought, how she fought against it! She battled until she lost consciousness, and then the struggle was over.

Marta's father Jan collected Marta's few possessions from the hospital bursar. He opened the velvet-covered box and puzzled over the ring. Why would Marta have such a thing? He shut the box with a snap. Brendan was waiting for him in the corridor. In faltering English Jan asked:

'Would you like something of Marta's? To remember her by?'

He handed over the box. Brendan, knowing what was inside, grimaced. He opened it.

'I'm sure I can find the right person to pass it on to.'

The ruby eyes of the skull stared into his, the newly-polished gold glinted in the harsh overhead light. Looking at the ring with new eyes he found he could appreciate the brilliance of the craftsman who had made it, the beauty of its line, the relevance of its purpose, the enigma of the inscription. . . .

And it had been Marta's. Perhaps he would keep it after all.

THE VOYAGER

The pub is empty except for a couple—man and wife, judging by her wedding ring—sitting in silence by the fire. Her back is to me; the corners of his mouth turn down. I'm pretty sure they're the ones I'm looking for.

I hitch myself up onto the bar stool. 'I'll have a large glass of your finest red.'

'There's just the house Merlot,' says the landlord, 'but we have twelve different ales. Most of my customers prefer a pint.'

'Merlot it is then,' I say. The landlord is burly and bearded with old-fashioned tattoos on his arms and neck, like a sailor in a story book.

'Right you are.'

He opens the screw cap of a half-full bottle and pours up to the line. I risk a sip—it's rank stuff.

The landlord picks up a glass and polishes it. 'Passing through?' he asks.

'I'm on my way to the festival,' I say. 'The classical music festival at Chichester.'

'Can't say I've been,' he says.

The woman gets up and adjusts her skirt before making for the ladies.

She's prettier than in the photographs, badly dressed though, and with that glum husband.

Two young men wander in, fresh from a building site—they haven't bothered to change out of their work clothes. Predictable pints of beer are poured and set in front of them. They seem cheerful, easy in each other's company. When the woman returns I join them in watching her. She has a beguiling gait, dragging her feet slightly as if reluctant to rejoin the husband. And who can blame her? The man has not said a word since I've been here.

I swallow more of the ghastly wine.

'I could recommend a few relatively inexpensive vintages which might fit the bill,' I say to the landlord.

'As I've said, there's not much call for it.'

'You could build up a reputation for fine wine, attract higher-spending customers.'

'I do all right the way things are.'

I can see I'm getting to him.

'Lots of country pubs are closing. You have to innovate to survive.'

He flares up, 'You run a pub, do you?'

'As a matter of fact I don't.'

The two young builders finish their beers and say their goodbyes to the retreating landlord, leaving only my couple, who are now conducting a desultory conversation. I move over to a table by the window so I can hear them.

'I didn't invite them,' he says. 'They just turned up.'

'I'm not accusing you of anything.'

'What are we going to do?'

'I don't know. We could ask for advice.'

'Who from? It's not a common problem.'

'We can't be the only ones.'

There's a pause. She contemplates the icy dregs of her gin and tonic. He says: 'I'm not sure anyone will believe us.'

THE VOYAGER

She puts on her coat and scarf. He takes their glasses to the bar, and they leave. A blast of cold air billows through the door. I follow.

I think I've lost them in the gloom, then I see them, arm in arm, turning into a side street. It's a cul-de-sac, Rowan Drive, and they let themselves into No.12, a small detached house. The lights in the living room are switched on and they have neglected to draw the curtains. I see her typing on a computer keyboard. He stands behind, staring at the screen.

I can think of no reason to explain why I might knock on their door, so I walk back to the pub: The Voyager—an unusual name. On one side of the pub sign is a picture of an old-fashioned sailing vessel, on the other a spaceship. The landlord is back behind the bar.

'What'll you have?' he asks through gritted teeth.

'An orange juice.'

He finds a bottle of warm pasteurised stuff, prises the top off and tips it into a glass. It's disgusting. The place is still empty. He busies himself wiping down the tables, lifting the condiments and sauce sachets.

'Do you have many diners?'

'We don't do too badly,' he replies.

'Home cooked fayre is it?'

'Chef makes most of the dishes. It wouldn't kill you to try one.'

'The concert's starting soon.'

I knock back the rest of the orange muck.

'Thanks,' I say. He mutters something and I head for the door.

The cellist and pianist are mediocre, the former sawing away, the latter bouncing up and down on the stool like a child at a party. During their pedestrian rendering of Bartok's Romanian Folk Dances my mind wanders back to my couple in the pub. I shall drive to the village again in a few days' time.

It's quiz night and there are tables of competitors eating chips from small baskets, talking and laughing. The landlord, ensconced behind the bar, laughs loudest of all. I catch his eye and he begins to smile. Then he recognises me.

'I'll have a glass of red.'

He sighs. 'The house Merlot.'

He opens a new bottle and this time the wine is at least drinkable.

'Going to another concert?' he asks, without much interest.

'I thought I'd sample your food. You were so persuasive last time I was here.'

He brightens up a little.

'I'll fetch you the menu.'

There are the usual unimaginative offerings—pies, pasta, mixed grill and fried fish, plus a few more adventurous dishes—curry, pickled salmon, goulash and risotto. I choose the curry. When it arrives it's steaming hot and very good. I compliment the landlord, who asks:

'Are you the hygiene inspector?'

The door opens and my couple walk in. He is as nondescript as last time, she is better dressed than before in a longish skirt and blouse. Her chestnut hair has been cut and falls gracefully to her shoulders. They sit at a table with an older couple, then the husband gets up and comes to the bar for drinks. He stands next to me. I can see the premature wrinkles, the defeated look in his eyes.

'Jim,' the landlord says.

'Owen,' says Jim.

'How's Meg?'

'She's well enough.'

'Getting over that business now, is she?'

Jim shrugs. 'She's okay,' he says unhappily.

He picks up the drinks and carries them to the table.

Soon afterwards the quiz sheets are handed round and the competition begins. There is much forced hilarity and a certain ritual quality to the proceedings. This is something that has happened many times before. I am a sociologist on a field trip, a voyeur of the ordinary. The eventual winners sit in the far corner, quieter than any other team apart from Meg and Jim's. I sense the winners take the quiz very seriously indeed.

'It's a good evening for you,' I say to the landlord.

'Not bad, though they don't eat enough,' he confides. He's slurring his words a little.

'Get your chef to cook a small range of simple quiz night meals. Macaroni cheese, that kind of thing. There's a good mark-up on food like that.'

He strokes his beard. 'You may be on to something,' he says. 'Are you in the catering trade?'

I change the subject.

'The good-looking woman, Meg, is it? I sense a story there . . . '

'Their child died a couple of years ago,' he whispers. 'Meg had a breakdown.'

'How did it happen?'

'The girl drowned in the village pond. She got out of their garden somehow. Meg has only been in here a few times since it happened. She stopped going out. I keep an eye on her.'

I look over at Meg; she's talking to the older couple at her table. Jim sits morosely, staring at his beer.

'Will they have another child to replace the one they lost?'

The landlord says, 'You don't have children, do you? Jim had a vasectomy after the little girl was born. It turns out it's irreversible.'

Jim stands up.

'Time to go,' he says.

Meg frowns. 'I haven't finished my drink!'

'We need to go home.'

Meg puts on her coat and they head for the door. I leave it a few seconds then follow them.

Outside, my breath hangs in the freezing air and I dig my hands in my pockets. Jim has taken Meg's arm. I walk a few paces behind them and they seem too preoccupied with their conversation to notice me.

'... and they'll come tonight,' Jim is saying.

'How do you know?' asks Meg.

'I have a feeling. I can't explain.'

Meg sighs. 'We'll wait up then.'

They turn the corner into Rowan Drive and let themselves into the house. I wait outside for a few minutes but the curtains are closed and there's nothing to see. I go back to the pub until late. It's well after midnight when I return, and the lights are still on. I stand behind a tree. After a few minutes the bedroom curtains open and Jim peers out.

I hear steps behind me and turn around. There are two men and two women, smartly dressed, walking towards the house. I haven't time to hide and they stop in front of me. The taller man says:

'We've found a snooper!'

'A dirty Peeping Tom,' says the woman with black hair.

They crowd around me.

'I'm concerned about my friends, that's all,' I say.

'Do they know you're here?' asks the shorter man.

'Because you look pretty shifty,' says the blonde.

I make a run for it but they catch me easily and push me up the drive. Meg opens the door.

'Do you recognise him?' asks the tall man.

Meg says, 'He's the eavesdropper from the pub.'

They bundle me into the house.

'How much does he know?' asks the blonde.

Jim comes down the stairs. 'You should've left him outside.'

The shorter man says: 'He may come in useful.'

We sit in the living room. The tall man opens his briefcase and takes out a sheaf of paper. 'Old technology', he says, and turns to Jim and Meg. 'We like to do things properly. This is a contract for you to sign. Our friend the eavesdropper can witness the agreement. . . . I assume you're happy to go ahead?'

Jim clears his throat: 'The thing is . . . '

'It's perfectly natural to have second thoughts . . . but last time we were here you agreed to everything, so there is already a verbal contract in place.'

Meg says, 'What happened to "twenty-eight days to change your mind"? I thought that was the law.'

There is polite laughter. 'It doesn't apply here, I'm afraid,' says the black-haired woman. 'The paper contract is just a record of an existing agreement.'

'Where will it take place?' asks Meg.

'I can't tell you yet, but it'll be an exotic location far from here. Somewhere new to you.'

'How much will it cost?' asks Jim.

'There's no charge,' says the shorter man. 'We operate on a "not for profit" basis.'

'But you must have expenses . . . ' Jim says, then stops.

Meg and Jim exchange a look.

'What do we have to lose?' Meg asks softly.

Tears start in Jim's eyes. 'We can't go on like this.'

The tall man signs the documents and hands them over. Jim scrawls his signature on the bottom of the two copies. Meg signs too.

The shorter man places the contracts on the coffee table in front of me. 'There's no requirement for you to read them,' he says. 'You're merely a witness to the signatures.'

'I think I should know what this is about,' I say.

'Ever the sticky-beak,' mutters the black-haired woman.

I take a moment to look at Meg, and then I sign. The four visitors applaud.

'Well done,' says the tall man to Jim and Meg. 'You won't regret it. Welcome to your new life.'

Jim and Meg hug each other and I am so busy watching I don't notice the others leave.

A few days later I return to The Voyager. The landlord pours me a glass of Merlot while he finishes talking to a man in country clothes at the bar.

'... Most people wouldn't know it's a slave ship. You can tell because it's so broad in the beam. They had to pack 'em in to make a profit. It was a hazardous voyage from Africa to America, for crew and cargo, but it was lucrative. Our local gentry, the Turner family, made their money that way. That's why the sailing ship's on the sign. They own the pub, I hold the lease.'

'What about the spaceship?' asks the country gent. 'That's pretty unconventional.'

Owen laughs. 'I'm interested in travel. I was in the Navy for twenty-five years. Space travel's the next step in exploration.'

The gent grunts. 'You could pressgang a few saddos and undesirables. Blast them into space.'

I finish my wine, walk round to No. 12 and knock on the door. Meg answers. She looks well, radiant even.

'What do you want?'

'I've come to see how you are.'

She raises her eyebrows.

'Why would you do that? You hardly know me.'

'I'm not sure you should've signed the contract.'

In the kitchen she sets the kettle to boil.

'Can't you tell me what it's about? I may be able to help. . . . '

'You're nosy, you mean.'

'I'm good at sorting things out. It's my job.'

There's a pause, then she seems to make up her mind.

'Owen will have told you about our child . . . Emily. He's very indiscreet when he's had a few drinks.'

She pours the boiling water into a teapot.

'They knocked on the door one day and said they were from a medical foundation that can help us conceive a child identical to Emily. It's an experimental procedure, not strictly ethical, so we have to keep it under wraps. I'm telling you because you're our witness and we need someone to know what we're doing in case anything goes wrong. Our families and neighbours think we're going on a long holiday.'

'But everyone knows Emily died!'

'We'll give her another name, have her hair cut differently. It isn't unusual for there to be a strong resemblance between sisters. Anyway, the house is on the market. We're moving away.'

'You can't! . . . ' It's out of my mouth before I can stop it.

'Why not?'

'Because . . . I don't want you to.'

We sit at the kitchen table and she tells me about her dead daughter—how everyone loved her, how bright she was. How funny.

'You can't blame us for wanting her back.'

Several days later I'm sitting at the bar in the The Voyager and the landlord pours me a glass of Merlot 'on the house'.

'What have I done to deserve this?'

'Drink some and see.'

I take a sip. It's wonderful—warm and spicy.

'I took your advice,' says Owen. 'We're stocking four reds and four whites. They're selling well, despite the fact that they're more expensive. The quiz night specials are taking off too.'

'Glad to be of service.'

'What is it you do for a living?' he asks.

'I investigate things,' I say.

At that moment Jim bursts in. 'Come quickly!' he says.

We hurry round to No. 12. The door opens and the tall man shepherds Meg out of the house. Owen and I wait for Jim to tell us what to do.

'I'm not sure I want to go with them,' Jim whispers.

'Come along,' says the tall man. 'You can't back out now. You signed the contract.'

'There's something wrong here,' says Jim. 'Where's the car to take us to the airport?'

'You don't have to go with him,' I say. 'He can't make you.'

'But I want Emily!' Meg says, her voice quavering.

Jim pleads. 'I don't trust them.'

The tall man says, 'If you'd read the contract you'd realise you gave us permission to transport you any way we choose.' He raises his arm.

There's a shimmer in the air and a loud roar. A wide-bodied spaceship materialises above the house, manoeuvres and hovers. The hatch opens and the smaller man, the black-haired woman and the blonde step out onto the road.

'It's a long journey,' the tall man says to Jim. 'Don't hold us up.'

He turns to me, 'I'm entitled to take them on board. You're a witness to that.'

'I wasn't allowed to read the contract!'

'You signed it nevertheless.'

Owen turns to the tall man, 'What about *me*!' he whispers.

'I'm afraid you're too old.'

The tall man guides Meg and Jim into the belly of the craft, and the three others follow them inside. There is a brief roar, the hatch closes, and the spaceship disappears.

'God damn it!' says Owen.

Dazed, we walk back to The Voyager, past the double-sided sign which swings in the displaced air. Owen pours me a large glass of Merlot, and a pint for himself. We sit morosely either side of the bar.

'They said if I helped with Meg and Jim they'd take me with them. The tall one came in here a few weeks ago. I don't know who they are; Government, maybe. Maybe not. He told me about the mission and practically promised I could go.

'Being in the Navy opened my eyes. I saw enough of the world to believe anything is possible. If this whole thing was a hoax then no harm done. All I had to do was work on Meg and Jim. Encourage them to think about Emily. Not that they needed much encouragement. They're going to do it, you know, give them Emily back, if the procedure works.

That's why they wanted them. They're looking at alternative methods of reproduction.'

'Are there many others on board?'

'Packed in like sardines—the cargo, anyway. They're waifs and strays. The crew are made to sign the contract, like Meg and Jim. It's their children's children that'll reach the destination. The cargo are for the experiments. . . . '

I think about Meg. Perhaps she'll be happy when she has her little girl back, even in the cramped confines of the spacecraft.

Owen says, 'I'd give anything to be aboard that vessel.'

'I'll be writing a report,' I say. 'I won't be able to keep you out of it.'

'You have nothing to worry about there. I'll keep quiet. The pub will be my last command.'

THROUGH THE STORM

It's unlikely you'll read this as it's hidden on my computer, saved under 'lists'. If it comes to light it will hurt you, Lars, and I'm sorry for that. There's another story, about me and you, that you already know, and I mean it when I say I have valued our life together above almost everything. I loved you from our first meeting. You'll remember that, like today, it was windy, the waves chasing each other up the beach, our dogs unsettled and whining for home.

The window is rattling. I tell myself that the flurries of air filtering through the gap are good for me, but I can't ignore the chill. I feel the cold so badly now. We never got round to repairing the window—there were too many other things to do—so I've retrieved my old shawl from its hook on the back of the door and draped it round my shoulders.

I can hear the fury of the sea. The beach will be burdened with a tangle of seaweed and debris, dividing the wave-soaked sand from the dry. Remember how we loved storms, safe in this house, watching the dark clouds scud by, the coals on the fire throwing out heat. We'd go to bed or read to each other while the tempest howled outside.

After the passion there was calm. Contentment curled around us. One evening I walked the dogs on the beach, slipping them off their leads. They frisked in the surf, mock fighting and happy, our tiny fragment of ocean bounded by the horizon. Tall clouds ballooned: another storm threatened. I called the dogs and we headed for the slipway.

A figure in dark clothing leaned against the wall.

'I saw you looking out to sea,' he said.

'Not very interesting for you.'

I made to walk past him, but the dogs lay down, heads on paws.

He smiled. 'Would you like an adventure?'

'What did you have in mind?' I asked.

'We can sail through the storm.' He pointed at the clouds rolling in.

I pulled the dogs to their feet. 'You'd willingly take a boat through something so terrifying?'

'Just once. We could turn back if you were frightened.'

The dogs came to life and loped for home, their leashes unspooling from my grip. He said: 'I'll be here tomorrow.'

I followed the dogs and reached the house as the rain began to fall.

You were reading, the lamp lighting the pages, the washing up dried and put away. You looked up.

'Another storm coming?'

Settling beside you on the sofa I picked up my book. The room was stuffy, the fire dead in the grate. Sleep overcame me, I nodded over the pages, the narrative continued senselessly in my head.

You touched my arm. 'Why don't you go to bed?'

Wind and rain slammed against the window. When I managed to sleep, I dreamt of the sea.

The following evening I walked the dogs on the beach. Litter was strewn over the smoothed contours of the sand. Perched on the cliff were herring gulls, their cries puncturing the twilight. I closed my eyes for a moment, inhaling the storm-cleansed air.

He was there beside me.

'You could hang-glide from the cliff.'

'No,' I said.

'We'd be harnessed together. . . . '

I thought of his body pressed against mine. Anger seized me, and guilt.

'I'm perfectly happy with the way things are.'

I strode up the beach towards the dogs. They were digging holes and sniffing the rubbish.

'You need adventure,' he called after me.

At home I shut myself in the study for as long as I dared and cried bitter, futile tears. I thought about the next evening, barely speaking until you asked what was wrong. I pleaded some minor ailment and, thoughtful and kind, you left me alone.

He was waiting on the slipway. I let the dogs off their leads and they fawned around him before running to the surf.

'You can have what you desire,' he said, and led me to the cave beneath the cliff, where I betrayed you, Lars, without a second thought. Afterwards, he and I walked along the beach.

'We can hunt with lions,' he said, and we crept through the savannah, the beasts' soft breath susurrating through the sun-bleached grass. 'Or look into a volcano:' the molten, fire-veined mass seethed in the crater. 'Anywhere on earth can be yours.'

Worn out, the dogs slept on the rug. I blamed my lateness on them.

'It's dark,' you said. 'I hope you're feeling better.'

Work, food, sleep. You tiptoed around me, waiting for the storm, but I stayed calm. Every evening I took the dogs to the beach, searching, my life on hold. You booked a doctor's appointment (I did not go). You bought the foods I liked. You covered me with blankets. I think you suspected I was sickening for something you'd find it hard to understand.

On the twelfth evening I found him on the beach, watching the terns swoop over the waves.

We kayaked down the broad brown ribbon of the Amazon, dived on the coral of the Great Barrier Reef. At home I slept, preparing for the next adventure.

But he did not come.

I could not eat or sleep; days merged with night. My head pounded and, wretchedly in pain, I tormented myself with longing. Without telling me, you arranged for the doctor to call. The diagnosis was confirmed by hospital tests.

The cuckoo tumour grew. Each morning you studied me, my face a barometer. You anticipated my needs, ministered to my whims. Every evening I shambled to the beach, revisiting the cave, pining for adventure. Do you remember one rain-lashed night you followed me there, guiding me home, a lifeboat in the storm?

One evening I found him waiting in the cave. I cried out with relief and flung my arms around him.

We stood on the summit of Everest, swam with whales, drove dog sleds over the Arctic ice.

'Now you must go home,' he said, and I lay on the beach, the tide licking my boots. I crawled along the road. You found me slumped by the door and carried me inside.

'No more excursions. You need your strength.'

Because of you, I underwent the treatment. The scans showed I was in remission. You were ecstatic, as if my recovery was assured. Carefully I resumed my evening walks. Even though I expected never to see him again, there seemed no way back to our contented existence.

One night, while you were out, I escaped into the storm. Buffeted by wind, drenched by rain, I screamed and shook my fist at the unseeing sky. You returned to find me shivering in the kitchen. Tenderly you undressed me, ran a bath. I sat on the sofa in front of the fire you had lit. Do you remember that I cried? I wept for the beauty of your gentleness, for the love I had betrayed. You knelt down and stroked my hair until the fire turned to ash.

Becalmed, I lived an undemanding life, garnering my strength. One morning I woke to pain, to garbled speech. You took me to the specialist—the tumour was growing again. To your dismay there was nothing that could be done.

I can no longer walk to the beach, so, while you are sleeping, or walking the dogs, he visits me here.

Our children are born on the Savannah, beneath the thorn trees. We run from our enemies into the cave beneath the rocks, where the fire frightens the fiercest away.

We see glaciers, the succession of forests, the wild land before the settlers come. He fashions the flints that can pierce the hide of any living thing.

Our ship sails from the Northlands to Newfoundland, beating thirst and starvation, building our longhouses on the sward above the shore.

I shall sail through the storm.
We await only a fair wind to set out on our final adventure.

DEAD LETTERS

When Lavinia's attention was fully engaged by the television, as often as not the pen would lower onto the paper and the words appear. She had no idea what they said until she read them afterwards, and even then they sometimes made little sense.

At the evening meetings of the Sudbury Spiritualist Church she would bring along the latest offering and read it to the congregation. Then they would discuss it. This week, the meeting was held in Lavinia's sitting room. There were only seven of them and they took it in turns to play host. After prayers Lavinia retrieved the sheet of paper from her handbag and paused for a moment. Silence fell. She cleared her throat and began.

'You don't know it, but I see you. I see you all the time. Whatever you do, wherever you go, I am there, watching. I see you with him in the pub laughing and drinking. I see him in my house, eating at my table, sitting in my chair. I see him in my bed.

'I am heartbroken, I am sick. Stop seeing him. If you don't I'll be watching you for as long as you live.'

There was a flutter of reaction.

Sean said, 'She found a new man too quickly. The spirit can't move on.'

Carol leaned forward. 'He must hate her, otherwise he would let her go.'

'Strong emotions,' agreed Frank. 'Any idea who he is, Lavinia?'

'He didn't make himself known.'

They sang hymns then closed their eyes and concentrated as Carol went into a trance. Lavinia's correspondent didn't emerge, but Carol's spirit guide, Lepanto, spoke through her.

'*Evil is close. You must root it out.*'

'Can you tell us what kind of evil?' asked Sean.

'*It is in the writing. Be careful, this spirit has great strength.*'

They looked at each other.

'He must mean Lavinia's writing,' said Wendy

'It's not *my* writing,' said Lavinia.

Eve, who was new, said nothing.

Lavinia made tea and brought out the biscuits. Afterwards, her guests left together, leaving her to tidy up. As she washed the china cups, saucers and tea plates she experienced the tingling feeling that presaged a spirit coming through. She left the crockery to dry, turned on the TV and found her pad of paper and pen. She watched a lioness chase an antelope, bring it down, and begin to feast. The lioness's cubs joined in. The pen was already moving over the paper.

'*I see you spending my money, driving my car, meeting him. You are provoking me. I am speaking through these dimwits but you don't show you're listening.*

'*I want you here with me. I still love you, despite your faithlessness. Don't bother trying to run away, I'm with you all the time.*'

'Is it bluster?' Frank asked.

Wendy said, 'Why has he chosen us?'

'Perhaps Lavinia is the only conduit he can find,' said Carol. 'He's threatening this woman, and you all know we should try to do something about it. Can we work out who she is?'

'How would we find her?' Malcolm said.

'Ask Lepanto,' suggested Frank.

But however hard Carol tried, Lepanto would not come through.

Lavinia was thinking, the cup of tea cooling beside her. If she concentrated really hard, could she persuade the spirit to give up the name of the woman? But she needed to be mindlessly watching the TV; surely, trying to influence what the spirit said would be counter-productive. When she had attempted to direct the writing before, it had refused to come.

She switched on the TV. There was a political discussion about the need for reforming the state education system. The two protagonists were arguing; voices raised. Lavinia became fascinated by the hairpiece worn by the spokesman, and the angry, reddening face of the woman. When she looked down, the page was covered with writing.

'I have seen you both in the forest, the fallen leaves your bed. Do you not understand the agony I feel? Do you think you can hide from me?

'I wish I could hate you but love is still there: your smile; those grey eyes; the curl in your hair. If I stopped loving you maybe I could move on. Being here without you is torture. I'm afraid I'll go mad.

'You should be looking over your shoulder everywhere you go. As for your lover, it is punishment enough that he will lose you. I know how that feels.

'Were you seeing him before I passed? Do you love him more than me? You must be frightened by now, and that is your punishment. It will only hurt for a short time. Through force of will my body is materialising. Soon, I'll be with you, my darling. Once we are together all will be well. We'll be in paradise.'

As Lavinia finished reading there was a brief silence, then Frank spoke.

'This is quite exciting.'
There was a loud sob. Everyone turned to Eve.
'Please help me,' she said. 'I don't know what to do. I hoped you would make him go away, but it's getting worse. I can *feel* him watching me.'
Sean put his arm around Eve.
'Careful, Sean' said Frank, 'we don't want anything to happen to you.'
Wendy said to Eve, 'So you joined us to sort out your love life?'
'I'm a believer. How could I not be,' replied Eve.

Carol rocked back and forth, her face contorted. It seemed an age before Lepanto came through.
'Help us outwit him,' said June.
'He has anger and that gives him power.'
'There must be something we can do?'
'If you can find a way to placate him, his strength will diminish.'
'What should we do?' asked Sean.
But Lepanto had gone.

Knowing they were all waiting in the adjoining room made Lavinia restless. She pottered around, smoothing the table cloth and rearranging the cushions. Finally, she turned up the volume of the TV and switched channels. She found a programme about Hitler's last days in the bunker. The voiceover's tone of grim righteousness caught her attention. The pen sped over the paper.
When it was over Lavinia felt very tired. She turned off the TV and the congregation filed back into the room. Eve sat at the far end of the table.
'Go ahead, Lavinia,' said Sean.

'These dimwits have been useful, but now it's time to wish them goodbye.
'My love for you, Eve, is stronger than ever. Soon I'll be powerful

enough to be with you again. What a moment that will be! I'm convinced that, when you see me standing next to you, you'll willingly follow me to the spirit world. You'll quickly forget about your lover. No need to be frightened anymore; I know we'll be happy.'

Eve let out a howl of despair. Sean climbed over the table and put his arms around her.

Frank said, 'How can we protect her?'

'He'll be here soon,' Eve whispered. 'I know it.'

Lavinia stood up.

'It'll have to be me then.'

'What do you mean?' Wendy scoffed.

'I'm going to write him a letter. Did you love him, Eve?'

'He was wonderful. I was devastated when he died . . . passed.'

'We'll help you draft it,' said Frank.

'I don't think so,' said Lavinia firmly. 'I'll let the pen do the talking.'

'This time we're staying in here with you,' said Malcolm. 'We don't want you coming to any harm.'

Eve moved to the sofa and sat next to Sean. The TV was tuned to a reality programme where celebrities vied with each other to be the last one voted off by the audience. Every kind of indignity was visited upon the contestants. Lavinia could not get into the right frame of mind, and sensed the impatience that was building in the group. She switched channels to a programme about a year in the life of an oak tree. The tree stood impassively as life hummed in and around it. A woodpecker drilled into its trunk, insects buzzed among its leaves. The pen lowered onto the paper.

Dear Paul,

Thank you for your letters, which we have read with interest.

Eve joined our congregation a few weeks ago, and we have very much enjoyed having a younger person as a member. We were concerned that the church might give up after we oldies have passed. Let's hope this is the beginning of a new era.

You will have realised that, although we have great empathy with the spirit world, we are not entirely on your side. I'm sure you feel that Eve has found a new love too quickly, but I think you underestimate how upset she was after your passing, and how much she needed someone to lean on. It would be an act of great love to forgive her, an act more powerful than any wish to cause harm. You are a particularly potent spirit and I think you have the strength to do this.

Your power is impressive indeed. Our little group has not before encountered a spirit who can re-manifest itself in the world. But surely your progression should be forward, not back. If you could stop hating, you would be free of the shackles that bind you. Your anger is disguised as love, and that is the worst kind. Eve loves you but she must be allowed to live her allotted span.

If you go ahead with your plan then the best that can happen is that the woman you say you love will be a captured butterfly, beautiful but pinned forever in the moment of her passing. The worst is that you will frighten her to death, and her spirit will be as lost as yours.

Talk to us, Paul. We can help you on your way to a happier place. Don't spoil your chances of a serene afterlife.

We wait to hear from you.

Yours sincerely
Lavinia (on behalf of the Sudbury Spiritualist Church.)

Frank cleared his throat.

'Well done, Lavinia.'

'I had nothing to do with it,' said Lavinia.

'Do we just sit around and wait?' asked June.

Wendy laughed. 'I don't think a stupid dreamt-up letter is going to achieve anything.'

Eve began to sob again.

The clock ticked on the mantelpiece.

'I can't stand this,' said Malcolm. 'Why don't we let Carol have another go?'

There was general agreement. This time, Carol fell quickly into a trance.

'Who's there? I sense someone close by.'

'*Why did she write that letter?*' said an angry voice.

'It's Paul,' Eve whispered.

'*What you don't seem to realise is that Eve has betrayed everything we had together,*' said the voice.

'It's not true!' shouted Eve. 'You're the one that left.'

In the corner of Lavinia's living room a man's disembodied head appeared.

Wendy turned to Carol.

'How did you do that?'

Carol shook her head. 'I'm not doing anything.'

Eve slid off the sofa and knelt on the floor.

The head said, 'I didn't want to leave you. It was too soon.'

'We all pass at our allotted time . . . ' said Frank shakily, his eyes on the head.

'I'm so lonely without you,' the head said quietly.

'Wait for me, Paul,' said Eve. 'I'll join you when I can.'

The head began to fade.

'I love you,' said Eve.

At the next meeting, in Frank's conservatory, everyone was very subdued. Instead of the usual activities the congregation sat in silent prayer. Eventually, Wendy turned to Lavinia.

'Can you teach me how to do the writing?'

Lavinia smiled gently. 'How can I? It's not something I learnt. It's a gift.'

That afternoon, she became intrigued by a documentary about shoplifters. A young mother explained that she could not afford to pay for the groceries she stole. The familiar tingle began in Lavinia's fingers. She reached for a pen.

Dear Lavinia,

I'm in a better place now. I've made some friends and things are much more peaceful here. I can't thank you enough for giving me another chance. I think I went crazy with loneliness. Please tell Eve how sorry I am that I frightened her. I promise never to visit her again.

I hope you don't mind, but I'd like to introduce you to my new friends. I trust you have plenty of paper. . . .

FEVER

I've laid down my plastic under-sheet but it doesn't stop the chill from leaching through my sleeping bag. At least it's sheltered here, the doorway set back from the pavement. My hat gapes on the ground, but the punters are in too much of a hurry to get home to stop and fish out their change.

A man in a padded jacket walks past and casually kicks my leg. Some people are just arsy—that's what Freda says—and I don't want to provoke him into anything worse. You'd think I'd be used to it by now, but sometimes I forget how bad I look. I do my best to keep clean, but I've not combed my hair for months and my coat is stained and faded. I used to go out of my way to avoid scum like me.

There's ice on the pavements—unusual for London. I unzip my sleeping bag, step out and run on the spot. A woman skirts round me, eyes averted, high heels clicking as she rushes past. It's a long time since I've felt the touch of a woman, other than Freda, or a man, come to that, except for the policeman who occasionally moves me on.

Viewing the world from the pavement gives you a permanent crick in the neck. I've never been one to bow my head when begging. I look the donor straight in the eye and say thank you. They give money if they're God-botherers or if they're scared; they know they're only one poor decision, one piece of bad luck, away from me. They're throwing a penny in the fountain to keep the demons at bay.

Freda wanders along the pavement, can in hand.

'Hello lovely!' she calls out. 'Give us one of your smiles and you can have a sip of this.'

I gurn at her and she passes me the can. I gulp the cider down and hand it back. She's too drunk to notice it's empty.

She sits down, so close she's practically on my lap.

'Get off, you great lummox,' I say affectionately. Actually, she's light as a feather. Freda shifts over; her musty smell all too evident.

'Where are we going tonight?' she asks. 'The Maldives?'

'Too fucking nice for the likes of us.'

'Language!' she says. 'Paris, then?'

'Too French.'

'You are a silly bugger. I like Paris.'

'You've been there?'

'In the old days.'

She quietens down, rocking back and forth. Her eyes glaze over. People stream past, pretending not to look. They feel less sorry for you if you have company. She lays her head on my shoulder and is soon snoring.

'Make your girlfriend shut up,' says a man in a smart woollen coat. 'It's bad enough having to look at you people.'

I do the usual beggar's trick of staring at the ground. The man gobs but his phlegm lands on the pavement and froths harmlessly in front of us. Freda snorts and wakes up, sees the gob and the bloke standing there.

'Fuck off!' she shouts, 'or I'll follow you home and tell your wife I'm your bit of rough!' Freda laughs like a drain. The man walks on.

'On your way, Freda,' I say. 'Get back in your box.'

'Ha, ha,' she says. 'The cardboard's gone soggy. I'll have to scrounge another one.'

She shuffles off back to her pitch under the railway arches.

I get up and jig around, clapping my hands above my head. A blonde woman stops, digs in her purse and puts a tenner in the hat.

'You don't have to dance for it,' she says. 'Spend it on a hot meal.'

They kid themselves their generosity is for my benefit, and assume that, without their guidance, I'll spend it on drink. I don't know what gives them that idea. I go round the corner to Bargain Booze and return with a four pack of Special Brew. I usually resist the lure of spirits, though on cold nights like this they'd be a good idea, but the aim is to get mildly pissed, just enough to make it easier to sleep. I zip myself into my sleeping bag and open the first can, attracting disapproving looks from some of the passers-by. Others quicken their steps as if they're afraid they'll catch whatever it is I am.

Darkness falls, or it would if the shop lights were not left on. The flow of pedestrians dwindles to a trickle. It takes two tins for the alcohol to kick in. A pleasant warmth floods through me and I find myself humming. My eyes close and I feel myself falling asleep. . . .

Freda strips off and wriggles into my sleeping bag. Her breasts jiggle against my chest. . . . I wake with a start.

A walking cane, wielded by a stout man in a long black cape, is poking me in the ribs.

'A gentleman of the road!' he says. 'Can I offer any assistance?'

'You could've left me to sleep.'

He bends down, looking me over.

'I was concerned you might freeze to death.'

'I've been through worse than a cold night.'

'How long have you lived this way?'

'I forget,' I say.

'Some considerable time, then. I'm sure you have a story to tell.'

Despite myself, I'm enjoying the attention.

'Everyone has a story.'

'Perhaps you would be kind enough to tell me yours.'

'The usual. Lost my job. Wife ran off. Lost the house. Lost the plot.'

'Brief and to the point.'

'At least I'm not beholden to anyone.'

'Independence is important to you?'

'I can't stand do-gooders,' I say pointedly.
The gent laughs. 'I don't wish to add to your troubles.'
He shuts up for a few seconds, then says, 'I often wander through the city. There are wonders to be found in the most unlikely places.'
'I stick to my own patch,' I say.
'Exploration is the stuff of life.' He raises his hat. 'I wish you goodnight. I hope our paths cross again.'
With that he strides off.
I open another can.

'You alright?' asks Freda. 'You sound a bit chesty.'
I cough up some mucus.
'I expect I'll survive.'
She looks particularly fetching in a bright red raincoat.
'I nicked it from a charity shop. Those old ladies don't notice anything.'
' "Shall I compare thee to a summer's day? . . . " '
'What are you going on about?'
'You look great. It suits you.'
She twirls round.
'Buy us some grub.'
'I haven't made much money this morning.'
'Let's go to the God-botherers then.
'No thanks.'
'Aren't you hungry?'
'I'd rather starve.'
'Suit yourself.'
She trudges off. A young boy and his mother stop in front of me. He's given a fiver and lets it float down into the hat. It lands on the pitifully small pile of coins. He stares at me with round-eyed curiosity until his mother drags him away. I buy chips and eat them with the last can of Special Brew. There is enough dosh left to buy a litre of cider for tonight. It's still freezing—I sit wrapped up in the sleeping bag.

I used to have a dog; a terrier. I found him, dirty and hungry, in a yard near the railway arches. He was too small to be of much use as a guard dog, but I made good money while he was around. A delivery van ran him over when he strayed into the road.

'You missed out. There was trifle.'
Freda pats her stomach and belches.
I'm overtaken by a coughing fit.
'You're skin and bone. You need to get some grub inside you.'
'I'm fine,' I say through the coughs.
'You're a stubborn git.'
'If you'd stop smoking that street shite I'd go to the Sally Army with you.'
'No way, Grandad.'
She sits down and puts her arms round me.
'I'll nick you some cough medicine.'
The stuff she comes back with is pink and sickly sweet. I neck it down.
'Can you get me some paracetamol?'
'They keep them behind the counter.'
I reach into the hat and hand over a few coins. I'm burning up, I feel like shit. I swallow the pills and eventually sleep. When I wake, my money has gone and so has Freda, but she's left behind the bottle of cider, bless her. It's rush hour. I shiver and cough. The punters keep away now I'm doubly contagious. My head throbs and the lights hurt my eyes.

The next thing I know the gent in the cape is standing in front of me.
'I see you've kept to the fields you know.'
I cough for a long time.
He takes off his cape and drapes it over me. He spots the cider.
'Ah, the wine of Eden. What will become of you, my friend?'
'Why should you care?'
'There but for the Grace of God . . . I would say we are of a similar age, and I sense you are a man of intelligence. . . . '

'Do-gooder,' I say under my breath.
'Forgive me, I've been remiss. How should I address you?'
'Crow.'
'And I, Mr Crow, am Arthur. How do you do?'
With a flourish he doffs his hat.
I try to sit up. He shakes his head and tuts.
'I'd like to offer you my help, Mr Crow, if you will accept it.'
'I'm fine.'
He sighs.
'Pride is all very well in its place. . . . I think I can be of assistance.'
What's in it for you?'
'I understand your wariness.'
'Are you some kind of perv?'
'All I can offer you is a leap in the dark. What is life without adventure? Will you take the risk?'
I'm burning hot.

He holds out his hand and I grasp it and pull myself up. Another coughing fit hits me. When it's over he puts his hand on my shoulder and points his cane down the street. We walk, and after a few paces he slows to match my shuffle. After a hundred metres or so, I stop. My breath rattles in my chest and the buildings crowd around me. I hear barking and see a small dog trotting along on the other side of the road.

'Rags!'

The dog breaks into a run. I start to cross the road but my knees buckle and I sprawl onto the pavement. Arthur helps me up.

'You must take more care,' he says.

'My dog. . . . '

'I saw no dog.' He looks at me thoughtfully. 'Are you well enough to carry on?'

'You promised me an adventure.'

We weave our way through the evening crowds. Arthur offers his arm and I take it. The fever has me in its grip and I burn and freeze by turns. We pick up speed and our feet glide over the paving stones. Faces flash past, hideous, beguiling, ferocious, blank, blurring into a whirl of multi-coloured light. I close my eyes and Arthur guides me through the throng. The noise of the street fades, and, as I pass out I hear the sound of bird-song and trees buffeted by the wind.

I open my eyes. I'm lying on a grassy bank and the sun is rising, peeping over a heather-clad hill. I am wearing Arthur's cape. Drained and weak, I'm overtaken by another coughing fit. On the ground is bread and cheese, and a metal flask of water. I eat and drink greedily.

I'm on the summit of a hill and below is a river plain and a small, picturesque town. The high grassy bank on which I lie is flanked by a deep, continuous ditch. I walk along the bank and find the earthworks curve round and follow the contours of the hill-top. It's some kind of enclosure.

What the hell am I doing here?
Arthur walks along the bank towards me.
'Where is this?' I ask him.
'My native county.'
'How long was I out? How did we get here?'
'Those are imponderables, I'm afraid.'
'Is this a dream?'
'If you wish it to be.' He gestures at the view. 'Come with me now to the green hills and a little church. . . . '
'I like the countryside, but I'm not into all that Christian stuff.'
'God and the spirit of the place are in equal parts the means of your salvation.'

I'm still wearing Arthur's cloak and we're walking along a country road up a long, steep hill. On either side, small fields interlock like the pieces of a crude puzzle. I'm beginning to remember the names of the birds we see in the hedgerows: goldfinch, wren, sparrow. A tower-less church comes into view. Arthur guides me through the orderly graveyard to the porch and thick oak door. Inside, the building is gloomy and scraped, the pews pitch pine, the walls a uniform white.

'This was my father's parish,' says Arthur, 'where I was introduced to the mysteries. . . . '

'My dad was a vicar, too,' I say. 'He was a vicious bastard.'

Arthur brushes his fingers against a pew. He walks to the pulpit, then the lectern, and strokes the head of the broad-winged, stern-eyed, eagle.

I say, 'He spoiled religion for me.'

Arthur gently takes my arm and guides me out into the sunlight.

We cross a narrow brook, jumping from bank to bank. The water tumbles over itself in its quest for the sea. Beyond is a dense beech wood with an understorey of bushes and brambles. The fallen beech leaves have made a tawny blanket on the ground.

I'm tiring; Arthur lopes ahead. A robin perches on a twig, twitches and flies away.

'Where are we going?' I call out.

'It is not far,' he shouts back.

We come to a clearing. Trees crowd round, their branches overhang the grassy glade. Arthur stands at its centre, his arms flung wide.

'See how the wild wood makes room for its mysteries,' he says.

Exhausted, I sit on the grass. Birdsong fills the air.

'What are we doing here?' I ask.

He sits down beside me.

'Close your eyes and listen.'

I hear birdsong and the rasping cough of a deer. I think of my childhood in the countryside; running through fields, catching sticklebacks in jam jars, going on adventures with my friends.

'Try not to think; just listen,' Arthur says.

The trees creak. All around are tiny rustlings. The breeze stirs the beeches; I hear their twiggy fingers tap against each other. From far away comes the sound of some instrument playing a trilling tune I do not recognise.

'The wood is a song,' says Arthur. 'A harmony of sound, light, shade and green. And the smooth grey bark of the beech plays its part, and the thorns of the briar. Hidden in every wood is a place where the trees give way to grass, where the birds can court and the deer graze, where a boy can worship at the altar of that which he barely understands.

'Every living thing is poised between earth and sky. The trees have deeper roots than most. Anchored to the ground they stretch their arms to Heaven and every autumn their leaves fall like tears. The birds have the freedom of the air, but they must return to the trees to build their nests. We have dominion over the world, and it is beautiful and good, cruel and unfathomable. When we do not know our maker, horrors are unleashed.

'You are sacrificed on the altar of those who despise you. "Blessed are the poor in spirit . . . " My faith has words to cheer you, if you could but listen. In the meantime, walk with me in this hallowed land . . . '

I open my eyes. Skylarks hover and the air shimmers around us. I see purple-flowered heather and feel the heat of the sun. Below the moor is the river plain and beyond, green hills rising and falling.

'What magic is this?'

'It is the sorcery of your five senses,' says Arthur.

'I mean, how did we get here?'

'Hope brought us. You have lost your faith, but hope is still with you.'

'And you're charity I suppose.'

'I am a curious and sympathetic friend.'

I unfasten the cloak and throw it on the heather.

'You're a bloody do-gooder.'

Arthur bends down and picks up the cloak. He folds it over his arm.

'I wish to do you good, and I hope that you are enjoying your adventure.'

The sun warms me. I hear the chuckling call of a grouse. I think about my patch in London and Freda in her box.

After a while the path winds through rocky outcrops, blocks of grey granite rising from the moor, sculpted into wind-smoothed shapes.

'God's sentinels,' says Arthur.

He is utterly sincere, a look of wonder on his face. Then his expression changes.

'The terror of ancient worship, the dancing and the singing of strange songs, the appeasement of the stone god with offerings and sacrifice . . .'

We walk on. He is silent for a while.

'I'm hungry,' I say.

'Then close your eyes again, Mr Crow. . . .'

We're in an old-fashioned pub; all dark wood and Axminster carpet; tucking into steaming platefuls of steak and kidney pudding. Full glasses of porter sit in front of us.

Arthur says, 'Good hearty fare.'

I am too busy eating to reply. He takes a great gulp of beer, and supresses a belch. We finish our meal and get up to leave.

'I bid you good day,' says Arthur to the landlady.

Outside are shops and houses. At the rear of the pub runs a river. Arthur stands on its bank and watches the brown water flow past.

'This is the town of my birth,' he says. 'It is a palimpsest of the centuries. Roman soldiers were sent here to a great stone fort. The buildings you see now lie within its dilapidated walls, and artefacts from Roman times have been dug from its earth. Shards of samian-ware and iridescent glass, intaglios loosened from golden rings, tegulae and imbrex fallen from the rooves of abandoned buildings. Clues to the lives of the distant past.'

We walk through the streets of the town. The fever has receded, but I feel drained and weak. Arthur sees that I am flagging and we sit on a wooden bench beside the river. I close my eyes for a few seconds . . .

It's night-time and the traffic roars past. I don't recognise the street. Arthur guides me into an alley between a restaurant and a shopping arcade. In the dim light from the single street lamp he points to the gable end of the restaurant. There, painted over the red bricks, is a huge mural of a lush green landscape. In the foreground, sitting on a Friesian cow is a lovely girl, naked to the waist. I recognise the girl . . .

Freda stands over me, clutching a steaming take-away coffee.
'Get that down you.'
I hold the hot cup in my frozen hands.
'You've been out for a day and a half! We thought you were a goner. Mikey was going to call an ambulance, but I said you wouldn't want that. Too much fuss. I'm bringing you some hot food, though, you stupid git.'
Someone has covered me in blankets. The fever has gone but I'm weak as a kitten. I struggle to sit up. Grey clouds have dimmed the light, even though it must be the middle of the day. My hat is full of notes, £190 worth. I stuff them into my coat pocket.
Freda returns with a polystyrene container full of sausages, baked beans and chips. I realise I'm starving, I haven't eaten since the steak and kidney pudding with Arthur. . . .
'This is from the Sally Army. Don't argue about it, Crow.'
I say without thinking, 'My name's Nick. Nick Evans.'
Freda raises her eyebrows. 'Blimey, it speaks.'
I eat the food quickly, its warm energy flows through me.
'You found your money, then. Nobody nicked any of it. We stood guard, you see. Me and Mikey.'
'Thank you. Perhaps I should get ill more often. I'll share it out when Mikey comes back.'
'He's gone on one of his wanders. With that gent.'
'What gent?'
'I don't know his name. He hangs about sometimes. Mikey says there ain't anything dodgy about him.'

Carefully, I shrug off the blankets and stand up.

'Are you sure you're up to it?' Freda says. 'We don't want an accident.'

'I'll be going walkabout soon, Freda.'

'You have to get better first, bird-brain.'

'Birds are wonderful and comical. Think of the green parakeets. . . . '

'Hark at you!'

'And the plane trees sigh for the want of purer air.'

'Is this Nick Evans talking, or has the fever come back?' Suddenly, she bursts into tears, her lovely, dirty face crumples. 'I don't think I could stand it if you went away.'

'I'll always come back, Freda. Because I'll never find anything as mysterious and beautiful as you.'

HOLY INNOCENT

I've seen you with the others, your little machine capturing their words, and now, it seems, you have come to me. They say you're a professor and must, therefore, despite your youth, be wise, so I suppose I should do my best to lay aside my misgivings and put my trust in you.

You want me to talk about my childhood. In my experience, keeping silent on that matter is best, but the elders have persuaded me to speak in the hope that the village will be blessed with some more of your cold, hard cash. Your university is rich, and we need a new water supply. In truth I suppose it will be little trouble to ramble on for a while and let your device hold my story in its belly until it sees fit to spit it out. You can switch it on now.

My name is Ebuyo, which means 'precious child'. You'll find it hard to believe that such an ugly old woman was once a young girl. When my mother first saw me she was afraid of the sickle-shaped birthmark on my cheek, until my father reminded her that it was the gods who had put it there. It was a blessing, he said, a sign that I had been chosen for a special purpose.

The gods saw fit to make me an only child, and perhaps because of that my parents showered me with love, spoiled me a little. I was given the best food and my father carved toys for me from the branches of the thorn tree. There was a stiff-legged doll, I remember, her hair plaited dried grass, a lion cub and a zebra streaked with charcoal. Because of my birthmark most of the other girls kept their distance, except poor lame Aluha, with whom I played long, complicated games, the toys having many adventures in the dust below the thorn tree. It was a sad day for me when Aluha caught the fever and died.

The sickness rampaged through the village, taking half the population with it, my beautiful, beloved mother among them. My father railed against the gods, shaking his fist at the sky, until the elders persuaded him such blasphemy would not help the living or the dead. In his overwhelming grief my father forgot about me, and for the first time in my life I was afraid.

Despite their strong bodies, many of the hunters succumbed to the fever, and the village, even in its shrunken state, soon ran short of fresh meat. Then came the drought. The antelope migrated in search of water and we were forced to slaughter the goats. When they had all gone, we began to starve. Many prayers were said, but the gods were busy elsewhere, so the elders decided that to reclaim the gods' attention a sacrifice was required.

They looked for the weakest, least useful person in the village. As Aluha had gone, they turned their sights on me. Not everyone, it seemed, saw my birthmark as a blessing. Brushwood was collected and stacked in a great pile in the corral. When they came for me I struggled and screamed for my father, but he, half-mad and cowardly in his grief, ran out into the bush. They bound my feet and hands and carried me to the corral. Grimly, the villagers circled around the bonfire. Prayers were said and speeches made. I felt my fear grow and, alongside it anger. I would find a way to defy the elders.

They carried me to the pyre and laid me on it. Thorns pierced my buttocks and back. Then Linopo, our chief, made the spark and the dry grass ignited. Soon the brushwood was alight, crackling and spitting, the flames creeping up to where I lay. Fear left me and rage boiled in its place. If this was what the gods expected of me, then I would not listen to them anymore. I cursed loudly and sang the defiant song of the women that my mother had taught me.

> 'You can break our bodies
> But our spirits are free
> We women are stronger
> Than the baobab tree.'

The flames licked closer and I could smell the burning and feel the searing heat. I shouted at the villagers, 'You should be ashamed.'

At first the rain fell in sparse drops, then in torrents, thudding onto the parched, cracked surface of the mud. The musty smell of newly-moistened dust mingled with the cries of the villagers: 'The drought is over! We are saved!'

Fire fought water, but the water won. The pyre was a sodden, smoking heap. Villagers danced around the corral in their joy, embracing each other, singing and laughing. I shouted 'I'm alive,' and one of the hunters lifted me off the remains of the pyre and cut away the twine that bound me. I stood alone.

Gradually, silence fell.

I said, 'The rains came and put out the fire.'

'The gods make the rain,' said Linopo thoughtfully.

Father never came back. From the morning after the fire, gifts of food and water were laid at my door. I sat outside the hut, touching my birthmark, its roughness rising above the smoother skin of my cheek. Mostly, I was left alone, but every few days someone would sidle into view and ask for help with a problem or curse. I told them, 'I'm not a witch. I am a girl.' At first only Linopo understood.

'Innocence is holy,' he said. 'We must cherish her, and that will please the gods.'

I sat cross-legged as the villagers lined up to prostrate themselves: they would not look at me. The gifts of food grew ever more elaborate and I gained weight as, unlike the other children, I no longer carried water from the creek. Was I indeed the holy child Linopo thought me to be? Pride took me in its grip and I became fickle and sulked when the food was not to my liking.

There was little enough for me to do because things went smoothly in the village. I became unhappy, imprisoned in my innocence: a child, but unable to live like one because the well-being of the village rested on my small shoulders. How I longed for someone to cuddle, or with whom I could play games! Every morning I woke up wondering what would happen to me if there was another drought; if the new goats were eaten by lions; if Mibora's baby was still-born. Linopo would be dismayed that I had not intervened. I thought of running away, like my father, but where would I go? How could I fend for myself?

Linopo came one day and sat next to me in the dust. I knew then that he had a favour to ask.

"I am respectfully suggesting that you should wear the fine clothes that Kikuyua has woven for you. It befits your status as our holy child that you should be covered.'

'I will be too hot.' I waved a hand to dismiss him.

He lowered his voice. 'Your body is changing. Soon you will be more than a little girl.'

I thought about what he said.

'Why are the gods allowing this? Surely they would have me remain a child.'

'We can hide your body in the robes. Then the gods will tell us what to do.'

So I sat every day, draped in the finery he had brought, and for two more years the villagers came to worship me, and in that time I became a young woman. But Linopo would not let me speak to the other young women my age, and he forbade the young men to come near me.

'For the sake of the village,' he said, frowning at my burgeoning body, 'you must keep your innocence.'

At night he placed guards outside my hut, and another guard stood by me every day.

'For your protection,' said Linopo. 'It behoves us to look after you and keep you safe from our enemies.'

As well as food and water, the villagers brought other gifts—necklaces and anklets, a new beaker. I lived in a gilded cage, a fat little bird that was forgetting how to sing. And the strange thing was that very little happened in the village during those years to cause anyone any concern. It was as if a spell had been cast, keeping us safe from harm. How could I be sure it wasn't all something to do with me?

Just before my sixteenth birthday, when my childhood would be formally left behind, everything changed. I was bored and lonely, sick of constant surveillance and empty worship. One day, I told Linopo that trouble was coming. I said it to see his face grow haggard, hear his breath come hard.

'What do you mean, my child? Tell me what you see?'

'The gods are fighting each other,' I said. 'There will be thunder and fire.'

Linopo swallowed. 'Can you prevent it?'

I stared at him. 'I think so. You must set me free.'

He shook his head.

'The elders will not allow it.'

'Don't you want me to stop the catastrophe?'

He considered, then said, with some dignity, 'We'll wait, I think. It may not happen. A real seer would never bear false witness.'

He had called my bluff and I was more miserable than ever. I sat outside the hut in my robe and sulked.

But later that week thunder clouds towered on the horizon. Linopo arrived at my hut.

'I'm sorry I doubted you, my child. Please forgive me. Show your love for us by chasing away the storm.'

I laughed angrily. 'It's too late.'

The clouds rolled in and thunder deafened us. Jagged lightning raked the sky. There was a shout. The lightning had set fire to the bush, and the wind was blowing in our direction.

'Make it rain!' screamed Linopo. 'My child, make it rain!'

But the dark clouds withheld their bounty, and the fire swept on towards us. As the flames threatened the thorny tangle of the corral, and the goats bleated their alarm, the wind changed and the heavens opened.

Linopo prostrated himself before me.

'Let me go free,' I said.

'How can I? You are more needed now than ever.' He was silent for a while. 'Perhaps we could find another little girl marked out for glory.'

For a brief moment my heart leapt, but then I thought of that new girl, and how she would be confined.

'I will make a bargain with you,' I said. 'If I stay, you can tell the village that although I go in the guise of a woman, I am still the same girl. I promise that I will not marry or have children. As for the gods, I truly believe they do not answer to little girls; they will have their sport whatever we do.'

So Linopo took away my guards and I could at last walk freely in the village. Sometimes I strayed out into the bush—this made Linopo bite his fingernails to the quick. I have kept my word and not run away, and the villagers have learnt not to fall down before me. I will never be one of them—In times of trouble I act out my part—and together, we have got through the bad times the gods have thrown at us.

I see your eyes have glazed over: you are thinking of other things. Of your wife and daughters, perhaps, in the cold northern city where you live.

And of what interest can an old woman's story be to a young man in the prime of life? You have switched off your machine, and every pore of you wishes to be gone. Have I outlived my usefulness so quickly? A holy woman who has shared her memories so freely is due some respect. Look at the birthmark on my face—you know what it means. I have enough wisdom to match your knowledge of the world, even though I have stayed in the village all my life. I have outlived Linopo and the others; I am by far the oldest person here.

Dusk has fallen, and I must go to my hut. Sleep is more precious now that I am old. I am so tired I spend my days sitting under this umbrella. Sometimes I get up and watch the little girls play their long, complicated games in the dust under the thorn tree, and remember my dead friend Aluha from so long ago.

You have taken my story and will weave of it what you will. How strange that you trade in memories. What value, I wonder, will you place on mine?

JOY RIDING

Selena lived on the other side of town, several miles away from Karl's house. Karl had not seen her for some days, and, however many times he rang, she was not answering her phone. Since his driving ban came into force he had been unable to take her out into the countryside and to pubs on the trips that had formed much of their romantic life. It was rush hour, and Karl weaved through the heavy traffic on his father's bicycle, ignoring the red traffic lights. Selena was soon to sit her 'A' level exams so he expected she was studying hard. Her parents had been talking about her going away to university later in the year, although Karl was doing his best to persuade her that there were alternatives.

The bicycle was somewhat old-fashioned: a road racer, with drop handlebars and six gears, but Karl decided that it was up to the job. It even had a small bag that strapped on behind the saddle. He had pumped up the tyres and oiled the chain and gears, which changed smoothly, and he ensured that the tyres did not catch on the mud guards.

In what seemed a very short amount of time Karl pedalled up the drive to Selena's parents' house, which was a good deal larger than his parents' semi-detached. He leaned the bicycle against the wall and rang the bell. Eventually, after several rings, Selena came to the door.

'Oh hi, Karl. Sorry, I was listening to some music. Come in.'

Karl wiped his shoes on the door mat. 'How's the revision going?'

'It's okay, I suppose.'

She led the way up the stairs and into her bedroom. Karl looked around the large messy room. 'I see you haven't tidied up.'

Selena frowned. 'I've been busy. I need all these books.' She went down to the kitchen to make tea.

Karl sat on the edge of the unmade bed. Selena, in his view, didn't know when she was on to a good thing. He would've made this a beautiful room. When she returned with the mugs he asked, 'We're still together, then, are we?'

'I don't see why not. Mum and Dad hate you so that's a plus point. My phone's on the blink in case you were wondering.'

Karl reached over, pulled her to him and kissed her.

'Mum'll be back shortly, so we'd better be careful.'

Karl kissed her more passionately.

'How did you get here? The driving ban's a real pain, isn't it?'

Karl explained about the bicycle. 'You know, Selena, I may lose my job.'

'No car and no job. What a drag!'

'Do you have a bike?'

'I hate cycling. It's way too much effort.'

'We'll have to take the bus or something, then.'

Selena grimaced, then took a sip of her tea. Downstairs, the front door banged.

'That'll be Mum,' she said, pushing Karl away.

Selena's mother came up the stairs and entered Selena's room without knocking.

'Hello, Karl, have you been here long?'

'I've only just arrived, Mrs Sandys.'

'Good. Selena, I hope you've been revising.'

'Yes, Mum.'

'Dinner will be ready at seven. Are you staying, Karl?'

'Yes please.'

She nodded briefly, then left.

Karl began picking up the clothes that were scattered across the floor. He piled them on a cane chair next to the chest of drawers. Selena laughed. 'What's wrong with being a bit messy? You're a control freak.'

'I hardly think picking up a few t-shirts makes me that.'

At 7 p.m., after Selena's father had returned home from his job in London, they sat down to dinner in the kitchen.

'It was unfortunate that you're banned from driving, Karl,' said Mr Sandys, 'but perhaps we'll see a bit more of Selena now.'

Karl explained about the bicycle.

'It's a shame it's not a tandem!' said Mr Sandys—his wife kicked him under the table. 'You'll not get Selena on a bike, anyway. You should've seen the trouble we had teaching her to ride one when she was a little girl. I don't think she's been on a bicycle since.'

'I haven't,' said Selena.

Karl sliced into his steak. 'Could you give us a lift out to the Clifton Arms tomorrow evening?' he asked Mr Sandys. 'There's a band playing that we'd like to see.'

Mr Sandys rubbed his chin. 'I suppose you'd want a lift back as well?'

'Yes please, Dad,' said Selena, wide-eyed. Her father soon capitulated.

'Do you have any lights on your bicycle, Karl?' asked Mrs Sandys. 'If not, you'll have to leave here early, before it gets dark.'

As soon as they had finished dessert Karl was hurried on his way. He cycled contentedly through the twilight. At home, his mother was upset because he had not come home to dinner. 'You should have rung,' she said, reasonably. 'Anything could've happened to you.' His father seemed pleased that his old bicycle was getting a new lease of life.

The next evening, after dinner, Karl cycled to Selena's house. Selena was dressed in her best psychedelic dress, leggings and sandals, her hair parted in the middle and tucked behind her ears. Mr Sandys was in his study, and Selena seemed reluctant to disturb him, even though, if they were to see the band, it was time for them to leave. In the end, Karl knocked on the door.

Karl and Selena sat in the back of Mr Sandys's vintage Jaguar. Mr Sandys had said very little since being persuaded away from his study. Outside, darkness was taking over from the day—a huge full moon hung in the pinkish sky. Mr Sandys pulled up outside the pub. 'I'll collect you at 11.30, no arguments,' he said, before driving off.

The Clifton Arms was packed with young people expecting to see the band, Black Cats, who would be playing after the support act. Karl bought Selena a vodka and orange and himself a pint of Guinness. They knew quite a few of the crowd, who were mostly ex-pupils of their school. The support act, Into You, turned out to be of an introspective cast, playing quiet love songs to themselves. Selena bought more drinks while they were waiting for the main act, who were very loud. Karl briefly lost Selena in the mêlée and eventually found her at the front, only a few metres from the band. It was impossible to have a conversation, so they danced, holding hands.

After the band had finished their set there was very little time before Mr Sandys would be collecting them. They waited outside in the starlight. Promptly at 11.30 p.m. the Jaguar arrived. Inside was Mrs Sandys. 'Your father received a phone call from work and he's bogged down in his study at the moment.'

Selena and Karl climbed into the back. Karl had drunk three pints of Guinness and was wondering how he would manage to cycle home. It seemed that Mrs Sandys had read his mind because she said, 'I will drop Selena off and then take you home, Karl. You can collect your bicycle another time.'

When they reached her house Selena kissed him goodnight and got out, and the car swept slowly on through the deserted streets. Mrs Sandys was careful to keep to the speed limit.

'Selena has applied to Oxford,' she announced. 'And even if she doesn't get in there, she will be going away to university. Her grades are expected to be very good.'

'Are you sure she wants to go to university? She told me that she would like to take a gap year at the very least.'

'That is not going to happen, Karl.'

'Doesn't Selena have some say in it?'

'She might, but you don't.'

'Now look here . . . you can't make her do anything . . . ' said Karl, then thought better of it.

There was silence for a few seconds, then Karl said, 'I know you don't like me . . . '

'It's not a question of liking . . . It's about suitability. I'm sure you've done quite well for someone from your background.'

'No I haven't. Plenty of people like me go to university. And I'm about to lose my job because of the driving ban.'

'Well, that's a shame, Karl. There doesn't seem to be any real harm in you.'

The car pulled up outside Karl's house. Karl got out and took a moment to breathe in the night air.

Selena's father opened his study door and called her back down the stairs.

'Have you told Karl that you're definitely going to university? You shouldn't keep him hanging on, it isn't fair.'

'I haven't even taken my "A" levels yet! Anyway, Karl and I can stay together even if I do go away.'

'It's very difficult to conduct a long distance relationship, especially at your age. You'll meet someone else.'

'What if I don't want anyone else? I'm happy with Karl.'

Selena went up to her room. She heard her father's study door close, and outside the low hum of the returning Jaguar. As so often before she wished she had a brother or sister to help dissipate some of her parents' unwavering, stifling attention.

———

Karl walked briskly through the deserted streets to the park. He climbed over the fence and made toward the trees—he had felt the changes coming over him earlier in the evening in the pub and knew it wouldn't be long before the full effect came into force. He had learnt that if he could get himself away from people he would be less likely to do, or come to, any harm. It had been unfortunate that last time it happened he had been in his car and the conviction for careless driving had resulted in the driving ban. He was hoping that he would learn how to manage the condition so that it did not impinge too much on his daily life.

Once under the cover of the trees Karl lay down and attempted to wait it out. The restlessness soon took over, however, and he got up and began to follow the scent trails. It would have been difficult to explain how, with a heightened sense of smell, the world took on an extra, delicious dimension. Before long he was racing through the woods, oblivious to the cold and the thorny briars in the undergrowth which caught at his clothes and skin. Later, near morning, he would wake in a pile of leaves or a ditch, needing to find his way home to change and shower before work.

It was no surprise to Karl that he was dismissed from his job at the Estate Agents. Without a valid driving licence he no longer met the requirements of the position. His boss was very nice about it, but it was clear that an exception was not going to be made.

Karl caught a bus that took him to Selena's road. She was surprised to see him so early in the day, and very understanding when he explained that he had been sacked.

'Poor you,' she said. 'Let's go upstairs. Mum and Dad won't be back for hours.'

Afterwards, they ate lunch in the kitchen.

'It happened again last night,' said Karl. 'After your mother dropped me off.'

'It's just as well for Mum's sake that it didn't happen while you were in the car with her.'

'What am I going to do, Selena?'
'I don't know. So long as you don't hurt anyone. . . . '
'I may do, that's the trouble.'
'Well, I'll have to keep a close eye on you. We could go away together after my exams and then I would be with you all the time.'
'What if I hurt you?'
'I don't think that's going to happen. You were very protective of me last time.'
'So are you going to take a gap year then, Selena? Shall we do some travelling together?'
'That's the plan, but I'll have to find a way of persuading Mum and Dad that it's a good idea.'
'Maybe if you get your university place sorted out first, and then tell them. If it's definite that you're at least going to uni they should be pleased.'
'Let's hope so.'
Karl was beginning to feel more positive about things. They booted up Selena's laptop and looked at some ideas for places they could travel to. The Far East—perhaps Thailand—appealed to them both.

In the afternoon Karl left Selena to her revision and retrieved his father's bicycle from the rear of the house. It had been drizzling and the saddle was damp. Karl rode back home through the heavy traffic. His father, who worked shifts at a local engineering works, was in the living room reading the paper.

'I've lost my job, Dad.'
'What are you going to do with yourself now?'
Karl explained about Selena's gap year.
'Well you're the right age for a bit of travelling. Do you have the cash? I suppose you can work while you're over there and pay your way.'
'I've a bit put by and we're hoping Selena's father will help out.'
'You'll not get much out of him, in my opinion. Listen, Karl, I've been meaning to say something. . . . I wondered if you'd been experiencing some unusual . . . symptoms . . . I think you know what I'm talking

about. I heard you come in last night, and saw the state of your clothes in the laundry basket. All I wanted to say is that it runs in the family. The good news is that it does wear off after a few years. At least it did for me, and for your grandfather. The trick is to learn how to keep yourself and others safe, and to enjoy it, if you can. Does Selena know?'

'Yes. She was there when it happened once. She's pretty cool about it.'

'Good. But don't tell anyone else.'

'So this is my inheritance?'

'Something like that.'

Karl's father got up and put the newspaper on the table.

'I need to get to work. Hopefully you'll be free of it for a few weeks. And the driving ban won't last for ever. You'll be back behind the wheel before you know it. Travelling abroad for a few months with Selena will be a good way of spending the time before then. You can look for another job when you get home.'

Selena sat her exams and persuaded her reluctant parents that a gap year was the price they had to pay for her agreeing to go to university. Karl got a temporary job in a pizza factory to earn some more money for their travels. While he was working there he experienced another episode. This time he had to lock himself in the gents and wait for it to pass. It was a horrible experience being cooped up in the small cubicle with all his senses blazing and his limbs twitching. When it was over he was relieved that he had been able to control the cravings. It boded well for future eventualities.

Selena's father was more impressed than he cared to admit that Karl was offering to pay Selena's travelling expenses as well as his own. But, wanting Selena to be safe and happy he eventually made a substantial contribution to their fund. Everything that could be was arranged, and they were set to fly out at the end of August.

The next time it happened, Karl experienced few of the usual warning signs. He was at home on his own and his car was parked outside. The changes hit him in a rush, and it seemed this time there was little he could do to mitigate them. The wanderlust was on him and he went outside and got into the car. He turned the key in the ignition and the engine roared to life—he let out the hand brake and drove into the traffic. Soon he was out in the country lanes where there was no CCTV, zipping past fields and farmhouses. Somehow he managed to avoid hitting anything. Gradually the changes left him. He slowed down and drove the car carefully back to his parents' house. Although he was in some ways horrified by what had transpired, he was buzzing and he felt truly alive. And it seemed that he had got away with it—after a few days there was no sign that anyone in authority was aware that he had been driving. He did not tell Selena or his father about it.

Eight days later, Karl and Selena flew out to Thailand.

REALITY TV

*15th February
Morning*

I have been looking forward to being here so much and now it hardly seems real. The view from my bedroom window is of fields and sheep and a hill that is almost a mountain. It is very much like the landscape we dreamed of when we first watched the Series, only on TV the fields are framed by the screen. Here they seem to flow on for ever.

Last night, near the end of our journey, we stopped for a pizza in the local town. It was dark, and there were few people about. When we arrived at the cottage I looked up at the sky and found that I could see the stars—really see them, I mean—and more of them than ever before. There is little light pollution here, and hardly any people. Once, we heard someone say on the Series that there are more sheep than folk in the Dales. And more stars than sheep, I could add.

I can hear Mum and Dad unpacking supplies in the kitchen. They sound almost cheerful. Yesterday, during our journey, they put on brave faces for my sake. It could be that it's too soon for a holiday, or maybe it's one that we really need; none of us are sure which.

I have a twin-bedded room, Mum and Dad have a big double bed in theirs. I have explored all the rooms in the cottage, and the outbuildings.

It is larger than our house, and there is a table tennis table in the barn. After breakfast we are going to walk around the village and then we'll have lunch in the pub. In the brochure it says that there is no shop or café and only one pub, so there is little choice about where to eat. Tomorrow we'll get back in the car and explore the dale and some of the nearby villages, and visit some of the locations for the Series.

Evening

The houses here are built of stone and have thick stone slabs on their roofs. They are unalike, having been built at different times, even though many of them are attached to each other. As well as the pub there is a disused church, a chapel, a garage and a village hall. Once there was a school beside the church, but it closed many years ago. The pub landlord told us that the children are bussed into a nearby village where there is a small primary school. The secondary school is in the town where we bought the pizza. That's the one I would attend if we lived here.

I've never stayed in a village before. If we lived here then I would come to know every stone, every clump of moss, every crow. I would attend each village event (domino drives, fêtes, carpet bowls, according to the notice board) and go to the pub nearly every night, as some people do in the Series.

Our pub lunch was very good, although Dad says it was 'not cheap'. He and Mum were quiet on the walk and over our meal. I did most of the talking, which is happening more than it used to. When there were four of us things were more even. I suppose there has to be some readjustment, a realignment to reflect the lack of symmetry.

It has been grey and drizzly all day, unlike in the Series, which they film mostly on dry days, although the people in it talk about the weather all the time. We first came across the Series one evening when flicking through the channels looking for something to watch. We thought it was a spoof reality soap set in an impossible world. It dawned on us after a couple of episodes that it was real, and we soon became obsessed with the people featured in it (Cliff the sheep farmer, Maggie who cleans the holiday cottages, John in the garage). Mum and Dad have never been able to see the attraction, but I think they were amused to find us enthralled by something so unlikely.

This afternoon I played table tennis with Dad until he grew tired of it. Mum read her book in the living room, stretched out on the sofa. There is no television here and in any case I am longing to get out and about, but Mum and Dad need to rest after yesterday's journey. Mum, especially, does not have the stamina she used to.

16th February

I have seen John's garage, and Cliff's sheep, but I found that I could not bring myself to approach any of our heroes. I felt shy and diffident, but it was more than that. Perhaps keeping the real people at arms' length preserves my appreciation of them? Unedited, would they live up to their on-screen characters? . . . I realised that I did not want to take the risk of finding out.

John was striding up the road from the garage, his unmistakable lanky form eating up the ground, but I would not let Dad drive past him. We drove instead to Cliff's farm, which is in a tiny hamlet twenty miles north of 'our' cottage. There was smoke rising from his chimney, but I would not knock at his door. I know from the Series that Cliff's sheep are those with the black faces, curly horns and long, straggly wool roaming over the coarse grassland and heather that we drove through to get to his farm. His sheep dogs were barking as we briefly got out of the car, and I smelt the sharp tang of coal smoke hanging in the stillness. There has been not a breath of wind today, but the sun is too feeble to break through the clouds. I know from the Series how fickle the Dales weather can be.

We bought pies from a butchers' in one of the larger villages near Cliff's farm. It was just warm enough to sit outside to eat them. Mum was impressed by the number of shops around the village green, although Dad pointed out that two of the four pubs had 'to let' signs outside. After lunch we drove to the village where Maggie lives. Her 4x4 was parked outside her house, and we could see all of her paraphernalia in the back—the famous feather duster and innumerable cans and bottles of polish and cleaning products. Her village is larger than most we had driven through, with a functioning school and a convenience store and post office. She's your favourite, isn't she—gossiping about holiday cottage owners, people in her village and her own family, while brushing out fireplaces and making up beds.

As we drove slowly past, Maggie came out of her front door and let herself into her vehicle. I took out my phone to take her picture and then thought better of it. Mum laughed good-naturedly at me, then was crestfallen when I explained.

'I wasn't thinking, Mum. I was taking the photo for Sara.'

We were quiet on our way back to the cottage. The evening has been spent playing Scrabble and gin rummy. We are tired after the fresh air of our day out and we are each afraid of upsetting the others by talking out of turn.

17th February

Mum has one of her headaches so we left her in bed at the cottage while Dad drove me to Richmond. There we found a tiny cinema in a disused railway station where we watched an old film called *The Innocents*. Dad wasn't impressed because he doesn't like plots to be so unresolved. This may be why he doesn't watch the Series.

We had lunch in a pub from which you can walk to a waterfall. It featured in the first season of the Series, when a brass band competition was held on the land by the beck. The rivers and becks are swollen with rain so the waterfall was very impressive, roaring over the high rocks and giving off a fine spray which dampened my hair and made it curly. Dad laughed at my attempts to straighten it with my fingers. He seems more cheerful when he isn't fussing over Mum. They fuss over each other, which is half the trouble.

Back at the cottage Mum was up and looking brighter. We decided to go to the pub for dinner. I put on my black dress and high heels, and even Dad made an effort, appearing in a clean shirt and a tie. There was a difficult moment when the landlord unaccountably asked 'a table for four?' as we walked in, but we managed to enjoy our meal without further upsets. You would've loved the young waiter, who made a brave stab at pronouncing some of the more elaborate dishes on the menu.

When we got back to the cottage Mum went to the living room cupboard and took out the urn.

'I think it's time,' she said. 'Come on, don't stand there staring. We'll do it now.'

So with the help of a torch Dad found in the kitchen we filed out into the back garden and tipped what is left of you onto a weedy flowerbed. It was almost a comical moment. Afterwards, Dad opened his bottle of whisky and we each had a large draught which, on top of the wine they'd drunk in the pub, made our parents drowsy. They went up to bed soon afterwards.

I suppose I should be glad that it has happened at last, even though it was something of an anti-climax. You have travelled so many miles with us, and now you will remain here, in the garden, and be a part of this place that we have loved for ever.

18th February

Today we took a trip out to a village in the southern Dales where there is a famous church with Mouseman pews and woodwork. J.B. Priestley loved it. We looked round the church interior dutifully and on coming out of the main door to walk around the graveyard we bumped into a small man in a dog collar. It was Rev Martin from the Series. He dropped his bag, and when he had picked it up he said hello and shook Dad's hand.

'What do you think of our little church?' he asked.

'It's lovely,' I simpered in my excitement. 'I just love all the little wooden mice.'

Mum put a hand on his arm. 'You mustn't mind Selma,' she said. 'She's a big fan of your Series. And we've had a bereavement in the family.'

Dad and I looked at her in surprise. Rev Martin's expression and manner changed.

'I'm very sorry to hear that. Please accept my sympathies. If there's any help that I can give? . . .

'I can't think of anything you can do or say. What possible help could you give someone who has lost a daughter?' she asked. 'I think it must be one of the very worst things that could happen to anyone. Especially when it makes no sense.'

Dad said, 'Rosalyn . . . ' then his voice gave out.

There was an uncomfortable silence while Rev Martin tried to think of something appropriate to say. He cleared his throat.

'Sometimes there is very little in life that makes any sense. I hope you can take some comfort that your daughter is now in a better place.'

Mum just looked at him. Dad put his arm around her shoulders and steered her towards the car.

I thought, until we had driven halfway home, that by 'a better place', the Reverend had meant the weedy flowerbed at the cottage. He at least tried to sound sincere, and he is more handsome in real life than he is in the Series. You would be envious that I have met him. What a pity that I made such a fool of myself and could think of nothing witty or interesting to say. It seems that now we're here we will bump into characters from the Series whether I like it or not.

When we arrived back at the cottage Mum found the whisky bottle and poured herself a large glassful. Dad unpacked the shopping and began taking out pots and pans while I laid the table in the dining room. We ate our meal in silence. I did the washing up and Dad dried the dishes. Mum had taken the torch and gone out into the garden.

19th February

I came down to breakfast to find Mum and Dad in each other's arms. When they realised I was there (which took some seconds), Mum smiled and Dad said, 'Don't mind your soppy old parents.'

Something seems to have changed between them, some shift in perspective. They have decided to pull together, rather than tear each other apart.

It has rained all day so we took a driving tour around the southern half of the Dales. Mum switched on the radio and we sang along to pop songs as we used to. Some of the roads were wide enough only for one car, and on the road to Settle, I had to get out to open and close a gate. We stopped for a pot of tea and a plate of sandwiches at an isolated café and stared at the stupendous, rain-lashed view. It almost . . . almost . . . felt like one of our old family days out.

In the Series the landscape can be brooding or indifferent or benign, like a god from one of the old religions. Today, we crawled over the face of the divine. Rev Martin is not averse to quoting from Greek philosophers in his sermons, so he will forgive me for a lapse into paganism, although I am sure as a Yorkshireman and a Christian he would claim this as God's country. If I had paid more attention in our geography lessons then I might understand the natural forces that formed this extraordinary place. I would not need to rely on religion to explain the coves and fells and tarns and caves and limestone pavements, the scree slopes and sink holes, although it is tempting to do so.

Now it is night-time and the stars are hidden behind the clouds. Our parents are talking quietly in their room next door. I think, Sara, they have 'turned the corner'. They have each other. They are going to be all right.

20th February

Tomorrow we are going home, and we will be leaving you behind. This morning we walked from the cottage down to the river. There is a ruined chapel and a sort of beach of cobbles on which we stood to skim flat stones across the water. Dad showed me how to do it. Afterwards we went to the pub. To my surprise Ivan O'Connor was there, drinking lemonade and talking to anyone who would listen about his vegetable garden. You'll remember that he was featured in season three of the Series as a sort of Holy fool, dispensing platitudes about the weather and his plants. I had not realised that he lived in the village. Mum asked him for his autograph and he gladly wrote it on a napkin. He was so pleased to be asked that I suspect he is not approached very often. After lunch he showed us his vegetable patch and talked about it as if he was unaware that we had seen him in the Series.

This afternoon I went out to the back garden and told you about Ivan. You laughed, and I asked you not to be so cruel. I said that he was a nice man with learning difficulties and you laughed at me some more. You said, 'I remember when you found him amusing too.'

I could still see your cold grey ash sticking to the damp mud of the flower bed. Soon the worms will drag you down into the soil. You will be here and I will have gone home. I plunged my fingers into your ashes and smeared them on my face.

I don't want to be back in dull Northampton with my bereavement counsellor and the friends who eye me warily. I don't want to live a life without you. Can I not stay here with you and be in the Series: surely I'd make a good character—the girl who does not want to leave her twin behind?

But one day the ratings will begin to slide, and the cameras will disappear from the Dales. What will happen to the people in the Series then? How differently will they live their lives when they are left to live on their own?

I washed your ash off my face before our parents saw it.

I have spent the rest of the afternoon in my twin-bedded room, writing this journal. I am noting down everything that happens—every incident, every piece of scenery, every person we have seen—nothing will be forgotten or missed out. It will be here waiting for you.

CHALLENGING BEHAVIOUR

I first came across the boy in the supermarket; he was eating an apple from the pile. I said, 'You are supposed to pay for that,' and then realised what a killjoy that made me. He looked me in the eye and crunched again into the apple, the juice dribbling onto his shirt. Averting my eyes I walked past him down the aisle.

My stomach was rumbling and I found it hard to ignore all the tasty fruit and the tempting chocolate bars at the checkout. The boy stood behind me in the queue, in his basket a packet of crisps, a can of Coke and a cream cake. He watched as each worthy item of my weekly shop rode the conveyor belt towards my waiting carrier bags.

As I lifted my shopping from my trolley into the car he sauntered past, swinging his carrier, swigging from the Coke can and munching a sausage roll. The latter hadn't been in his basket. The little thief waved at me and grinned.

He was slim, about fifteen, with an elfin face: the school uniform made him seem younger. As I got into the car I saw him turn right into the school road. I considered driving to the school and asking to speak to the head teacher. . . . Instead I turned the car for home, unloaded the groceries and drove back to work.

I didn't see the boy for several weeks, until bonfire night, when I attended the town's official display. He brought his own fireworks. He stuck them in the ground and lit them one by one with a cigarette lighter, well away from the designated fireworks area, in amongst the crowd. No one else seemed particularly concerned. His fireworks were of the relatively harmless variety, but that was not the point. Did he do it, I asked myself, for the sheer hell of it?

Once his fireworks were spent, he lit a cigarette, strode up to me and blew smoke near my face, then disappeared into the crowd.

I found myself taking home a pen and a box of paperclips from the office, secreting them in the bottom of my briefcase. I returned them, unused, the following day. I stole a cheap paperback book from the newsagents, but donated it to a charity shop because I couldn't bring myself to read it.

A couple of weeks later I attended a concert at the school. The boy was in the audience, throwing little pellets of paper at the stage and into the crowd. I stood up and sidled along the row towards him, but by the time I got there he had gone. Angry glances were aimed at me by other audience members—I went back to my place and sat down.

The next day was cold and dreary. In the evening I turned up the central heating and opened a bottle of beer. It was time, I decided, that I should live a little more recklessly.

I handed in my notice and booked a holiday to Venice. My colleagues were concerned, but I told them I was taking a break from work. I bought some clothes and a new pair of brogues.

I went to Venice and found that I disliked the dirty canals, high prices, and the general air of decay. I was glad to get home to my neat little house and garden.

My boss agreed to give me my old job back, provided I promised not do anything so stupid again. I turned down the heating and lived within my means.

I was content.

A few weeks later I was in the supermarket buying a sandwich for lunch. The boy appeared in front of me. He grinned and took an ice cream from the freezer, peeling off the wrapper and began ostentatiously to eat it. He ate as if he had never eaten an ice cream before, licking and sucking and generally behaving in a disgusting manner. And all of it aimed at me. When he had finished he pocketed the wrapper and the wooden stick and sauntered off towards the exit.

I found myself heading for the manager's office, then thought better of it. Why put them to the trouble of checking their CCTV over one ice cream? So I went to the checkout and paid for my sandwich. I ate it, fuming, at my desk.

The things that had given me pleasure—gardening, cooking, painting watercolours—now seemed worthless and tame. My dreams were full of lurid encounters, loving embraces, frantic couplings. I was tormented by my own imaginings. I, who had prided myself on my equanimity, was now in a hot bed of longing. With no outlet, I succumbed to a breakdown, and was advised by my doctor to take some time off work.

I agreed to see a counsellor, and I told him about the boy. He frowned and said, 'You are projecting your own desires onto this revenant.'

'No,' I said. 'He is a real boy, doing exactly what he wants.'

'Is there anything wrong in doing what you want from time to time?'

'Good behaviour is very important to me.'

'It wouldn't do any harm to let yourself go occasionally.'

After a few weeks of enforced inertia, I went back to work. Colin said, 'Are you okay now or should we still be worried?' Just to spite him, I asked Sue in accounts out for a meal, because I knew he had a soft spot for her. To my surprise she agreed, and we had a very pleasant time in the Chinese restaurant near the office. She said she had never had a more polite escort. I had no idea how to proposition her, so I simply drove her home and we wished each other good night as she got out of the car.

When I told my counsellor that I had enjoyed an entirely chaste date he said, 'What's wrong with telling her how you feel? Do you find her attractive?'

'Yes,' I replied, 'she is a nice-looking woman.'

'On your next date you can say, "I find you very attractive." That's pretty unequivocal. Then you take it from there.'

I was steeling myself to ask Sue out again (Colin was gratifyingly annoyed), standing outside the florists wondering if I had the courage (and funds) to buy her an extravagant bunch of flowers, when the boy walked past. He was wearing a dark t-shirt and jeans and when he saw me he stopped and took from his back pocket a large roll of bank notes. He waved them under my nose, then, laughing, ran off. Where could such a young boy have come across so much money, I wondered? I was struggling to make ends meet after my enforced period of sickness; my mortgage repayments were cripplingly high. What japes he could get up to with no responsibilities and all that cash.

I bought the biggest bunch of flowers in the shop and presented them to Sue in front of Colin and the rest of the office. She was embarrassed but I could see that she was pleased, and the receptionist found her a vase to put them in. Later, I asked if she would like to go out for a drink. After work we went to a nearby pub. I bought her a glass of wine and said, 'I find you very attractive'.

'Thank you,' she said, 'but I would like to take things slowly, if that's okay. I broke up with my boyfriend recently.'

'Oh. Right,' I said. I was annoyed that I had spent a lot of money on the flowers. 'Just the occasional date then?'

'Yes,' she said, 'for now. That would be nice.'

We drank our drinks in silence. Then she said, 'I do like you, David. It's nice of you to be so understanding.'

When I had finished my drink I made an excuse and left.

My counsellor pointed out that Sue in fact had been quite encouraging.

It was probably inevitable that I should next see the boy when I was with Sue. We had gone to a wine bar in town, and were sitting on high stools at the counter when he walked in. He was dressed smartly in black jeans and what looked like a silk shirt. Although he was obviously too young to be served, he sauntered up to the bar and asked confidently for a pint of bitter (I do not like wine but was drinking it to keep Sue company). He grinned at me as he sipped his pint, then carried his glass to a table in the corner. My blood was boiling. I said to Sue, 'This place is really going downhill now the underage drinkers are moving in.'

She looked at me quizzically. 'What do you mean?'

'That boy,' I said, waving my hand in the direction of the corner table.

'What boy?' she asked.

I looked over but he had gone.

I took Sue to see *Othello* at the National Theatre. She said she enjoyed it and afterwards we went out for a meal at an Indian restaurant. It was very expensive (I am not used to London prices) but afterwards as I held the door open for her to get into my car I kissed her on the cheek. She smiled and then reached up and kissed me on the lips. I was so surprised I took a step back. We got into the car and began the long drive home. It was late when we arrived and so I thought it best that I drop her at her flat. She was very quiet on the journey.

During our lunch break the next day Sue and I went for a walk down by the river.

'Look,' she said, 'I don't know where I am with you. I know I said I wanted to take things slowly but not like this. When I kissed you yesterday you jumped like a frightened rabbit. Are you sure you want to go out with me?'

At that moment I caught a glimpse of something white in the river. It was the boy, completely naked, paddling in the freezing water, bending down and splashing it with his hands. There were several notices warning people against bathing in the fast-flowing river.

I yelled, 'Get out of the water, it's dangerous.'

Sue gasped, 'What the hell? . . . '

'Don't look, Sue.' I tried to put my hand over her eyes but she broke away from me angrily.

The boy was capering and cavorting through the water, laughing and shouting, ignoring my gesticulations.

'There's no one there,' she said.

I turned to remonstrate with him again, and saw that she was right. He must've scuttled up the bank into the trees, where no doubt he had left his clothes. I was all for going into the wood after him, but Sue stopped me. 'What good would it do,' she said.

As we walked back to the office she said, 'I think we should take a break. I'm happy to be your friend, but let's stop seeing one another for a while. It's for the best.'

I told my counsellor what Sue had said, expecting him to find the positive in it but instead he said, 'She's finished with you. I don't think she was quite your type. Tell me more about this boy.'

I said, 'I don't want to talk about him.'

I took to carrying around a small video camera in the hope that I could film some of the boy's exploits and so have proof for the authorities of his behaviour, but I didn't see him for many weeks. In the meantime I went to work each day, and tidied my garden. Colin asked Sue out and soon they were an item. I found I did not mind very much after the first few days.

Christmas came and went, and we were into the cold, grey days of January. One evening, I saw the boy on the local television news. He had won a prestigious art competition—his painting a garish jumble of abstract acrylics—and he was being interviewed. He was wearing a grungy t-shirt.

'I went for something bold,' he said, 'none of these prissy little watercolours for me.' He gestured at some of the other entries. 'Big, brazen and beautiful. My painting's about life and how I live it.'

His insolent face filled the screen. He'd won a considerable amount of money. I fetched some of my own watercolours. I had been pleased with them but now they seemed prim and unremarkable.

I realised then that I was never going to escape him. The boy would grow up and obtain some impossibly glamorous job, or become a world famous artist or rock star. I took the camera with me to the supermarket for some months, but I never saw him there again. In fact I mostly came across him on the television. There he'd be, grinning in a crowd or studio audience, playing guitar in a band, being interviewed in a student union about the first show of his paintings. After a while I took my television to the municipal tip and learned to live without it. It means that I have even less to talk to my colleagues about. Sometimes I catch a glimpse of the young man (as he is now) in the street, and when I visit the cinema, he's there throwing popcorn at the front row, and jeering at the film.

    I have been waiting for another reckless moment in my life, but it seems that I am not that kind of man.

CHANGE

I said something silly, I forget what. He smiled, shook his head and whispered, 'Don't ever change.' I was charmed, even though part of me knew it was a cliché, and, if I was honest, a little bit patronising. But in the muzzy warmth of our mutual passion, I didn't much mind what he said or did.

He dressed quickly and let himself out and as I lingered in bed a worm of doubt wriggled in my brain. Did he really want me to remain a naïve twenty-year-old forever? Were we not to grow into a mature, loving couple, sharing the good times, the middling and the bad? For the first time it occurred to me that he might have a very different view of our relationship. I shivered, pushed back the duvet, and spent a long time in the bath, thinking.

He was some years older than me, (I only found out how many after several weeks). As far as I was concerned he was a man of the world, and that was part of the attraction. He was earning good money (I was a student) and he took me out to restaurants and the theatre. Sometimes we stayed at country house hotels, going on long muddy walks and using room service profligately. I couldn't get enough of the smell of his skin, the touch of his fingertips. Outside, nature seemed aligned with us, the long summer grass dancing to our tune, the deer in the park raising their nostrils but not shying away. We sat under the trees and drank cider from the bottle: on those trips we sustained an alcohol-induced haze. We were wholly indifferent to the presence and needs of the other guests. I suppose it was the arrogance of love. As far as we were concerned, we were the most important people in the world.

As I dried my body with the towel I told myself that loving someone was as big a risk as several other things in life: buying a house, choosing a career. It was a form of gambling, taking a chance that the input of emotion, time and effort would result in a meaningful bond. I was sure he was the one for me; that he was worth fighting for. Surely, he was worth it?

If he wanted me to stay as I was now, would he discard me as soon as I showed signs of aging—bags under my eyes, lines from my nose to the corners of my mouth? I looked in the mirror. Good skin. Would he watch with growing horror as that bloom faded? If I displayed any degree of worldliness would he recoil in disgust? trade me in, as they say, for a younger, prettier model?

I was desperate. All that came afterwards stemmed from this. I shed hot, angry tears, then rallied, wiped my eyes and resolved that I would do everything in my power to keep him.

The instructions in the book I found in the British Library were precise, unequivocal. They guaranteed success only if they were followed to the letter. There was an incantation to learn and a philtre to drink prepared from all manner of hard-to-find-things—unfurled fern fronds, morning dew, the hair of a fox—crushed together with a pestle and strained into a silver beaker. Another drawback was that the spell must be cast and the philtre consumed while dancing naked in a forest clearing at midnight. The fox hair was the most difficult thing to find, but eventually I located a stuffed vixen in the Natural History Museum. For an exorbitant sum I purchased a hallmarked beaker from a stall on the Portobello Road. The fern fronds I stole from Kew Gardens, along with the morning dew.

I made the philtre, careful to add each ingredient in the correct order. It was a warm, clear night when I took the bus to Epping Forest. I had prepared thoroughly the week before reconnoitring for a suitable clearing. As per instructions, the full moon hung swollen under the glinting stars. I checked the time on my watch and took off my clothes. I unscrewed the top from the flask and poured the philtre into the silver beaker. I began to dance in slow, sinuous windings, offering the beaker up to the moon. Exactly at midnight I sipped the sour potion, being careful not to spill a single drop.

Afterwards was an anti-climax. I shivered, despite the warmth of the night, and dressed hurriedly. The walk back to the bus stop seemed interminable and the night bus was late, the other passengers dressed for an evening out and mostly worse for wear. Back home I lay on the bed in my clothes and fell into a troubled sleep.

A week later, I met him at a newly-opened restaurant (he had been to a conference in Paris). The waiting staff were keen and buzzed around us. He presented me with a bottle of expensive perfume, expertly wrapped, a luxury he knew I would treasure, eking out each drop. Fleetingly, I saw myself as others might: a spoilt young mistress kept sweet with meals and gifts. But it wasn't like that. We were in love. He was generous and kind.

'You look lovely,' he said. 'I like the way you style your hair.'

'Then I'll keep it this way,' I found myself saying.

'And your make-up is perfect. I'm a lucky man.'

He smiled a touch smugly.

'I'll always be your girl,' I said.

A year passed and I finished my degree. I moved in with him; he said there was no need for me to work. My time was spent looking after the house and shopping for clothes. I went often to the hair salon and the beauty parlour, having my hair set and my nails painted. The staff could not understand why they never seemed to grow. I said that I cut them myself at home.

He liked to show me off to his friends, buying me a new dress and jewellery each time we went out. I loved him passionately and I was content with my life. Why should I not be?

After a few years I noticed the first traces of grey in his hair. There were lines on his forehead and the beginnings of wattle on his neck. At first I didn't mind. They were signs of maturity and experience, the very things I lacked.

On my thirtieth birthday he decided that he wanted children. By then he was forty-seven. I went along with it but of course I didn't conceive. My body was in stasis. He brooded for a while then seemed to accept it.

He said, 'You're so lovely, you're all I need. You don't look a day older than when we first met.'

When we encountered new people they often assumed I was his daughter.

Not long after he reached fifty he began to feel tired in the evenings, sometimes falling asleep on the sofa. I looked after him, massaging his feet and concocting nourishing meals. He began to put on weight. I effortlessly stayed the same size, eating as much as I liked.

Gradually, subtly, so that at first I was hardly aware of it, he became less appealing. It was not so much the physical changes, more the coarsening of intellect, the death of mental vigour. I suppose he began to bore me: the long rambling grumbles about his colleagues, his discontent with the achievements of younger rivals, a falling off of his engagement with the world. He complained often about the aging process. He grew resentful.

'It's all right for you,' he said. 'You can still pass for twenty. I don't know how you do it.'

Our friends began to look at us strangely. Eventually I realised I could no longer live with him: as he slipped into old age I would be mistaken for his granddaughter. I broke it to him gently, or at least I tried to: there was no easy way of saying it. He showed little surprise.

'It's because you look so young,' he said. 'You've spent enough of my money keeping yourself that way. I suppose you could have anyone you desire, you no longer want to be chained to an old man like me.'

Some years before, I had opened my own bank account and saved a sizeable sum from the allowance he had given me. I set myself up in a flat in Pimlico and got a job as a receptionist, lying about my age. They asked few questions, happy that I looked the part. The job was relatively undemanding and I earned enough so that, with my savings, I was comfortably off. As I had left him, I lost most of our mutual friends and neglected the rest, those who knew my true age. I began dating and enjoyed a number of encounters with middle-aged men. They were flattered that so young-looking a woman was interested in them.

Inevitably, perhaps, I fell in love. He was thirty-nine and looked very much like a taller, younger version of my first lover. Like him, my new boyfriend worked in a merchant bank. In the early days we spent most of our time in bed. Late one night, after we had been out for a meal washed down with a great deal of champagne, he said he wanted me to move in.

I gave up my job and he kept me well supplied with money. For quite a while it was fun—he introduced me to his friends and we were often invited to functions and dinner parties. It seemed he couldn't get enough of me. But one evening, when I had dressed carefully for a night out with friends—elegant, but not too glamorous—he said: 'You always style your hair the same way. Why not ring the changes?'

My blood ran cold.

'I like it the way it is.'

'It's a bit old-fashioned.'

He began to find fault with me more and more. Character was as important as looks, he said. Why didn't I take a course, broaden my interests? I was so innocent and . . . shallow. After the first flush of attraction, being with someone so naïve—brainless, even—was becoming tedious.

I had retained my flat and moved back in to it. From then on I indulged exclusively in one night stands.

It was difficult to find another job. I couldn't offer my degree as it dated from so many years before. Questions in interviews left me struggling for an answer, I knew so little of the world. My savings began to dwindle.

One day on the Tube, I caught the woman sitting next to me staring at my hands.

'I hope you don't mind me saying so, but you have beautifully-shaped fingers and wonderfully smooth skin. I could find you work as a hand model.'

Within weeks my hands were featuring in television adverts for a well-known brand of washing up liquid and a high street jewellers. The money was good and the working conditions bearable, despite a lot of waiting around while the sets were arranged and lights positioned. My hands seemed to take on a life of their own, getting into character and enacting each role—the perfect housewife, the newly engaged young woman, the thirty-something looking after her hands by smoothing in cream. Before long I was one of the top hand models in the country.

But I couldn't stay in any job for long. Sooner or later my colleagues would notice that I never seemed to age. In my time, and it has been a long time, I have enjoyed many careers, none of them terribly taxing or intellectually challenging. I have moved flats often for the same reason. It has been an itinerant life, and would have remained that way, if it hadn't been for Doris.

For an old lady she was game. She had many callers and I admired her gregariousness, but over the first year our acquaintance did not progress beyond a smiled 'hello' whenever we met on the stairs. Then, after another of those anodyne encounters, she asked if I would like to come to tea. It seemed this was to be of the afternoon variety, with triangular sandwiches and daintily iced cakes. Her flat had the same layout as mine, but with more chintz.

I enjoyed the tea and said so. She showed her pleasure in a fluttery, old lady sort of way. I asked her why she had invited me and she lay her hand on mine. 'You're very pretty but I can see there is something wrong. Your smile is fixed, your eyes are troubled. Your make-up and hair are old-fashioned. I thought it might do you good to talk.'

Something inside me broke. I wept, copiously. Doris patted my hand and offered me a beautifully laundered handkerchief.

'There, there, my child. Don't take on so. Tell me all about it.'

So I did; the whole sorry saga.

'Do you mean to say,' she said, 'that it hasn't occurred to you that the spell is reversible?'

I stared at her open-mouthed.

'It's a standard spell from the 1650s. The sisterhood have modernised the reversal a little, but it's essentially the same. You can find it on one or two of the more comprehensive websites. I'm surprised you haven't looked. The thing to bear in mind, though, is that you require a willing partner.'

'How do I go about finding one?'

She smiled. 'When you're as old as Methuselah and death is camped outside your door, you will understand why I'm happy to volunteer. Remember, though, that if you decide to go ahead, you'll begin to age from the moment the reversal comes into effect.'

We collected the ingredients and intoned the sacred words. I will not describe the nature of the rites; suffice it to say that the gravity of the spell called for a lengthy and onerous procedure. When it was over, I knew that something had changed. But what I hadn't expected, was to find myself inside the body of Doris!

How I ached! How feeble I felt! I looked over and there she was, young, lithe and beautiful, in my twenty-year-old body.

'You should have read the small print,' she said. 'I used a slight variant of the spell.'

With that she got up and left. I never saw her again.

I moped for a while. It was easier to move into Doris's flat. Visitors kept arriving at my door with problems they expected me to solve. At first I concocted my own responses, and I found that Doris's clients paid me well. Then I discovered her laptop (in the chintz-covered ottoman) and taught myself to use it. It has proved a powerful tool, an invaluable source of information. Now, I take pride in the efficacy of my work; I believe I have a real flare for it. Doris, by contrast, was rather slipshod in her ways, and, as I found to my cost, a somewhat unprincipled character.

There is no need to seek to reverse her spell because I find that, in my new line of work, age equates to wisdom and I am treated with respect. I have begun to remedy my own aches and pains and ensure that I have the strength to lead an active and fulfilling life for many years to come. There is even a new man in tow.

He's a good few years younger. . . .

WAITING

All through August Abigail looked out for the ship, counting the masts on each vessel and reading their names before they reached the harbour. But, as summer faded to autumn she could no longer face standing for hours each day on the harbour wall with the other women in their shawls and clogs, their anxious camaraderie draining into one common pot of longing. It was enough that, every few days, she came to the harbour to wait.

The company relied on shipping tea back to England as soon as the leaves had been picked, dried and rushed from the Chinese hills to Shanghai. In the first tea of the season lay the biggest profit. But the clipper, *Challenger of the Seas*, was several weeks late: the opportunity had passed, and Abigail could not prevent her mind from wandering over the ocean, searching the waves for whatever could have happened to Karsten.

They had come to an understanding the previous summer, secretly, as Abigail's father did not approve of Karsten, even though he was a captain, the youngest in the company. Karsten had at first talked of taking her back to Norway and told her stories about growing up there with his friends. Before he left for Shanghai he promised that he would talk again to her father, although neither of them admitted to the other that they doubted he could change his mind. As the time of the voyage approached, Karsten began to meet her less often on the shore: when he did, his eyes focused far out to sea.

At any moment the missing ship might scythe across the bay and tack into the harbour. In that instant, all the longing, the hoping, the waiting would, she prayed, be over and forgotten. Abigail had written a letter to the company. The reply confirmed that *Challenger of the Seas* left Shanghai laden with its valuable cargo at the appointed time. There was no news of any shipwreck or other incident that might have befallen her.

A woman already stood on the harbour wall: it was Ellen, wife of one of the crew of *Challenger of the Seas*. She nodded a greeting.

'There's a ship,' said Ellen.

The sun was setting and dusk would soon fall. Abigail scanned the horizon but could see no sign of a vessel.

Ellen said, 'I saw it. It was a long way out. I couldn't count the masts.'

Abigail took Ellen's hand and squeezed it. The tide was in and the sea beyond the harbour wall eddied and swirled as the currents met. It would be easy to jump in and let the water take her under. Turning away, she forced herself to walk back toward the town, the gulls mocking her with their cries.

The inns were spewing customers out onto the pavements. Abigail dodged through the mayhem of the evening and strode on to her parents' house. It was in a suburb of the town, a red brick villa, one of several in a quiet street. As she walked up the steps and opened the front door her mother came out of the parlour.

'Where have you been?'

'I went for a walk. I lost track of time. Sorry, Mother.'

'It's not good enough! A young woman out on her own! Your father is beside himself, and what will the servants think?'

'I'm perfectly all right.'

Her mother's expression softened. 'Won't you tell me what's wrong? Perhaps I can help.'

'There's nothing that can be done.'

Abigail climbed the stairs to her room. As she undressed, beyond the curtains the remaining daylight ebbed away. The maid brought up a jug of hot water and, pouring it into the bowl whispered, 'Michael saw you at the harbour, Miss. Is there any news?'

'No, Freda. No news.'

Her mother and father had yet to find out about her visits to the harbour, even though the servants knew. Abigail suspected that she would be faced with impossible choices when they did come to know about it. Already her mother's friends were matchmaking on her behalf. At twenty-three she was considered too old to be unmarried.

The next day Abigail went to church with her parents. Sitting on the pew in front of them was David Milton, a clerk from her father's bank. He smiled at her and, out of the corner of her eye she saw her mother nudge her father. The sermon was tedious. Abigail spent the service silently praying for Karsten and his crew.

In the afternoon Abigail was drawn again to the harbour. The women were already there, shawls folded over their heads. They greeted Abigail, then went back to watching the bay. After a while a cry went up.

'A ship! A ship!'

As the speck sailed closer Abigail could see that it was three-masted, but too bulky for a tea clipper. The faded paint of its name resolved itself into *Mary-Anne*. The schooner steered into the harbour and moored against the western wall, the crew crawling over the rigging, stowing the sails. Ellen and the other women began softly to keen. Abigail fought hard not to abandon herself to grief.

When Abigail returned home her father was waiting for her; it was obvious from the anger in his face that he knew she had been to the harbour.

'Milton saw you with those women. Have you no shame?'

'We are waiting for our ship.'

'*Your* ship?'

Abigail could not find the words.

'Sailors always have another port, Abigail.'

She burst out, 'And what do you know about it?'

His face drained of colour. 'Milton was shocked to see you with those fishwives; you sound just like them.'

'I'll never marry Milton.'

Her father slapped her hard. 'You will marry him if I say so!'

Abigail wrenched open the door and ran down the steps. She raced through the town to the harbour wall, where the women still waited. She sank to the ground. They crowded around her and the older woman, Sheila, stroked her hair.

The afternoon still had some warmth in it. The four women sat so they faced out to the bay.

'I can remember,' said Sheila, 'when Jem first went to sea. He was on the whaling ships. It was hard, sailing the ship to the hunting grounds and harpooning the great beasts.

'When he returned he was weary, and sometimes I persuaded him to spend a day at home, resting. On one of those days, he told me a story.

'They had sailed out further than usual, up towards Norway, where the Minke whales feed and the hunting was good. But they had a cruel Captain who made it his business to taunt the crew and put them in more danger than was necessary. One of the whales they harpooned dragged a sailor into the sea and the Captain refused to send out a rescue boat. Instead he finished the hunt and made a note of the man's death in the ship's log as an accident.

'Jem was furious, but it seemed that there was nothing he could do. It would be his word against the Captain's if he reported the man's behaviour to the company.

'So Jem and his shipmates fell to talking, and they resolved to get their own back on the Captain. Over the next few days, on the return journey, one by one they removed items of clothing and personal possessions— his razor, a vesta case—from his cabin, and threw them overboard. The Captain was a superstitious man, and he could not believe that his crew would dare to defy him. Jem told the captain that he had seen the ghost of the man who had drowned, and that it had sworn vengeance on the ship. From that day the Captain grew haggard and ill and by the time they got to shore he had taken to his bed. Jem never sailed under him again.

'Jem is resourceful, and under a good captain, like your Norwegian boy, trials can be overcome.'

Ellen wiped her hand across her eyes. 'Perhaps they are marooned on a lovely island, with fruit trees and turtles, and plenty of driftwood for a fire. And maybe a passing ship will see their signal and send out a boat to rescue them. Maybe they are already on their way back home.'

Josie continued, 'On a full-rigger, at full sail.'

Abigail smiled. 'Or maybe the company is wrong and they are still in China. The tea is late due to bad weather, and they are waiting at Shanghai for it to arrive.'

'It's the not knowing that is the worst . . . ' said Josie, wringing her hands.

Abigail rose and walked slowly back through the town. As she let herself in to the house, she found her mother sitting on the stairs, her head in her hands. When she saw Abigail she rushed over and took her in her arms.

'My poor girl.'

'I'm all right, Mother.'

'Your father has gone out.'

'I don't care about that.'

'Your life can go on. Your young man would want that for you.'

Abigail broke away and ran up the stairs to her bedroom, tears coursing down her cheeks.

The next day she visited a dressmaker in the town and had herself fitted out in a mourning gown of black silk. She went again each day to the harbour and the fishermen, who grew used to her presence on the wall, began to call her The Waiting Widow.

Abigail's parents were beside themselves with worry. David Milton had lost interest in her because of her strange appearance and behaviour. They began to think that she would never find a husband.

Standing on the harbour wall one day, Abigail realised that she could no longer remember what Karsten looked like.

Autumn became winter, and one mist-shrouded December morning, just as she arrived wrapped in a black woollen shawl, *Challenger of the Seas* sailed into the harbour. Abigail, her heart thudding, watched as the sails were stowed and preparations made for taking off the tea. The ship looked in good order, the paint fresh and everything in its place. There was no sign of Karsten.

Abigail didn't know where the other women lived, so she asked one of the fishermen if he would fetch them. His eyes brightened and he gave her a mock salute as he ran off, happy to be the bearer of good news.

'Your ship's come in, Miss!' he shouted.

Karsten appeared on deck. Abigail did not know whether to wave or laugh or cry. He didn't seem to notice her. Sheila, Josie and Ellen arrived together on the quay, almost overcome with joy and excitement. Sheila soon spotted her Jem, who waved at her, and Ellen could see her Frank, and Josie her Will. At last the crew were allowed to disembark, and the three women disappeared with their men. Finally, Karsten walked along the harbour wall to where Abigail waited.

'You are here.' The Norwegian lilt in his voice was stronger than she remembered.

'You've grown a beard.' She smiled at him. Karsten looked back at the ship.

'I have to go over some of the paperwork with the company . . .'

'What happened to you?' she asked.

'What do you mean?'

'Why are you so late?'

'I don't think we made bad time,' he replied sullenly. 'The weather was against us.'

Abigail almost shouted. 'You've kept us waiting nearly five months! What will the company say about that?'

Karsten would not meet her eye. He strode off towards the shipping office. Abigail followed him and stood outside. After a while he came out and asked her to wait for him by the Ship Inn. It was another hour before he arrived. They sat on the wall outside, Karsten thoughtful and silent. Abigail talked a little of her battles with her parents, and her vigil on the harbour wall. At last he spoke:

'They're taking my command away from me. I'm to work in the head office for a year. In Liverpool.'

The relief was almost overwhelming. 'Did they not accept your explanation?'

'What explanation?'

'I thought you said the weather. . . . What happened, Karsten? Can't you tell me?'

He looked out to sea.

'Tell me, please!'

'There are things I have seen . . . things I have done . . . that you would never understand.'

'Why not?' she whispered. 'Why not?' He got up and walked away.

Two days later Karsten took the train to Liverpool. Abigail followed him. She rented rooms near the company's head office, and every evening waited for him outside. He was embarrassed to see her there, but they walked together to his digs. Abigail noticed that he took great care not to touch her.

'Talk to me, Karsten.'

'There is nothing to say.'

'Why won't you trust me?'

After a few days, Abigail's money ran out. She took the train home and asked her father for more: he had grown used to her vagaries and gave her what she asked for. Putting the bank notes carefully in her reticule she walked to the shipping office at the harbour and paid for a passage on the fastest clipper to Australia.

TOUCHSTONE

It was nearly midday when, bleary-eyed, Paula struggled up the last few metres of the slope. Lawrence's leaving party had drifted into the early hours, even though it was the middle of the working week, and in the morning, when he kissed her goodbye and got into the taxi, she had felt the first surge of panic. It was only the knowledge that she was already behind in her programme of archaeological surveys that prevented her from calling in sick.

On the high ridge, the outcrops loomed. Everything seemed to have conspired to make her late, (a neighbour complaining about the party, slow farm traffic), and even the brightness of the sun in the almost cloudless sky could not disperse the sense of unease that dogged her. Lawrence was gone and would be on the flight to Mumbai by now, perhaps drifting into a light doze, while she was expected to carry on as if her life had not changed irrevocably. She had always known that, despite what he said, he would not be coming back.

As soon as she reached the first rock she could see that the prehistoric carvings were far more impressive than she had expected them to be. The whole northern face of the rock was covered with small, shallow, bowl-shaped depressions encircled by concentric rings, some with snaking 'tails', the overall pattern aesthetically pleasing in a random sort of way.

Paula pulled out her field kit and began taking photographs and measurements. Somewhere, the commonplace accuracies of her survey, the mysterious purpose of the carvings lay.

And it remained a mystery, despite decades of expert research and amateur study. Prehistoric carvings had been identified on all three sandstone outcrops along the high ridge. Buffeted by five thousand years of wind and rain, they were still recognisable as the 'cup and ring mark' type, dating to the Neolithic or early Bronze Age. Some archaeologists argued that the almost ubiquitous siting of the rock art on high ground had some as yet unidentified ritual significance in the landscape. A more prosaic explanation was that the symbols served as way-markers on long distance routes along which precious goods, such as gold, had been traded. Several more fanciful notions elaborated on these two basic theories.

Such flowery speculation was frowned upon, however, in the archaeological reports Paula was employed to produce. Anything that strayed beyond the prescribed house style, honed over four decades of government-sponsored project, was excised by her eagle-eyed supervisor. Fresh from university, Paula had adapted quickly to the austere methodology expected of her, and after a year was seen by the management team as something of a success in the job.

But all her training did not stop her dreaming. . . . The breeze had died away and the mid-day sun warmed her. Skylarks trilled above the moor. In the lee of the western outcrop Paula drank from her flask of strong coffee. To the north, brown heather blanketed the plateau, to the south was the broad, green scoop of the dale with its tawny ribbon of river. The prehistoric carvings' siting on the ridge was on the border between the two, very different landscapes, a liminal area, where everything was subject to change. . . . Paula closed her eyes for a moment and let her mind wander freely. . . .

She woke suddenly, disorientated by the dream and dismayed to find, on looking at her watch, that a large portion of the afternoon had passed. This time the dream had been troubling, if perhaps understandable in the circumstances. Lawrence, after failing to get in touch, went missing in India, leaving no sign that he had ever been there. She had gone to Mumbai to find him, had wandered alone through the teeming streets. . . . It took her some minutes to readjust to the quiet of the landscape, and to prepare herself for the surveys of the other two outcrops that she needed to complete before the end of the day.

Paula gulped some more coffee, cold now, then hurried along the stony path to the central rock. This was smaller, its cup and ring marks less extensive and distinct. She took measurements and photographs and made more notes, concentrating on the details while bearing in mind the overall pattern. It was hard not to speculate. Could the carvings represent some constellation, a propitious alignment of the heavens? To the early farmers of the Neolithic, the progression of the seasons and the vagaries of the weather could mean life or death, and ways of divining or influencing them must have been attempted. They would be a powerful form of magic, in the hands of the holiest of men. . . .

The eastern outcrop proved to be the largest of the three, its nearly vertical northern face densely covered with cup and rings. There was a marked variety in the designs, and perhaps because of the steep angle of the rock, the carvings were less eroded. Paula thought as she worked methodically over the face of the rock that she could distinguish subtle differences of style between the various groups of motifs. They had, she began to see, been executed by several carvers, perhaps at different times. She was sure this wasn't a wholly original observation, but she would be able to document it fully with reference to her notes, drawings and photographs of these particular examples . . . her mind raced ahead. . . . There was an article for an archaeological journal here. . . .

Before Lawrence left for the airport Paula promised him that she would try not to stay out after dark. She knew she should be glad that he still worried about her. The car was parked four miles away, down near the river, so she would have to leave immediately if she were to get home before the sun went down. As she slung the bag over her shoulder she stumbled, her foot caught on a rock and she sprawled onto the heather. Her head hit something hard. . . . As she came back to consciousness, her temple was throbbing, and the pain in her ankle when she tried to stand made her wince. The discomfort was so intense she knew that she would be unable to walk back to the car. There was little choice but to call mountain rescue. She took the phone from the rucksack and pulled her coat over herself. After speaking to the operator, who reassured her that they would be with her within an hour or so, and feeling very slightly nauseous, she rested her head on a hummock of heather and closed her eyes. . . .

When she came to again it was getting dark and deathly quiet. Her head pounded; she could feel a lump already the size of an acorn swelling on her temple. The smooth flat stone on which she had hit her head lay nearby and in frustration she kicked it. It moved a little. She leaned forward. The stone was heavy but she managed to pick it up and examine it more closely. It was black, fine-grained, and as she turned it over she could make out scratched markings, columns of crude geometric designs; diamonds and triangles, some hatched; separated by vertical lines. To the side was a panel of circular patterns, almost identical to the cup and ring carvings on the rock outcrops.

She knew at once that the stone was of great significance. It could have been brought across the sea, deposited or lost by a holy man or trader? Or was it a relic, or some kind of tally connected with the conveyance and exchange of metals and gold? Could it even be a prehistoric Rosetta Stone, a way of translating the two pictorial scripts? If so, it might be the key to a new understanding of the transition between late Stone Age Neolithic culture and the Bronze Age. The possibilities spiralled and Paula felt her heart beat faster. Here, lying in her hands, was something that could revolutionise the discipline she worked in . . . and perhaps her own life with it. . . .

The correct thing to do would be to put the stone back in its original position, note its location and report it to her supervisor the following day. It was too big and heavy to hide and carry in her rucksack. She took some photographs, but the scratches did not show up well. Pleased with her resourcefulness, she took a piece of blank A4 paper from her notebook, laid it over the etched face of the stone, and rubbed a pencil over it. The result was a good representation of the markings. Then she replaced the stone, face down, in its peaty indentation.

It was dark when her rescuers lifted her onto the stretcher and carried her down the track to the car park.

'You've sprained your ankle,' the paramedic said. 'Here's some paracetamol for the head injury, and take it easy for the next forty-eight hours. Someone should be there to keep an eye on you.'

He bandaged her ankle and the ambulance driver drove her home. She would have to collect her car later. . . .

The house was silent and dark. Switching on the light revealed the debris from Lawrence's party. Plates of half-eaten food sat alongside smeared empty wine glasses. Paula unfurled the pencil rubbing and laid it out beneath the lamp. Her head and ankle still throbbed, but adrenaline was coursing through her, dulling the pain. She opened her laptop and began a long night of online research. . . .

In the morning, as soon as she decently could, Paula called her supervisor. He agreed that, in view of her injuries, she should take some time away from field work and stay at home to write up outstanding reports. There was a moment when she almost told him about the stone tablet, but she let it pass. Paula read through her survey notes and typed into a new Word document, which, after some thought, she named 'Touchstone'. The pencil rubbing, despite being weighted at the corners, repeatedly sprang free, rolled up and fell onto the floor amongst the trodden-in party food. Retrieving it, brushing off the soggy crumbs, she reaffixed it to the desk again and again. Finding correspondences between the curvilinear and angular etchings was proving difficult. Staring again at the disparate shapes yielded no new insights. Paula thumped the desk in frustration, then turned back to the computer screen.

It was dark again when the phone rang. At the last moment, she decided to answer it.

'Are you all right, Paula? None of us have heard from you since Lawrence left.'

Paula, recognising the voice of Joanna, Lawrence's sister, continued to tap on the computer keyboard.

'I had an accident at work. Nothing serious. I'm housebound for a few days, that's all.'

'But you're okay? It's just that you seemed a bit "off" at the party. . . . '

'I'm right as rain.'

'So you won't be able to come out with us tomorrow evening?'

'Tomorrow? . . . '

'Friday! Are you sure you're all right?'

'I have to stay in. . . . '

'Shall I come over?'

'There's no need, I'm fine. . . . '

'You are eating properly? Lawrence would want you to look after yourself . . . '

. . . And so the conversation limped on. Lawrence, Paula realised, had not yet been in touch, and she was sure he would not be. She did not feel sleepy now, and the mania of the quest fuelled her onwards through another night and into the dawn of Friday. The pencil rubbing had once more rolled onto the encrusted carpet, but this time she let it lie there. She had no need to consult it—every single mark on the paper was etched into her brain.

Lawrence rested his head against the train carriage window and watched the fields rush by. He hadn't been able to tell her. He had meant to, but at the last moment his courage failed him and they kissed and he left. They all thought he was going to Mumbai. Paula would find out soon enough that the house was about to be repossessed and he had spent every penny of their joint savings trying to recoup his losses. It sounded so sordid and old-fashioned, 'lost it all on the horses', but it was a fact. He'd lost her too, although she didn't know it yet. He supposed he was an addict and a hopeless one at that, and he knew he would take the same risks again, given half a chance. Starting over would not be easy but he would have to. He could no longer look her in the eye. She was better off without him.

After ringing the bell several times, Joanna tried the door and opened it. There was a pile of untouched mail on the lobby floor.

'Paula?'

The smell hit her first. Mouldy food festered on discarded party plates and had been trampled into the carpet. There were unwashed glasses on every surface. 'Good Luck, Lawrence', drooped on a banner from the ceiling.

'Paula?'

She carried out a careful search of each room, ending at Paula's desk. The laptop had gone, and there was a folded note addressed to Lawrence. Joanna considered for a moment, then opened and read it.

'It's what I've always wanted. A way into the mysteries.'

First Lawrence's flight to Mumbai had arrived without him on board, now Paula seemed to have disappeared, leaving only this enigmatic scrawl. What were the pair of them playing at? Fetching a bin bag from under the sink, Joanna began to clear up the mess. A creased, filthy piece of paper with smudged pencil markings on it was first into the bag.

Paula got out of the taxi and unlocked her car—she was lucky, she knew, that it hadn't been towed away, probably because the car park was so remote. She stowed the laptop carefully in the boot, then made her way to the bottom of the fell, where the footpath began to climb. She'd brought her field kit in the rucksack, even though she was not sure if she'd need it. Her clothes were the same (she hadn't changed out of them), and she'd filled the flask with coffee, as before. The hike up to the ridge was just as challenging as the first time. Halfway up she began to fell faint, and had to stop and take a sip of coffee. Food and sleep were the last things on her mind. . . .

Up on the ridge the outcrops were basking in the spring sunshine. A stoat zigzagged from a crevice and scuttled into the heather. Paula took off her rucksack and examined the eastern outcrop, poring over the circular carvings, looking for the thing she was sure must be there. And it was, the very faintest trace of angular etchings between the largest concentric circles. Paula breathed deeply, savouring her moment of triumph. She had been right; she could picture the scene, the holy man and the trader meeting on the ridge to exchange gifts; gold and the dark stone tablet, perhaps; the mason ready to carve the tally and the votive motifs so the people would understand the importance of the encounter, the reverence with which the tablet was passed between the elders. Afterwards, there would be feasting on flat bread baked from the wheat they had grown, fish from the river caught by their guests, and beer brewed from barley. . . . Then came the rituals, the offerings to the stars, the solemn incantations. Afterwards, Paula danced between the two peoples beside the great fire, her belly full, drunk and joyful in the moment as the stars wheeled overhead. . . .

The dog jumped up at him as he overtook them. Lawrence blinked as the woman apologised profusely. He stroked the hound's silky russet fur.

'He's a real beauty, isn't he?'

She relaxed and smiled. 'Yes he is.' The rangy dog suddenly pulled at the lead, nearly dragging the woman off her feet.

'He takes a lot of exercising.'

Her body language was easy to read. It was difficult to be sure of her age, but she was well-dressed and attractive. He could do worse.

'Why don't you let me help you with him?' he said, taking hold of the dog's lead in what he hoped was a masterful, rather than aggressive movement. 'How far are you going? I'm on my way back from the races. Did rather well, in fact. . . . '

In the light of early morning Paula woke alone next to the embers of the great fire. Everyone else had gone back to their farmsteads, she presumed. Her face was caked in ochre and charcoal from the rituals, her clothes saturated with dew, but she was not cold. In fact she was warm to the core, and sleep had done her the power of good.

It was easy enough to find the dark stone. But when she turned it over there were no scratches on its underside, just the smooth sheen of close-grained rock . . . empty, as if it were all about to happen again; the party and the leave-taking, Lawrence's desertion, the meeting of the tribes, the great fire. It was as if she was being given another chance to re-write the past.

THE GROUP

Although not compulsory, it was made clear to me that I was expected to attend the group.

I could find no good excuse to avoid going to the first meeting. As it turned out, it might have been worse. Mia brought along a fine array of supermarket-bought cakes, and made cups of tea. You could just sit there and feed your face if you wanted to. There were ten of us, and I knew most of the attendees from previous courses or hospital admissions. The group was something of a flagship for the Mental Health Care Trust and had already featured on their leaflets and website as a successful exercise in inclusion for those of us in recovery and living in the community.

The group was very much Mia's baby—after just over a year of meetings and memos, promises and foot-dragging, she had finally extracted the funding from some Trust budget or other.

'The whole Outreach team has worked hard for this,' she said.

Mia herself had earned a lot of brownie points, and I was afraid that she would be promoted beyond our parochial circle. There was always the chance that the Trust would not fill the resulting vacancy and my care would be shared by a team of strangers. Mia had been my case coordinator ever since my initial 'breakdown' eleven years ago.

At the first meeting there was a lot of grumbling about the latest review of mental health services. Ashley was service user representative on several committees and reported back their machinations. He had on occasion even been allowed to chair Trust meetings, and was attempting to explain the labyrinthine paths of public sector decision making to the rest of the group. Alice got up and helped herself to three miniature chocolate Swiss rolls.

'The committee rejected the proposal,' Ashley was saying, 'on the grounds that it contravened departmental guidelines. I suggested convening a subcommittee to look into mistakes made and this was accepted.'

After Ashley's report we were supposed to stick to an agenda designed to encourage the discussion of wider issues, but while Mia made tea in the kitchen, the conversation narrowed predictably.

'I'm having trouble sleeping,' said Matthew. 'Should I ask for some Zopiclone?'

Ashley frowned. 'We oughtn't to discuss our medication . . . '

'You should ask for some,' said Alice. 'You don't want your sleep pattern disrupted. You know where that can lead. . . . My problem is food.' She eyed Mia's table of delights. 'I can't get enough of it.'

'It's the pills,' I said. 'I'm hungry all the time. And sleepy.'

'We're all on different tablets,' said Jean, 'and they all have awful side-effects.'

'They keep us out of hospital,' said Ashley.

Mia returned with a tray of mugs.

'Why so glum? You know how important it is to stay positive.'

We drank our tea in silence for a while, then Mia cleared her throat.

'Any ideas for our first outing?'

'How about the cemetery?' said Matthew.

Mia managed a smile. 'We'll all end up there eventually.'

'The ice cream parlour?' suggested Alice.

'Newharbour Fort,' said Jean. 'It has a tea room.'

'That's a great idea!' Mia said. 'We could walk around the battlements and then have coffee and something to eat.'

'Forget the history lesson,' said Alice, 'let's cut straight to the cake.'

Ashley, Alice, Matthew, Jean and myself were the only group members who showed up for the first outing. There was an undercurrent of discontent.

'You know it's not appropriate for me to discuss the others' circumstances,' said Mia, 'but you can rest assured that they have good reasons for not attending.'

'They can't all be manic at the same time,' said Matthew.

A few russet leaves clung to the trees. The red-brick ramparts of the Victorian fort loomed through a miasma of drizzle.

Alice said, 'At least the café gets a good write-up.'

Mia led us around the battlements, casemates and armament stores, reading excerpts from the guide book.

'"The defensive capabilities of Newharbour Hill have been recognised for many centuries: the 1850s fortifications were built on the site of much earlier, Iron Age ramparts. . . . Newharbour Fort saw little use and soon fell into disrepair, its upkeep being taken over by Newharbour Historical Society volunteers in 1953."'

'Fascinating', said Matthew.

We stood in a loose huddle on the central lawn, beside a desultory half-barrel of pansies. Low cloud had settled over the tops of the battlements. The drizzle was turning to rain.

'Can we have cake now?' asked Alice.

Mia smiled. 'I think we've earned it.'

The café was cosy, with jam pots of flowers and frilly cushions, and almost empty. We crowded round the counter, then sat down with our choices.

'This is nice,' said Jean, guiding a sizeable forkful of devil's food cake into her mouth.

In the far corner were the only other customers: a well-dressed, middle-aged couple. The woman glanced at Alice with ill-concealed distaste.

Alice, still wearing her enormous pink raincoat, was cheerfully mashing cream cheese icing into her carrot cake.

Jean put down her coffee cup. 'Do we pass for normal, Mia?'

Mia, said 'You have as much right to be here as anyone else.'

'That's not what she asked,' said Matthew.

The elegant middle-aged woman got up and walked towards the lavatories. Her partner turned to look at us. His lips curled.

Ashley caught his eye. 'It's a shame about the weather.'

The man grunted and looked away.

We're quite harmless, you know,' said Ashley, sotto voce.

When the woman returned, the couple put on their coats.

Alice said, 'I bet they're both married to other people.'

Jean giggled. 'Funny place to come for a tryst.'

'Oh I don't know,' said Mia. 'I think it's rather romantic.'

When we went back outside, the sun was making a brave effort to break through the clouds. It had stopped raining.

'Let's walk down to the sea,' said Mia. She had won the funds for these outings on the understanding that we would get some health-giving exercise.

The walk from the fort took us through the town centre; a dispiriting mix of chain stores and amusement arcades; to the small area of imported sand around the pier. Phalanxes of seabirds perched on the iron superstructure. We watched the weak white surf lap the dirty gold of the beach.

Matthew sighed. 'I suppose we should be grateful.'

'You have to get out and see the world,' said Mia. 'It's a vital part of your recovery.'

Alice was looking at the birds. There were few people on the pier. I spotted the couple from the café, arm in arm: at least, I thought it was them.

The fort reared up above us, dominating the town, despite its demotion to tourist attraction. Jean shuddered.

'Why is it so cold?'

Ashley laughed. 'There's no easy answer to that.'

Matthew said, 'When will something happen?'
I had been studying the sand and when I looked up the elegant couple were standing in front of us.
'We're claiming the beach,' said the man.
'Someone has to make a stand,' the woman sniffed.
They linked arms.
'There will be more of us shortly, so you'd better leave.'
Mia looked as if she was going to cry. Ashley straightened up.
'It's Mental Health Awareness Week!'
The man snorted. 'We don't want any of that sort of thing here.'
Alice took a step forward. 'We were here first. What are you going to do about it?'
The woman laughed unpleasantly. 'People like you should be under lock and key.'
Alice launched her bulk towards them. The seabirds began to squawk, then rose as one, hanging above the couple in a frenzy of flapping wings. The couple, assailed by a shower of guano, retreated towards the pier.
Mia, putting a restraining hand on Alice's arm, said shakily, 'We'd better get back to the mini-bus.'

'I don't see why I should regret what I did,' said Alice when we arrived back at the centre. 'They started it.'
'I'm not asking you to,' Mia sighed. 'I just wanted you to think about what we've learnt from today.'
'That there are some funny people about?' suggested Jean.
I said that I had thought we would blend in better, that no one would notice the semi-institutional nature of our group.
'Fat chance,' said Matthew, 'and it's about time you faced the fact that some people will never accept us.'
Ashley was quiet for once, busying himself with his phone.
Alice said, 'The best thing to do is confront them head on.'
'Literally, in your case,' said Matthew.

'There are some advantages to being big,' Alice grinned.

We agreed, after Mia had presented us with a number of suggestions, that the next outing should be to the petting zoo. The zoo was used to catering for groups of visitors, and Mia said she would see if she could arrange for us to have a special visit.

It turned out that the special visit involved a talk by the head keeper in the insect house. We were encouraged to stroke giant cockroaches, all except Jean, who refused point blank to have anything to do with them. The cockroaches were clean and shiny, their carapaces warm to the touch. The more conventional petting animals were outside in small pens, washed, groomed and docile. A goat munched on a wisp of hay, staring into the distance with its peculiar eyes.

'We might as well be a group of toddlers,' said Alice, who nevertheless cuddled a lamb and had her picture taken with it. Even Matthew was not immune to the charm of the animals: he bent down and scratched the ears of a dopey-looking rabbit.

Mia was starting to say something about the therapeutic properties of touch when the elegant couple from our previous outing walked around the corner. They did not seem surprised to see us.

'Here you are again . . . ' said the man sarcastically.

' . . . Spoiling the zoo for the rest of us,' continued the woman. 'Why we should have to put up with degenerates like you at every turn is beyond me.'

Alice carefully placed the lamb back with its mother in the pen.

'I don't like you,' she said to the couple.

'Now, Alice . . . ' warned Mia.

But Alice was already heading towards them. This time the couple stood their ground.

'They're not worth it, Alice,' said Ashley.

'What can have made you so nasty,' Alice whispered, her face growing pale.

The man laughed.

Alice blinked. The goat bleated again. We realised then that it had escaped from its pen and was trotting towards the couple. Bypassing Alice, it put down its head and charged. The elegant woman let out a sharp cry and the man stood in front of her, taking the full force of the butt. One of the keepers ran over, grasped the goat by its horns, and wrestled it back to its enclosure.

'Are you all right?' he called to the couple as he refastened the catch. 'I don't know how it managed to get out. I can't apologise enough.'

The man was dusting down his elegant trousers. 'You shouldn't let these people loose in the zoo.'

'We're just saying,' said the woman, 'that you should be a little more selective, *if* you know what I mean.'

They walked off towards the café. The keeper raised his eyebrows and patted the goat's rump. The goat chewed contentedly on another hank of hay.

'I can't think how it got out,' said the keeper again.

Alice smiled.

Matthew said. 'They got rid of people like us in the gas chambers.'

I asked Alice, 'How did you do that?' but she was petting one of the pot-bellied pigs and didn't answer.

There was a lull in the discussion. Only four of us: Ashley, Matthew Alice and myself had turned up.

'The trouble is,' said Mia, 'that if our numbers keep on dwindling the Trust will withdraw funding.'

'I can raise the matter at the next service user advisory meeting if that's any use,' said Ashley.

'You can't force people to attend,' said Matthew.

'So the next outing may be our last,' I said.

'Then let's make it a good one,' said Ashley.

We sat in silence for a minute or two.

'We could walk the Nightjar Trail, along the old railway line,' I suggested. 'Well, some of it.'

'What about cake?' asked Alice.

'There's a tea room in Bisley. We could start at Horfield. It's only a couple of miles,' Mia said. 'The spring flowers will be out. It'll be beautiful.'

'We'll have to dodge the cyclists,' said Matthew. 'And the dog turds.'

Mia parked the minibus alongside Horfield village green and we emerged into the clear blue of the morning. Birdsong heralded the burgeoning of new growth: the leaves of the young trees on the embankment were a vivid green. We set out along the trail. I suppose we were a motley looking crew.

An early butterfly zig-zagged across the track.

'At least they haven't stopped us breeding yet,' said Matthew.

'Your son's at university, isn't he?' asked Mia.

'He has his mother's brain,' Matthew said.

A group of cyclists passed us, ringing their bells in friendly warning.

Alice was very quiet.

Ashley said, 'So we've lost our funding.'

Mia sighed. 'Yes, I'm afraid so. There have been more cuts in the mental health budget. This is definitely the last meeting of the group.'

'I'm going to lodge a formal complaint,' said Ashley.

'It's not your fault,' I said to Mia.

Two people approached. Mia moved next to Alice, who was staring at them, head up, nostrils flaring. As they drew nearer we could see it was the couple from our previous outings. They were dressed in expensive walking clothes. The woman whispered in the man's ear and they laughed, their eyes on Alice.

'I'm surprised you can move,' said the woman, 'carrying that much weight.'

The man snarled. 'If you're well enough to be walking you're well enough to have proper jobs.'

Alice stared at him.

Before any of us could react, a fox bounded up the embankment and ran onto the trail in front of us. It stopped next to Alice, sniffed the air, then lunged forward and bit the man on the thigh. He crumpled to the ground. Quick as an arrow the fox leapt down the other side of the embankment and disappeared into the undergrowth.

'Vermin!' the woman shrieked at Mia. 'Can't you keep them under control? That's what you're paid to do.' The man rose with some dignity.

'He'll have to have a tetanus injection at the very least,' said the woman. She glared at Mia. 'I've a good mind to sue.' They headed off in the direction of Horfield, the man limping and leaning on the woman's shoulder.

Mia gathered us together and we agreed to carry on towards the café at Bisley. When I looked back along the trail there was no sign of the couple. A class of primary school children stood on the edge of the embankment, drawing pictures of flowers.

Clive was in the kitchen, pouring out glasses of wine. He had made dinner. I sat down and told him about the couple.

He shook his head. 'You shouldn't have to put up with that sort of thing.'

'Is it really so easy to tell us apart from everyone else?' I asked.

'I suppose it's the group aspect,' he said, after some thought. 'With Mia obviously in charge.'

'There is no more group,' I said. 'It's just you and me now. You know, Clive . . . I think I *am* a freak.'

Clive smiled and kissed me. 'You're *my* freak,' he said.